KU-351-313

STEFANIE DE VELASCO lives and works in
Berlin. In 2011, she received the Literature Prize
Prenzlauer Berg for the first chapters of *Tiger Milk*
and was shortlisted for the Aspekte Literature
Prize for Best Debut 2013. This is her first novel.

TIM MOHR has translated such authors as Alina Bronsky,
Charlotte Roche, and Wolfgang Herrndorf. His own
writing has appeared in the *New York Times*, *Daily Beast*,
and *Playboy*. Prior to starting his writing career he
made his living as a club DJ in Berlin.

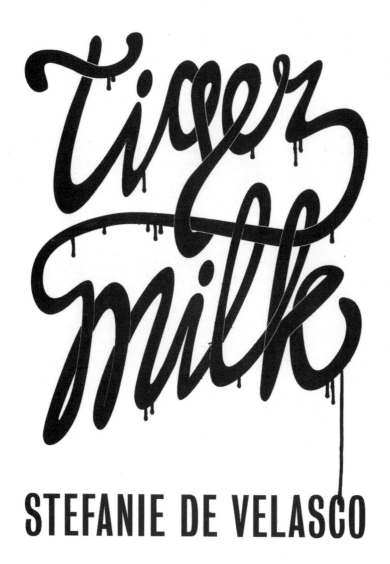

STEFANIE DE VELASCO

Translated by Tim Mohr

HEAD
ZEUS

Originally published in the German language as *Tigermilch* by Stefanie de Velasco.
Copyright 2013, Verlag Kiepenheuer & Witsch GmbH & Co. KG,
Cologne/Germany (2013)

First published in the UK in 2014 by Head of Zeus Ltd.

Copyright © Stefanie de Velasco, 2013
Translation copyright © Tim Mohr, 2013

The translation of this work was supported by a grant from the Goethe-Institut
which is funded by the German Ministry of Foreign Affairs.

The lines from *The Modern Witch's Spell Book* (p. 84)
are reproduced by kind permission.

The moral right of Stefanie de Velasco to be identified as the author
of this work has been asserted in accordance with the
Copyright, Designs and Patents Act of 1988.

All rights reserved. No part of this publication may be
reproduced, stored in a retrieval system, or transmitted in any form
or by any means, electronic, mechanical, photocopying, recording,
or otherwise, without the prior permission of both the copyright
owner and the above publisher of this book.

This is a work of fiction. All characters, organizations, and events portrayed in this novel
are either products of the author's imagination or are used fictitiously.

9 7 5 3 1 2 4 6 8

A catalogue record for this book is available from
the British Library.

ISBN (HB) 9781781857441
ISBN (XTPB) 9781781858134
ISBN (E) 9781781857434

Typeset by Palimpsest Book Production Ltd, Falkirk, Stirlingshire

Printed and bound in Germany by GGP Media GmbH, Pössneck

Head of Zeus Ltd
Clerkenwell House
45-47 Clerkenwell Green
London EC1R 0HT
WWW.HEADOFZEUS.COM

For girls

In a cool and airy mead
There turns the wind a wheel;
My beloved she did leave,
Who lived there in that field.

She pledged her love forever
Gave me a ring therewith;
She broke her pledge asunder,
My ring did split in half.

When I hear that wheel still turn,
I don't know what to do,
Death is that for which I yearn,
Then quiet would it be too.

Joseph von Eichendorff

I WOULDN'T HAVE EVEN NOTICED IT IF MAMA HADN'T RUN INTO Frau Stanitzek on the street. I know it was Frau Stanitzek because she already owned the convenience store in the building where Jameelah lives now. I can still remember how they stood around talking and laughing forever, and then they talked some more and then came more laughter. I wasn't paying attention to them, I was bored and I remember I was holding onto the baby carriage to brace myself because the pavement was so icy.

Jessi was lying in the carriage, she was still a baby then, an accident. Mama had cried when she found out she was pregnant again. She was sitting in her room, on the corner of the bed, the corner of the same bed she used to share with Papa. Rainer was sitting next to her and then he took her in his arms and suddenly they both began to cheer up. I remember that I watched all of this through a slit in the doorway and that I had to pee really bad. The pregnancy test was still sitting next to the bathroom sink, it was one of the cheap paper ones and the ends were curled up like a dried-out slice of cheese on a sandwich put out for display at the bakery.

And then I saw it. It was lying in the snow, it was green, and it was steaming. Someone must have just spat it out. It looked like a little balled-up lump of pizza dough, about the right size for my Barbie doll to make a pizza out of, except it was green

1

and it had teeth marks in it. I was still holding onto the baby carriage, I had mittens on and they were connected by a cord that ran up each sleeve of my jacket and across my back. My Barbie was stuffed into one of the mittens. And as Mama and Frau Stanitzek chatted away, the upper body of my Barbie crept out of the mitten and bent down. With an outstretched arm she speared the gum and then stuck it into my mouth. It was still a tiny bit sweet, and it tasted like Waldmeister syrup with a hint of cigarettes. Later, when I was eleven and took a drag on a cigarette for the first time, I immediately thought of that piece of gum and then today, again, I had to think of that piece of gum, the way it was just lying there in the snow, and the taste of it, because today for the first time I put a condom on using just my mouth. An old hooker's trick says Jameelah, guys love it. I'm only explaining all of this because I think I had a childhood memory for the first time today, and you can only remember something as a childhood memory once you're no longer a child. Jameelah says she can't remember anything from her childhood. Then maybe you're still a child, I said to her. Then she thought of something, she remembered how she found two bunnies in a dumpster once, how they weren't quite dead but almost, it was one summer in Iraq when I was still little, and my cousin killed them with a tennis racket but other than that I don't have any memories, Jameelah says, which is probably for the best, I don't want to grow up anyway, at least not really, not all the way, just enough so that I can get into all the clubs and so guys don't think they're going to get thrown in jail if they fuck me.

The two of us, me and Jameelah, we really are grown up now. Which is why we buy striped thigh-high stockings with our pocket money. When you start to buy your own clothes, you're grown up. After school we lock ourselves in the girls' bathroom and take off our trousers, underneath are the stockings. Our t-shirts hang down just enough to cover our asses, and the stockings come up to the top of our thighs, it drives guys crazy. I always get milk from the cafeteria during our lunch break, I have a calcium deficiency, you can tell by the white flecks on my fingernails. At the discount supermarket we've bought cheap Mariacron brandy, maracuja juice, and a wide-mouth plastic container of chocolate Müller milk. The cashiers don't usually care that we're not eighteen. We dump the chocolate milk down the toilet, chocolate milk is for children. We drink Tiger Milk and this is how you make it. Pour a little of the school cafeteria milk, a lot of maracuja juice, and a decent slug of brandy into the Müller jar. Jameelah stirs it with her fingers, she has really long fingers and wears lots of rings, all of them stolen. She doesn't steal just rings, she swipes perfume, nail polish, basically anything that doesn't have one of those things on it that sets off the alarm when you leave a shop.

We take turns drinking from the Müller jar while we ride the U-bahn toward Kurfürstenstrasse. As we cross the city on the elevated steel rails, the train rocks us back and forth and Jameelah starts making up stories again. Just imagine, she says, looking at me with her huge dark eyes, picture it in your mind. It sounds like *once upon a time*. . . but it's not once upon a time, it's more like this is how it could be. I close my eyes and everything starts to spin a little. I imagine the train is a flying carpet and now, any second, Jameelah will start to tell some story or other.

Just imagine that when you're seventeen or whatever, when your breasts have stopped growing, just imagine, that for a few days

3

each month they filled up with Tiger Milk. How crazy would that be? I mean, how crazy would guys go over that?

Shut up, Jameelah, you're the one who's crazy.

Jameelah giggles loudly.

No, seriously, think about it, the same way you get breasts and you start to get your period, what if you got Tiger Milk once a month?

TMS?

Tiger Milk Syndrome. Miger Silk Tyndrome.

Jameelah loves switching letters around. Word-crunching, she calls it. She makes lust out of list and sex out of Beck's. Put a six-pack of sex on your shopping lust. We also talk in our own O-language. Forget saying someone took a hit off a pipe, they take a hot off a pope.

You know, I always used to think that being a teenager just meant you were old enough to drink tea, what about you?

Jameelah laughs and shakes her head and her long earrings jangle.

What's the Arabic word for teenager?

No idea, says Jameelah, who cares? What do you think about the idea of getting Tiger Milk for a few days a month as a gift from nature, a gift from god, from some god of sex, as, you know, a celebration of ovulation.

You're wasted. And I don't know. Every month for your whole life? Wouldn't that end up being a pain in the ass?

Jameelah squints her eyes and thinks it over for a second. Okay, she says, how about only until you have a kid? Only up to then, right, that's the way nature planned it, because by then you'd have a husband anyway.

I nod and Jameelah looks at me conspiratorially.

In that case, she says, you can never have kids, because then it would stop.

4

Nobody in Germany has kids anymore anyway. I saw it in a magazine.

They do in Iraq.

But you're not in Iraq.

Yeah, but I might be soon, in three months.

What? Why?

I don't know, my mother got a letter from the immigration department.

She gets stuff from them all the time.

Yeah, but this was different.

What do you mean?

It was a different colour.

For some reason this makes me laugh.

What, like a pink slip, I say.

Jameelah glares at me.

It's not funny. They might deport us or something.

Deport you? Why?

Jameelah looks at the floor and fidgets with the Müller jar, squeezing the plastic sides and making them loudly pop back out.

No idea. But my mother's worried.

They can't just kick you out.

You have no idea how it works, says Jameelah, it can happen just like that.

You don't even know any Arabic, I say.

That's not true. I can understand it. But even if I didn't, it doesn't make any difference to them. They don't care.

So, what now?

We just have to wait now, says Jameelah, they'll send us notice one way or the other sometime in the next three months. Though my mother wanted to try to get us naturalized.

Naturalized? You mean become actual German citizens?

Exactly.

Is that difficult?

Pretty difficult, yeah. You have to fill out all kinds of paperwork and take a test. If you pass the test you get a real German passport instead of the stupid residency card we have now, and then we wouldn't have to constantly run around to all these government offices anymore, we wouldn't have to get our residency permits extended all the time. Man, if that ever happens, if I ever become a German citizen, I'll throw a huge party.

Sounds good to me, I say.

Yeah, says Jameelah, but it won't be just any old party. I'll throw a potato party.

A what?

A potato party. Orkhan and Tayfun did the same thing, like in that one movie, you know, where the guy serves nothing but things made out of potatoes.

I look out the window of the subway car and think, three months. I don't want to think about it, I don't want to think what it would be like if Jameelah wasn't around anymore so I grab her hand and hold it tight.

Things are always changing, even if you don't want them to, says Jameelah.

No, I say, everything will stay the same if we want it to. When you're grown up, you can keep things the way you want. You decide everything as an adult, that's the good part of being grown up. And anyway, three months, do you know what that means?

Jameelah shakes her head.

Three months means we have the whole summer in front of us.

I have a pebble in my shoe. I kind of like it when I have a pebble in my shoe. It's like someone's there, like someone's accompanying me through the world. I can play with it if I get bored, roll it around with my big toe, round and round like a circus horse being paraded around the ring. I don't know why, but when I have a pebble in my shoe I never feel like I'm alone.

Jameelah and I put our feet up on the seat bench opposite us. The pebble tumbles down toward my heel and diamond-shaped clumps of dirt fall from the soles of our Chucks onto the seat. The dirt is from Tiergarten, sometimes as part of detention we have to go to the park and do stuff. Jameelah kicks her shoes against each other and the dirt rains down on the seat. She smiles and takes a big gulp of Tiger Milk.

Leave some for me, I say.

We still have the bottle, she says, kicking her backpack. Dangling from the zipper is the luggage tag I gave her back in elementary school, the one with the cartoon mouse. The mouse used to be white but it's grey now, that's how long me and Jameelah have been best friends. On the front of the backpack, handwritten with a sharpie it says *Love you my angel, from Anna-Lena*. Anna-Lena is full of it. It's a load of shit that she loves Jameelah. And a load of shit that Jameelah's an angel.

Some old man, typical senior citizen, walks past us.

Get your feet down, he says.

We're getting out at the next station anyway you old Nazi, says Jameelah.

The old idiot stands there with his mouth open. Jameelah chugs the rest of the Tiger Milk and drops the container on the floor. At the station we get out and sit down on a bench to mix another round in an empty soda bottle I have in my bag.

Crazy, says Jameelah as she pours brandy into the bottle, there are some words with magical power in Germany. When you say one of them the world comes to a complete halt. Nazi. The world just stops and stares at you.

7

More like words that are cursed, I say. The old bastard felt insulted. You know how it is with the word Nazi.

Yeah, okay, that's true, Nazi is a bad example, but if you think about it there really are words that make people stare at you, whether they feel personally insulted or not. I mean, forget the old guy, imagine what would happen if I just said Nazi out loud, not even at anyone. Everyone would stare. Or Jew. You can't say Jew. Even though it's really just a normal word.

That's another bad example.

Jameelah puckers her lips, thinking it over.

True, true. But you know what I mean, like. . . I can't think of a good one right now.

The last few drops of school milk trickle into the soda bottle with the brandy.

Vagina, I say.

What?

Vagina's one of those words, I say.

Jameelah looks at me blankly for a second.

Vagina, vagina, she shouts, exactly, that's what I mean! It's just a normal word.

No reason to shout, I say.

What, you, too? You said it first, she shouts, that's exactly what I mean, you can't say it, you just can't say it.

She jumps up and the mouse on the tag on her backpack swings around like it's gone crazy.

New game, says Jameelah and the millions of bracelets she's wearing jangle in my face, let's try to think of all the totally normal words in the world that you're not allowed to say.

Only if you come up with the next one, I say.

She thinks.

Nazi, Jew, vagina, it's not that easy to think of another one.

Jameelah grabs a pouch of loose tobacco out of her backpack and starts to roll herself a cigarette. She tries to sprinkle the tobacco out smoothly and evenly on the rolling paper, precision work she's doing. Neither of us says anything for a while, maybe because we both know what's coming and we both know we could still reconsider it. But I don't want to reconsider it. And anyway, it was Jameelah's idea originally.

We're going to do it again aren't we, I ask.

Jameelah doesn't react, she just sits there calmly, rolling her cigarette.

Come on, I say.

Jameelah licks the edge of the rolling paper and shoves the finished cigarette in her mouth and then looks at me.

You think we should, she says, pulling her Zippo out of her backpack.

I think we should. It was a good laugh last time.

More like crass, that's what it was last time, crass. Or cross.

Yeah, it was cross. But it was fun, too, right?

Her dark eyes bore into me. She takes a drag on her cigarette and blows the smoke out the side of her mouth. I grab the cigarette from her and take a drag.

Why else did we dress like this?

Jameelah cracks a smile.

Fine, she says, you wouldn't have it any other way.

Give me a break, you sound like our teacher.

I hand the cigarette back to her.

But today I get to put the condom on, Jameelah says, the red one.

We hop down the stairs of the subway station together, two steps at a time, down to Kurfürstenstrasse.

* * *

There's a lot happening on the street, as always. People are racing from one shop to the next. It seems like everyone on Kurfürstenstrasse has a bit of tuna salad or ketchup stuck to the corner of their mouth. That's because every third storefront is a place to get cheap food. I counted one time. Department store, optician, bakery; clothing store, office supplies, sandwich shop; more clothes, bed linen, fish and chips. On and on. The further down the street you go the cheaper the places get, that's where the mobile phone stores and ninety-nine-cent shops are and loads of Turkish bridal shops and nail salons. Just beyond the discount baby store is where you start to see the women standing around.

I'm hungry. You have any money?

No, really, none.

With our last few cents we buy a packet of Yum Yum ramen noodles at a ninety-nine-cent shop and then stroll on down the street all slick and cool, crunching away on the dry noodles like potato chips. Further down there's nothing but peep shows, porn theatres, and kebab shops. There are lots of women standing around down here, but none of them are wearing striped stockings, they're in shiny leggings or leather skirts that lace up the side.

Tasty. That's what Jameelah said last time. The laces look just like strands of black liquorice. I'm not so sure I think that's funny.

Sometimes there are girls the same age as us standing here. Today one of them looks familiar to me but I can't place her. She's wearing one of the skirts with the liquorice laces, striped tights, and a tank-top with spaghetti straps. She's holding a leash that's dangling in the gutter, soaking up water from a puddle, and on the other end of the leash is a huge black dog. The dog has on a red handkerchief instead of a collar and its mouth is hanging open. I'm pretty sure that if it could talk it would hit us up for spare change. The girl is sitting on the kerb rummaging through her army rucksack and she looks up at us suspiciously.

She has dark makeup around her eyes and her dyed-black hair is parted in the middle and her arms are covered with scabs. I'm letting the last few Yum Yum noodle crumbs dissolve in my mouth when Jameelah grabs me by the t-shirt. A car comes around the corner and the girl with black hair quickly jumps up and pulls her dog out of the street. The driver leans out the window and grins at us, his face is all red. Jameelah gives him the finger, but the girl runs after the car and together with her dog jumps into the backseat.

Shit, I think looking at the ground. The pavement is dotted with old pieces of gum.

Give me the tobacco.

Jameelah reaches into her jacket pocket and then walks over and leans against the wall of the nearby building, she tucks one knee up and props her foot against the wall behind her. I crack a smile. Now we really do look just like all the other girls around here. Jameelah winks at me and nods at a guy across the street who's leaning against a signpost and looking across at us. He's tall and thin, wearing skinny jeans and a pair of those idiotic-looking horn-rimmed glasses. He looks kind of sweet though and I can't imagine he could possibly be waiting across the street because of us.

I shake my head at Jameelah.

I'll bet you, says Jameelah, I'll bet you he comes over here.

She waves at him and I see his eyebrows arch. He hesitates for a second and then crosses the street with an awkward grin on his face.

Him, I ask.

Jameelah nods without taking her eyes off the guy.

Watch this, she whispers.

* * *

11

As the guy gets closer I start to feel a little strange. But that's normal, you always feel a little strange at first, it happens every time, it's just part of the whole thing. Jameelah takes my hand and we saunter toward him.

Hey, says Jameelah.

The guy looks us up and down and grins.

What are you staring at, says Jameelah.

I'm not staring, he says.

He's pretty old, he must be thirty. He looked younger from far away because of his clothes. He's barely got any hair left, with just a bit of fluff above each ear.

Our last two classes of the day were cancelled, says Jameelah.

Aha, he says, so what are you up to then?

I'm Stella Stardust, says Jameelah, and this is my friend Sophia Saturna. I'll bet you have one of those apartments with wooden floors and stucco moulding and all that stuff, right? And tons of old vinyl? You definitely look like the type of person who collects records.

No vinyl but a lot of CDs, the guy answers, shoving his hand into his jeans pocket, do you know what CDs are?

Nah, we're walking talking MP3 players you know, at night we plug giant thumb drives into our ports, kind of like in the Matrix, you know? We keep them on our nightstands right next to our kiddie cassettes and the music is downloaded automatically onto our internal hard drives along with everything else, like our homework assignments, telephone numbers, French vocabulary lists, everything.

The guy looks at Jameelah and laughs out loud.

What's so funny about that, says Jameelah, barely able to keep from laughing herself.

Shaking his head, he stares at her like he's watching the climactic scene of the most interesting movie ever. For a second

I think he might actually believe Jameelah's bullshit. Belief is wanting things to be true that you know are impossible. And this guy is one of those people, the type of guy who wants to believe everything because he spends all day taking care of boring shit, emailing and crunching numbers and sucking up to clients, yeah, he probably has to meet with clients constantly and once in a while when he's running back and forth to the copier he stops and asks himself why he bothers with it all. He'd much rather lose himself in our lies.

What do I have to do to see these ports, he says folding his arms across his chest.

It'll cost a hundred euros, I say.

Jameelah winks at me and her eyes guide my gaze to her left hand. She forms a circle with her pointer finger and thumb.

I actually never do this kind of thing, he says as we climb into the backseat of his car which is parked at a nearby garage.

We never do this kind of thing either, Jameelah says giggling. She picks up a pile of glossy magazines on the seat and tosses them into my lap.

Are you rich, I ask.

He laughs.

No, not really, he says adjusting his rearview window so he can see us.

There's no such thing as not really. Are you rich or not?

I don't talk about money, he says trying to sound all slick and cool.

Jameelah looks at me and rolls her eyes.

What an idiot, she whispers.

The apartment is incredible, exactly the way we imagined it would be, gigantic, full of beautiful furniture, kind of like what you see at Ikea except more expensive, and there's not a speck of dust anywhere. He must have a cleaning lady I think to myself.

Do you guys want ice cream, he asks.

I don't like ice cream, I say, though it's a lie.

Right, we don't like ice cream, says Jameelah opening her rucksack, where's the kitchen anyway, she asks, and do you have any milk?

There's a tall CD rack next to the bed. The guy really does still buy CDs. From the far corner of the place I hear the sound of utensils clanging. Jameelah and the guy are in the kitchen. Then Jameelah slides across the wooden floor in her stockings and stops in front of me.

Hey, she whispers, Sophia Saturna.

She smiles, nods at the silk scarves hanging from the rungs of the cast iron bed frame, and looks at me inquisitively. I nod and push play on the CD player and the music is decent so I turn up the volume. Jameelah slides back toward the kitchen, balancing herself like a newborn foal taking its first steps across the pasture. I have to laugh because I know that couldn't be farther from the truth. All of a sudden the apartment goes dark. A disco ball hanging from the ceiling starts to spin and tiny flecks of light dance on the walls. The guy must have taken off his t-shirt in the kitchen because his upper body is naked when he reappears. The tiny points of light spin across his skin and it reminds me of Friday nights at the ice skating rink. There's no hair on his chest, I bet he shaves it. He holds out a glass for me and smiles. He looks like a nice guy somehow, but that just makes me feel kind of sorry for him.

Jameelah takes off her top, hops onto the bed, and starts jumping up and down on the mattress. I toss my t-shirt on top of Jameelah's things and join her. Our heads bob up and down as we jump. The guy stands in front of us and takes cautious sips from his glass of Tiger Milk.

Come on up, Jameelah shouts, the air's much nicer up here.

He gingerly tests the mattress with his big feet and I notice that his second toe is longer than his big toe. He says something but the music is so loud that I can't understand it. I grab his hand so he doesn't fall over and as I do I ask myself whether the length of your second toe plays a role in keeping your balance. Mama had said something once about people with long second toes, I can't remember what it was, but it was something bad, something like people with long second toes die young, that wasn't it but it was something like that. Mama often says things that sound wrong. Mama says that back when Papa left he took her engagement ring, the one with the green gemstone in the middle, it was real, she says, it belonged to his mother, she says that every time she starts going on about the ring, it was real, she says, and Papa took it to give to his new girlfriend, and then she starts to cry and says that you just don't do that, and the way she says it makes it sound as if the fact that the ring is gone, that Papa took it with him, is much worse than anything else about Papa leaving.

We jump around on the bed to the deafening music. The guy pulls me close.

You have such beautiful hair, so blonde, he shouts in my ear so loud that it hurts.

He tries to grab my hair as it flies around and I kiss him and he grabs my ass. Jameelah drops to her knees and pulls the guy down with her and opens his belt and pulls down his jeans and he's wearing boxers and they get pulled part way down with the jeans but it looks kind of nice, even the bulge where his hard-on is sticking out. Jameelah takes a big swig of Tiger Milk and dribbled it all over the guy's chest. She leans over him and starts to slurp up the milk from his body and he wraps his long legs

15

around her and I take two of the silk scarves and tie his hands to the bed frame. We take turns kissing him and take off the rest of our things until we're naked except for our stockings. Jameelah ties his feet to the other end of the bed, her stockings are rolled most of the way down, I don't know why and I want to pull them up for her but she does the opposite and takes them all the way off. She's hidden the condom somewhere inside, and when she finds it she rips open the package. The condom's bright red and I wonder what flavour it is, must taste like something red, I think, maybe strawberry or cherry, but then Jameelah puts it in her mouth tip first and things get serious. We take the big white sheet that's crumpled at the bottom of the bed and lay it around the guy so that only his cock, which is all red, is showing, like during surgery, when everything is covered with that green fabric except the spot where they are going to operate. The guy lays there completely still, as if we've given him anaesthesia.

Jameelah says you can learn something from these guys, just like when you study medicine. First you cut up a frog, then corpses, and only at the end do you get to work on real, living people. That's how you learn something. We need to practise, for later on, for real life, at some point we'll need to know how it all works. We need to know everything so nobody can ever mess with us.

It's still the middle of the day, meaning it's a little too early to go to the planet, but going home now would be weird so we head toward Wilmersdorfer Strasse U-bahn station and wander through the pedestrian zone, into the mall, and then downstairs to the supermarket. We grab all kinds of stuff, Yum Yum noodles, marble cake, Pixy Stix, tubes of sweet Milchmädchen condensed milk, and butter rum flavour Riesen, which Nico likes so much. We pay with Jameelah's fifty euro bill and then walk over to the planet.

The planet is a big ugly concrete ball right next to the mall at Wilmersdorfer station. There are a bunch of smaller planets or moons around the big one, all of them made out of concrete too. In summer, when it's hot, foamy yellow water sometimes shoots out of the small planets, but most of the time the whole thing is dry. I have no idea who decided to put it here. I guess it's supposed to be art but it just looks like shit. I think they wanted mothers to sit around the planet with their kids and eat ice cream and splash around in the fountain or whatever. But you never see mothers and children at the planet, only alcoholics and crazy people and us.

Nico says the city didn't build it for mothers at all, he says it's for us so that we have a place to meet after school and on weekends. There's a phone booth next the planet. It's an old yellow dinosaur and I've never seen anyone go in to use it except for Nico when he's smoking up. But it's actually in the perfect spot. It's covered from top to bottom with writing. We leave each other messages on it about when we're going to meet or where a party or concert is. It may be old fashioned but it's cheaper than calling or texting and everyone who comes to the planet checks the phone booth for messages anyway and luckily for us the city cleans it as soon as every inch is covered with ink.

Kathi and Laura are sitting at the planet. Kathi is fussing around with Laura's bangs with a razor blade, just like earlier today at school during the twenty minute morning break, when we were down in the basement in the bike storage area, where we always smoke, she was working on Laura's hair too. She wants her bangs to be straight, perfectly straight, but to run at an angle from left to right and it's not so easy to cut them at an angle and make the line perfectly straight.

So what's going on today besides hair cutting, asks Jameelah.

S-bahn party I think, says Kathi, Nico was just here and said something about it.

Where is he anyway, I ask.

Under the railway bridge. You guys have anything to drink?

Jameelah pulls out the bottle of Tiger Milk and the bag of butter rum Riesen from her rucksack. Viovic are next to the phone booth. Viovic are always in the same outfit, all in black, with the same hair, dyed black and cropped at the chin, and when it rains they have the same black umbrellas, which is why we just call them Viovic, like it's just a single entity, even though that's not true, there are two of them, they're twins. The only time you can tell them apart is when they are on stage, because Viktoria plays bass and Violetta plays guitar. Their band is called Viovic and they're crap, everyone says so, not just me. I don't understand why they are so bad since they have a rehearsal space in their parents' basement, with egg boxes on the wall and every-thing, and they practise almost every day because there's also a music room at the private school they go to, but maybe they don't practise as much as they say they do.

Nini, Viktoria calls, do you have a sharpie?

I shake my head.

I do, says Kathi and tosses it over to Viktoria.

Violetta scrawls something on the phone booth.

You guys coming to the S-bahn party?

Viktoria and Violetta shake their heads.

We're going to Rotor, they say.

I wonder to myself whether they practise saying everything simultaneously like that, it's almost creepy.

Here comes Nadja, says Laura with her mouth full. She points toward the S-bahn tracks.

She looks awful, whispers Kathi.

She was already looking bad at school earlier, says Jameelah.

Hey, have you guys seen Tobi, asks Nadja as she walks up.

Is everything okay with you, asks Kathi.

Got my period, where's Tobi?

He's with the others under the railway bridge.

I look in the butter rum bag. Only one left.

This one's for Nico.

We run past the entrance of the U-bahn station and cross Stuttgarter Platz toward the raised S-bahn tracks. Apollo and Aslagon are squatting next to the underpass. It looks like Apollo is drawing something on the ground with his wooden sword. His Viking helmet is tossed to the side, lying in the dirt. Apollo believes he's a Viking and Aslagon thinks all humans are divided between bird people and lizard people. I'm a bird person and so is Jameelah, he says, but he himself is a lizard person, just like the royal family of Saudi Arabia. Apollo and Aslagon only hang out with us at the planet during the summer because they spend winters in the Auguste Viktoria mental hospital.

What's that supposed to be, asks Jameelah.

It's Naglfar, says Apollo, the ship that has to be built out of human fingernails before the end of the world can finally come.

And that's why you two can't pass, says Aslagon, peering at us with his kohl-smeared eyes.

Why not?

Anyone who wishes to pass beneath the railway bridge must have their nails cut by Apollo, he says, so we can build the ship and bring on the apocalypse.

Why would you even want to bring on the apocalypse, asks Jameelah.

Yeah, says Nadja, maybe we don't want the world to end.

God's earth is rotten, says Apollo as he gestures at us with a rusty set of nail clippers.

Nadja rolls her eyes.

Fuck it, she says, taking the clippers and snipping one nail from each of us.

The walls of the underpass are covered with spray paint from floor to ceiling. The crappy graffiti is Tobi's. Tobi tags his stuff *animaux*, which means animals in French. But for a graffiti tag *animaux* is too long, Nico explained it to me. It's the last two letters that make it too long, you need to spray quickly and then get the hell out of there. Maybe that's why Tobi gets caught all the time and maybe that's why you see the tag *anima* all over the city.

The good stuff is Nico's. *Sad* is his tag, written in English.

Sometimes he writes *Sadist*. He writes it in soft funny-looking letters, like clouds. It's comforting when I'm riding the bus around town and see a *Sad* Nico has tagged on some random wall. It's like the sensation I get when I have a pebble in my shoe, in that moment when I see one of Nico's *Sad* tags I'm not alone.

At the far end of the railway underpass, Tobi and Nico are standing around smoking. Nico's leaning against the wall. He's big. Everything about him is big actually, his hands, his blue eyes, his mouth, and his feet, which are always in the same pair of trainers which he throws into the washing machine just as often as he washes his clothing and hangs to dry along with the clothes. Even his shaved head is big and really the only small thing about him is the kiddie lunchbox he always carries around. It's plastic, with bright stripes and on the side of it a clock that doesn't work because it's out of batteries. I used to have one just like it from when Nico and I were kids. We were at the carnival one day and the lunchboxes were on display on the top shelf of a raffle ticket booth. Nico and I wanted them so bad, one for each of us, but both of our mothers just wanted to keep moving. We began to cry and Nico's father started buying raffle tickets, more tickets than anybody else. Nico's mother cursed at him and the man at the booth laughed as he handed Nico's father one ticket after the next, pulling them out of the clear wrappers like meal worms and shoving them at Nico's father until he had enough points for two of the lunchboxes.

So that's how we're going to spend our money, Nico's mother had said to his father pointing to the slips of coloured paper littering the ground, but she was just in a bad mood because Nico's father was drunk and so were my Mama and Papa but she couldn't drink because she was pregnant with Pepi then.

I don't think it's right either, my Mama had said to my Papa, say something, she said, but Papa just rolled his eyes.

21

Nico has carried that thing around with him ever since. He used to carry his matchbox cars back and forth to the playground in it but these days he keeps his pot in it and uses the smooth plastic face of the clock to blend the pot with tobacco. He even takes the lunchbox to Schulze-Sievert, where he's doing his apprenticeship. Everybody jokes about Nico and his lunchbox, but he doesn't care, he laughs right along with them. His lunchbox is his lunchbox. Mine got destroyed the same summer I got it. Dragan threw it against the wall of a car park after I told him the clock on it was shockproof.

Hey, says Nico, so did you let Aslagon cut your nails?

I nod.

Poor guy, says Jameelah as she reaches for the joint.

What do you mean?

I mean seriously, she says, *God's earth is rotten* has got to be the saddest sentence I've heard in ages.

Nico spits on the ground.

Yeah, maybe it is sad, he says, looking up at the sky. Sad but true.

All of a sudden there's a commotion at the planet. A bunch of skaters are riding around the fountain, shouting and clapping as they fall down and hop back up and their boards smack loudly against the concrete. It looks like the diagram Herr Wittner shows us in physics class, with the planet as the nucleus of an atom and the skaters whizzing around the nucleus like electrons, everything is made out of atoms, says Herr Wittner, the whole universe.

It starts to drizzle. We sit down next to the fountain. Just for a laugh, Kathi and Laura start asking people for spare change. The nearly empty container of Tiger Milk sits between me and

Jameelah. I wrap my arms around my knees as the summer rain falls around us and soaks into the parched concrete, giving off that unique smell.

I'm pretty wasted, I whisper.

Jameelah nods.

Me too, she says, I was already completely wasted at that guy's place, she says and then she reaches into her shoe, pulls out my fifty euro note, and hands it to me.

It was a good fucking laugh today, eh?

Yeah, I say, stashing the money, but it was fucking cross, too.

I look up at the sky, which presses down on us with that eerie yellow colour it gets before a big storm, like it's trying to scare us.

Look, I say, it really looks like the apocalypse is coming.

I guess the ship must be finished, says Jameelah.

That was quick.

Yeah. Maybe God's earth really is rotten. Maybe there really is a God and maybe his earth really is rotten. I'd believe it.

Wait, why? I thought you said it was the saddest thing you'd ever heard?

Yeah, but sad things are usually true, says Jameelah, Nico's right about that.

She closes her eyes, opens her mouth, and catches the raindrops on her tongue. Beyond the S-bahn tracks there's a flash of lightning, then we hear the thunder and a few seconds later the rain starts to pour down as hard as in a rainforest. Laura and Kathi come running over and grab their backpacks, which are on the ground next to ours.

Fucking global warming, shouts Laura and we all hold hands and run for cover shrieking but by the time we reach an awning we're all soaking wet. Jameelah puts her hand on my shoulder and braces herself as she pulls down the wet stockings that are

23

clinging to her legs. Her hand is warm and I close my eyes and listen to the rain, the way it falls out of the sky, the way it plunks into the gathering puddles, the way it drips from the awning and soaks into my shoe and joins the pebble. I'm tired and drunk, I think, and I still have to go shopping, bread, Leberwurst, noodles, ketchup, but then Jameelah's long nails dig into my shoulder. I open my eyes and am about to complain when I see him. He's coming toward us. His dark hair is all wet and drops of rain hang from his long eyelashes, and beneath the lashes his dark Bambi eyes and pale face, so pale it looks like he's suffering from some elegant disease. It's Lukas. In his right hand he has a bottle of wine and a tattered book is sticking out of his jacket pocket, which is just one of the million things Jameelah loves about him. I can't understand why anyone would read so much, I don't see what's so great about it, I think it's somehow abnormal.

Hello, he says, staring at Jameelah as she stands there barefoot with her wet stockings in her hand. I crack a smile and think to myself, either he thinks she's incredible or he thinks she's disgusting, but that's how it always is with Jameelah. As if in slow motion she stuffs the stockings into her backpack, gently, purposefully, every movement carefully considered, like a hunter trying to position herself without scaring off a wild animal. She slips back into her red Chucks and smiles.

I have to tell you something, she says looking at Lukas, I dreamed about you, I dreamt that you captured some kind of mythical beast, it was see-through with two heads. It was like a cross between a dragon and a kangaroo but it lived in the water and could purr like a cat.

Lukas laughs.

You should write that down, he says, that's really poetic imagery.

I already did, says Jameelah.

24

He is really good looking somehow, at least when he's listening to Jameelah tell him something, though maybe we all look nice when she is telling us something. Lukas wants to say something but two hands come from behind him and cover his Bambi eyes. The hands belong to Anna-Lena, Anna-Lena whose hair is always freshly washed – only freshly washed hair moves like Anna-Lena's.

There you are, she says and kisses Lukas on the cheek. Anna-Lena who always smells like flowery perfume and writes *Love you my angel* on everybody's rucksack but doesn't really mean it. You can't say I love you if you don't actually mean it, that's against the rules.

Behind her come Nico, Nadja, and Tobi.

S-bahn party, shouts Nico throwing his hands up and starting to run across the plaza toward the station. I can hear the beer bottles clinking against each other in his backpack. We run after him toward the S-bahn. As Lukas plays around with Anna-Lena a few steps ahead of us, Jameelah stares at him as if she's in a trance.

She loves him, Jameelah whispers.

Yeah, I whisper back, but he's her cousin.

So, says Jameelah, it's not illegal.

Still, you just don't do that, I say taking her hand, which is ice cold.

The creature in my dream, says Jameelah, he captured it for me, he showed it to me, and then he kissed me, he captured it for me and not for her.

I know, I say.

MAMA LAYS ON THE SOFA BASICALLY ALL THE TIME. MOST OF the time her eyes are closed, but when I come home she sometimes opens them and asks, where were you. When she opens her eyes she always looks horribly tired, like she's just arrived from some faraway place and only flopped down on the sofa here in our living room by blind luck. I don't think she's really looking for an answer to her question. Me on the other hand, I'd love to know where she was, where she always goes behind her shuttered eyelids, all those hours she spends alone on the sofa. Mama's sofa is like a remote island she lives on. And even though that island is in the middle of our living room, a thick haze obscures it from view. You can't dock on Mama's island.

Lately Jessi's been lying on the sofa with Mama more and more often, she lies next to her with her head buried in her breasts, motionless, like she's in a coma. Maybe Mama's disease is contagious, though Mama isn't even really sick, I just always think she is because that's how it looks. I know that Jessi drinks. Out in the hall above the goodie cabinet, where all the sweets are stored, is a glass-front cabinet. Jessi gets into that and drinks the Eier liqueur. I bet if Mama knew she would slap Jessi in the face. I only know because last week when I was in the kitchen I heard the click of the glass-front cabinet. You can open the goodie cabinet silently, but the glass-front cabinet has a magnetic catch that clicks, that's how I heard it. And also you can see the remnants of Eier liqueur stuck to all of Mama's JOY glasses. Jessi drinks the liqueur out of the dusty glasses and then just puts them right back on the shelf in the cabinet, like nothing ever happened. Then she lies in her bed like she's dead. Her room reeks of alcohol, like alcohol and little girls, like the gym when the fifth graders have been in there right before us.

Once a week I sit down with Mama on the sofa and brush her hair. Rainer went out of his way to buy an expensive brush for that at Spinnrad, all organic materials, just like Mama said it should be. Sometimes Mama cries when I brush her hair but I act as if I don't notice, I think it's better that way. Jameelah's mother says you can wake someone who's asleep but someone who's only pretending to sleep you can never get to wake up.

When I look out the window in my room I see the playground where I played as a child. We've lived here forever, just like Nico, who lives directly across the courtyard from us, on the same floor. I learned how to walk and how to ride a bike on the pavement in front of our place. Once I roller skated on the sandy path that leads from the playground out to the street where Jameelah lives. Jameelah was coming the other way, also on roller skates, the same kind as mine, only in red. I traded her my blue left skate for her red left skate and we roller skated until the ball bearings were clogged with sand. Then we climbed the old oak trees and tied pieces of yarn onto the branches. One oak belonged to each of us. Actually, no, that's not true, Amir's tree was the one linden tree right in the middle of the oaks. Nico was allowed to climb in my tree and I was allowed to climb in Jameelah's, but nobody was allowed up Amir's linden tree except Amir. The trees all had names but we all forgot them except for Amir. I

27

haven't climbed my tree for ages but Amir says the yarn is still hanging from his. Over the years the bark has grown over the yarn, but the ends of the strands are still visible, which is proof that we didn't just dream the whole thing up, at least that's what Amir says.

When I go to Jameelah's I always cross the playground. The playground's pretty big and right in the middle of it is a huge sandbox. Somebody drew an invisible line through the middle of the playground and the German and Russian kids never go on the slide and the Arab and Bosnian kids never go on the swings. Back when Jameelah and I roller skated around the playground there wasn't yet an invisible line.

Amir lives in the same building as Jameelah, right behind the playground, down the path and out to the side of the building that faces the street. In front of the door to the building I see Dragan standing around. He's smoking. Well, actually, smoking doesn't really describe it. He's sucking on his cigarette like he's trying to hurt it, and every now and then he spits violently on the pavement with a loud splat. A dark pool of spit has formed at his feet. The name Dragan says it all. It sounds evil, like dragon or Dracula. I mean, there's a lot of Serbs named Dragan but maybe Tarik is right, maybe all Serbs are evil, I have no idea, but this one is for sure. I slink toward the door to the building, trying not to draw attention. I push the doorbell for Amir's apartment.

You, says Dragan but I don't acknowledge him, man, why doesn't the stupid door buzz open.

Turn around when I'm talking to you, girl.

What is it, I say.

Dragan flicks the butt of his finished cigarette into the pool of spit and it sizzles as it sinks in and he smiles and spits again. I feel sick. And Jasna is in love with this guy, disgusting.

Are you going up to Amir and Tarik's place, he asks.

I nod.

Tell Jasna that I'll wait down here for her no matter how long it takes, I'll wait for her.

How romantic, I think as the door finally buzzes open.

The door to Amir's apartment is open and inside it smells like coffee and dirty nappies, just like it always does.

Hello, I call wondering whether I should take off my shoes. In the entry hall is a folding drying rack hung with men's underwear that must be Tarik's.

Hello, I say again then I walk into the living room and find Tarik and his mother sitting there. She never says guten Tag, she just nods and smiles. Maybe because she can't speak a word of German, seriously not a single word. Jameelah says you can't even borrow an onion or an egg from her because she doesn't know the words onion and egg.

Hello, kiddo, says Tarik.

If I had a big brother I'd want him to look just like Tarik. He should have the same dark blue eyes, the same strong shoulders. I used to have a serious crush on Tarik. I'd listen to the lambada all day and imagine dancing with Tarik. In my daydreams he was bare-chested and wearing just a ripped up pair of jeans. I told Jameelah about it once and she just about died laughing and said Tarik couldn't dance the lambada because he has only one leg because he lost the lower half of his left one during the war, as a kid. It's true that he limps a little but I still can't believe that he's missing part of his leg, I mean, when he stands around he always looks so solidly planted, with his legs spread confidently.

Tarik can be really funny, no matter what Jamelah says. Just because she doesn't get it sure as hell doesn't mean he's not funny. He does a great MC Hammer impression, for instance. Maybe he doesn't do it in front of Jamelah because he knows she thinks he's an idiot, that only makes sense. But he can also be really strict, which I actually think is good. On the back of Tarik's jacket it says *Teddy Dragon*, which kind of sums it up perfectly. I think he tries to look out for me, for Jamelah, for Jasna and for Amir, all of us. Of course Jamelah hates the idea that he looks out for us.

I don't need anybody to look out for me, she says, Teddy Dragon, what the hell is that supposed to mean, have you ever stopped to think what a teddy dragon would look like?

Jameelah says Tarik was only ever useful when he was still reading *Bravo* magazine and Amir could steal copies of it for us, and that was a long time ago, about as long as the bark has been growing over the yarn in those trees.

Amir comes down the hall holding Selma in his arms, she's crying and Amir's face looks funny too, like maybe he got smacked again. Loud music is coming out of Jasna's room.

We want to go to the planet, you want to come, I ask, but Amir isn't listening.

Jasna, he says tapping his finger on his forehead, she's gone crazy.

What's up, I ask.

Dragan bought her a bikini and she wants to go with him to the pool, he says banging his fist on the door to Jasna's room.

Turn the music off, he yells, we're all going to get in trouble otherwise.

The door flies open.

Get out of the way you dwarf, says Jasna, shoving Amir aside.

Hey, girl, she says to me coming right up close, her breath smells like Slivovitz. She dances off in the direction of the bathroom. She's not wearing anything except a bright yellow bikini. There's no question that it's cool, along the hips and neckline it's covered with bling and it sparkles as Jasna moves. Her impossibly long hair hangs down to the top of her impossibly long legs and it looks great no matter what Amir says.

Tarik hops up, walks over to Jasna, and grabs her by the arm.

Let go of me, shouts Jasna as the bling sparkles, let go of me, you cripple, and as she says the word cripple Tarik loosens his grip.

Jasna rips herself free of Tarik, runs into the bathroom, and slams the door shut behind her.

Selma cries and squirms in Amir's arms.

Come out here, shouts Tarik banging hard on the door, but Jasna just curses, she curses in Bosnian and the curses fill the hallway. Amir looks at me as if to ask for help.

Come with me, I whisper dragging him out into the staircase.

What's going on?

Amir sinks wearily onto a step.

Selma's crying is getting louder and louder.

Give her to me, I say putting Selma in my lap.

Last night, says Amir, after I'd already fallen asleep, Jasna and Tarik had a fight, it woke me up. She told him that she wants to marry Dragan.

Bullshit.

It's true, Amir says, she even has a ring, a real engagement ring, that he gave her.

Really?

Really.

The fight was so horrible that Tarik locked her in the living room but this morning she was gone, she'd broken the front door and gone to Dragan's place.

Then what?

I took Selma into my room, she was crying because Jasna wasn't there. At some point later in the morning Jasna came back and said she was moving out, she was going to marry him, can you imagine?

Seriously?

I'm serious. She says he's really smart and all that, but you know he never even finished middle school. The worst part is that we can't go anywhere since she got together with Dragan. They'll never invite us to a wedding, you know. But Jasna doesn't give a shit, she's already packed her things and I know for sure that if she leaves she'll never come back and when I say never I mean never, and now I'll have to look after her all the time, Amir says motioning to Selma, and it has to happen now, right when the summer holiday is about to start. I'm not a girl!

Big tears roll down his cheeks and Selma starts to cry again.

Dragan, I say, you remember when he used to throw rocks down at us from the parking garage when we were little? One time I was bleeding all over the place.

He killed his dog, says Amir, he gave it so much Slivovitz that it went into a coma. That's the type of guy he is.

I know, I say.

Amir sniffles.

Do you have cigarettes, he asks.

We sit next to each other for a while, smoking. Nobody says a word.

Are you coming to the planet?

Amir shakes his head.

I'll call you again later, I say.

I still don't have a phone.

Still?

No, Jasna sold her old one on ebay for three euros, Amir says tapping his finger on his forehead, three euros, it cost more than that to mail it, can you imagine. The point was not to give it to me, and really, as far as I'm concerned she can leave and never come back.

Here, I say handing the pouch of tobacco to Amir, you can keep it.

Thanks, says Amir and Selma calms down again too.

Where were you, says Jameelah when I go upstairs and ring at her door.

I was at Amir's, I say, I wanted to see if he was coming.

Noura comes toward me in the hallway in her nurse's uniform and kisses me on the cheek.

My little one, she says, you want to eat something?

What's going on down there, asks Jameelah.

Dragan, I say, he proposed to Jasna and she wants to move out now. That's why she's fighting so badly with Tarik. She came out of her room wearing nothing but a bikini and went dancing through the apartment.

Jameelah laughs out loud.

It's not funny, says Noura, they were screaming at each other all night, do you think that's a good sign? I'm so tired, I couldn't sleep at all. I have to go to work but some people just don't seem to care, they think only of themselves.

Amir says neither of them talk to him anymore because of the whole thing and Tarik looked really sad.

Tarik, says Jameelah, he's just jealous.

Jealous about what?

Jealous of Jasna. Because he can't dance with his fucked-up leg. Because he doesn't have anyone to give a bikini to because he's just everybody's big brother. Teddy Dragon will never find anyone, that ugly troll.

33

Stop, I say, that's mean. Tarik isn't a troll.

He is so, says Jameelah.

Enough, says Noura, you two shouldn't get involved, I'm telling you I don't want either of you to get involved, got it?

But Amir is our friend, says Jameelah.

I know, but there are things even friends can't help with and it's best not to get involved in something like that.

I'm not getting involved anyway, says Jameelah, I'm just giving my opinion.

I don't want you to give your opinion either, says Noura, I want you to stop talking about it, she says as she glares at us like our teacher, Frau Struck.

Fine, says Jameelah.

WE HAVE TO STAY FOR DETENTION AGAIN. DURING ETHICS CLASS, Jameelah kept making comments the whole time. It was about Christmas, and whether Jesus was really born on 24 December. Jameelah said that there was no way sheep would be standing around outside a manger in the middle of winter like it says in the Bible.

In Bethlehem everyone goes skiing, Jameelah said, and to be honest if I were God or the Messiah I would be totally insulted if my birthday was celebrated on a completely different day than the actual date of my birth.

Frau Struck had replied that Jameelah shouldn't speak to her in that tone and that she shouldn't carry on about such things.

I disagree, Jameelah said, it's not verboten, but that's when Struck went off.

Why are we talking about Christmas right before summer break anyway, I asked at some point, but that was a mistake because Struck said we should both be quiet or else we'd be kicked out of class and she had no desire to discuss the matter further. Struck hates it when anyone tries to discuss anything with her.

We were quiet for the rest of the class, we thought up good O-words, poke instead of puke, shot instead of shit, coke instead of cake, and we also played city-country-AIDS. Frau Struck realized what we'd been up to when she collected all of our notebooks.

Detention, she said then, detention for both of you.

Detention meant going to Tiergarten and gathering leaves with leaf-miner moth cocoons on them. We have to gather chestnut leaves because those are the ones the moths use. The pupae bite into the leaves like little pit bulls and then spawn like crazy when they come out. This year they've arrived early, so to keep the plague from getting any worse we have to gather leaves. Nobody seems to care that there's no point, that the whole city is full of the moths, and that it just gets worse every year, with more moths and more damaged trees.

It's just an arbitrary task, Rainer always says, they have to make you do something.

They're a bit like us foreigners, says Jameelah, you just can't get rid of them.

What Frau Struck doesn't get is that we actually like to go to Tiergarten. There's a boy there I like. He's a gardener and he sits in front of the shed where we have to go to get the bin bags and rakes we use to gather leaves. He always smiles so sweetly at us when we show up, once again, and sometimes he smells of Weleda lotion, which I like.

So what did you guys do today, he asks.

Nothing, says Jameelah, we were just playing city-country-AIDS.

City-country-AIDS? What's that?

It's the same as city-country-river, only we use diseases instead of rivers. We don't know the names of too many rivers, you know.

It's nice and cool in the park. We walk around the lawn barefoot and collect leaves while trying to come up with more normal words that you're not allowed to say.

UFO, says Jameelah.

36

UFO doesn't count, I say.

Why not, says Jameelah, UFO is a normal word but you can't say it too loud or believe in it or else everyone thinks you're crazy.

Yeah but saying something and believing in it are two different things, I say.

Not at all, says Jameelah, words only exist because people believe in them, otherwise the word wouldn't have been thought up, UFO is like the word God, the only reason we have the word God is because people believe in it.

Bullshit, I say.

Really, says Jameelah, do you think you would know the word leaf-miner moth if there was no such thing? Admit it, it's just too deep a concept for you.

No it isn't, I say.

They come from the Balkans by the way, says Jameelah, just like Amir.

Who does?

The leaf-miner moths, Jameelah says holding up the bag full of leaves, they emigrated just like Amir.

No way.

It's true, I read it the other day in the free paper on the U-bahn.

All the things Jameelah knows. Sometimes it can be really annoying because it makes it difficult to say it's bullshit when she says, for instance, all that stuff about belief and the existence of words. You can never tell someone they're wrong when they think they know everything, especially when they actually do know everything.

* * *

We head to the outdoor pool. I love it there. I love everything about it, the smell of the chlorine you get as soon as you walk in the gate, the suntanned boys, the noise of the splashing water, the way the girls shriek when the boys do cannonballs, I even like the mouldy showers and the way little twigs and pebbles press into my back through the towel. But the thing I like the most is the food. Sometimes I think I would go to the pool for the food alone.

As we're walking across the lawn, Jameelah suddenly stops.

Back there, she whispers digging her fingernails into my shoulder, Lukas is lying there all by himself.

I smile.

Come on, I say taking her by the hand. As slick and cool as possible we stroll on across the lawn.

Hi, says Jameelah when we stop next to Lukas, and her shadow falls across his face.

As if he's just woken from a deep sleep Lukas suddenly sits up and yanks the white earbuds out of his ears. Strange that he even has an iPod, I think, considering that he learned how to count using dried peach pits at that crazy school of his. Laura told me that, and also that they hang tapestries in the corners so the kids don't see right-angles and that instead of learning vocabulary words they build pizza ovens.

Hi, says Lukas and when he sees Jameelah smiling at him he smiles back.

I look at his earbuds again, which have dropped into his lap. They're almost as white as his skin. Hopefully he's put on a lot of sunscreen, I think, but then again people like Lukas are always conscientious about putting on sunscreen because they know when things are dangerous, whether it's to do with the sun or just life in general. So people like Lukas rarely get burned by the sun or anything else in life.

I see Amir farther back on the lawn, he's walking toward us and waving. Jameelah lays her towel down next to Lukas.

38

I have an *Aladdin* towel, Jameelah has a Coca-Cola towel, and Amir has no towel. It doesn't matter, though, because I almost never go in the water and Amir just uses mine. I'm afraid of the water. Laura, Kathi, and the others from the planet sometimes laugh at me for it, but Jameelah and Amir understand even though they aren't afraid of the water. Jameelah and Amir are afraid of firecrackers, but I never laugh at them for it. That's how it is with friends. Which is also why I always get something for them at the snack kiosk with the money Mama gives me, she gives me money whenever I say I'm going to the pool. I walk over to the kiosk and buy a bulette for myself, a pair of chicken sausages for Jameelah, and french fries and Kinder chocolates for all of us to share.

Last year there was a stabbing at the pool, so this summer it's crawling with security. I think it's good because now people are afraid to steal things. But it's not really as dangerous a place as it sounds.

What are you doing, I say watching Amir take alternating bites of fries and chocolate.

It tastes good, he says, try it.

No way.

Seriously, Amir says, it tastes kind of like meat, but sweet.

Steak and Kinder pie, says Jameelah.

I laugh.

If you barbecue beefy sweets for too long, says Jameelah, you get *cinder* chocolates.

Jameelah jumps up.

And if something goes wrong and your garden goes up in flames you'll be left with a cindergarten.

Lukas laughs out loud. We lay around on our towels and continue to crunch words and then Laura, Kathi, and Anna-Lena show up. Once again Anna-Lena looks like she's been freshly laundered on the gentle cycle.

Hey, she says to me, your sister is getting off with some guy back by the changing rooms, the brother of that girl Mareike Mauel.

Oh God, says Laura, that's the girl with the see-through bikini.

Anna-Lena nods.

Got to be at least sixteen years old.

The see-through bikini?

No her brother, says Anna-Lena giggling, but maybe the bikini too by the looks of it.

Kathi and Laura giggle too and I turn bright red.

I'd love to have something cool to say right now but nothing pops into my head, which always happens in moments like this. Instead I watch as Anna-Lena lays down a huge flower-pattern towel next to Laura. I realize immediately she's got her period, she doesn't even take off her shorts, that's how scared she is it might leak out. What's the point of her even coming to the pool if she's so worried. She reeks of flowery perfume, and now this towel. What kind of idiotic parents does she have, I wonder, buying her perfume like that and expensive shampoo and a towel like that, I mean, Anna-Lena, who would call their kid that, what a perverse way to welcome someone to the world, as if that's necessary, such a long name, as if children haven't been produced since the dawn of time, all sorts of things like that rush through my head but of course I can't say any of that or they would all think I'd completely lost my chador.

Come on, says Jameelah taking my hand, let's go over to the diving platforms.

Nico and Tobi come through the gate and head across the lawn toward the others. Nico is wasted, you can tell from across the yard. I sit down on the warm stone tiles next to the pool and watch as Jameelah climbs the steps to the ten-metre platform.

40

With her arms stretched wide she lifts herself up and down on the balls of her feet.

Can someone put on Carmina Burana, she yells, I'm going to do a double Rittberger.

The security guards look at her blankly. Jameelah springs head first into the air, arms and legs fluttering like rags. The way she hangs in the air, just like on TV, when people were jumping out of that tower in America, it scares the shit out of me, and I'm relieved when she finally hits the water with a splash. I watch her swim beneath the surface until she reaches the edge of the pool by me.

So how was I, she asks grinning as she climbs out of the water. Her right thigh is bright red.

It looked pretty dangerous, I say.

Above, on the diving platform, Amir stands staring down into the depths.

Don't look down, yells Jameelah.

Amir stares into the water as if there's some sort of beast waiting below to eat him, until finally the pool superintendent says something to him and points at the people waiting behind him.

Oh no, says Jameelah as Amir steps aside and the waiting kids push past him and splash one after the next into the pool below. Amir goes back out to the edge of the platform.

That's not how you do it, says Jameelah, you have to just jump, you can't think about it or you'll never do it.

A couple of boys start jeering him.

Loser, loser!

I look up at Amir, who looks much smaller up there, smaller than he really is, he looks down at the water, up at the sky where his father apparently is, then down at the water again, but then he turns around and climbs gingerly back down the steps.

41

The boys start jeering him again.

Chickenshit, says Jameelah smiling when Amir makes it down to us.

Cut it out, he says.

What, she says, it's not a crime to be chickenshit.

You don't know anything, says Amir, you're a girl, you don't have balls that can burst on impact.

Burst on impact, says Jameelah laughing out loud, who told you that bullshit?

It's not bullshit, Tarik told me.

Tarik talks shit.

Oh, fuck off, says Amir.

You fuck off, says Jameelah.

Cut it out, I say, who wants an ice lolly?

Eating sweets together always helps end a fight.

I run into Nico at the snack kiosk. He has a currywurst and fries in one hand and at least four ice cream bars in the other and under his arm is a giant bag of crisps. His eyes are hidden behind sunglasses.

You got the munchies, I ask smiling, but Nico just smiles back and kisses me on the cheek.

Always, he says.

His kiss is just right, warm and a little bit moist.

They're sold out of ice lollies so I buy slush puppies, and as we cross the lawn I keep an eye out for Jessi in case she's standing around somewhere hooking up, but I don't see her. Instead I see Jasna and Dragan lying down kissing. Jasna is wearing the bright yellow bikini and she has her long legs wrapped around Dragan, he's running his hand up and down her thigh, it's almost like in a porn film the way they're going at it as if the rest of the world

42

doesn't exist but then suddenly Dragan sits up and looks over at me.

What are you looking at, he yells.

I'm not looking at anything, I say.

Look somewhere else, got it?

Shut up, says Nico, and Dragan actually shuts up.

Tobi and Nadja have spread out their towels next to ours. Jameelah sits down at the foot of Lukas's towel and has him spread sunscreen on her back. A victorious smile spreads across her face and she makes a V with her fingers. Anna-Lena, Laura, Kathi, Tobi, and Nadja play Taboo, Anna-Lena brought it, I don't feel like playing Taboo with Anna-Lena so I start to squeeze blackheads on Nico's back, it's fun.

That's disgusting, says Anna-Lena, cut it out or I'll have a herpes outbreak.

You get outbreaks from everything, says Lukas, you even get it when people talk about spiders.

Spiders are totally disgusting, says Anna-Lena.

What a load of shit, says Jameelah, spiders are the protectors of sleep.

Exactly, says Amir, they crawl into the corners hunting evil. It's the only reason people are able to sleep in peace.

That sounds beautiful, says Lukas, so poetic.

Hunting evil, says Anna-Lena looking at Amir with her best just-bit-into-a-lemon face, what's that supposed to mean? Sounds like something out of the Middle Ages, she says.

Shut your trap, says Jameelah.

Right, says Amir, watch what you say.

I'll say what I want, says Anna-Lena to Jameelah, and by the way your tampon string is hanging out of your panties.

Impossible, Jameelah answers all slick and cool.

Joking, says Anna-Lena even though it wasn't funny.

43

Stop it, says Lukas, rolling toward Jameelah and whispering something in her ear.

The one from the animal, asks Jameelah laughing.

Lukas nods.

What about an animal, asks Nico, looking at me, but I shrug my shoulders and look at Lukas and the way he wraps his arms around his knees and listens to Jameelah. He really looks like Bambi sitting on that green towel with his dark eyes, a Bambi who learned how to count using dried peach pits and a towel as green as the forest Bambi runs into when someone's chasing him. I could never fall for someone like that, I think to myself, but such a green home I'd like to have, a home I could run to when somebody was chasing me. But I don't have one and neither does Jameelah, we just have the trees in the playground, and we can't even remember the names of those. Nico doesn't have a forest home either though he sure has a lot of grass, and whenever he rolls a joint I'm the first one he passes it to. I look up at the cloudless sky, close my eyes, and fly away. The sun burns. Everything smells like french fries and sunscreen.

The boy in the purple swimsuit, yells the pool superintendent, dive in from the side of the pool again and you get a lifetime ban.

Life vests squeak against wet baby fat and a baby cries somewhere in the distance.

Where did you hurt yourself, asks someone.

On the wee wee, says a child crying more loudly.

Wasps buzz by, Jameelah laughs, Lukas laughs, Nico laughs.

Shit, mutters Amir suddenly.

A shadow falls across my face. I open my eyes and see Tarik standing in front of me with Jasna in her yellow bikini next to him. Her hair is wet from swimming and glistens like the bling on the bikini. Tarik is holding Jasna by the arm but she's not

44

struggling against him, she's just standing there next to him with a slight grin on her face acting like she doesn't care.

Tarik shoos Amir off the towel.

Get up and give it to me.

Amir tosses him my towel.

This is Nini's towel, says Jameelah, standing up.

Jasna laughs.

When my fiancé sees I'm gone, he's going to kill him, says Jasna nodding at Tarik, he's going to kill him sooner or later anyway if he doesn't leave me alone.

Shame on you, says Tarik.

Shame on *you*, Jasna says and then she spits in his face, making me wince. Anna-Lena stares at Jasna with her mouth open.

Let's go in the water, says Kathi to Laura.

Tarik throws Amir his clothes.

Come on, get dressed, I'll wait for you out front.

Amir dresses hurriedly.

Just like I said, I hear Anna-Lena say, like the Middle Ages.

Should we come, asks Jameelah.

Amir shakes his head.

No, he says, squeeze some more pimples, then he grabs his backpack, which has nothing but notebooks and pens and *fussball* cards in it since he's still wearing his wet bathing suit under his jeans. He walks slowly across the lawn toward the exit, the green grass looks suddenly yellow and Amir like a thirsty wanderer staggering across the desert.

A blond guy in a purple bathing suit sprints past us in the direction of the exit. It's Dragan.

* * *

It's insanely hot in the S-bahn. Jameelah and I practically doze off as we suck on our monster slushies. It's so hot that it makes

45

your skin look as if you have a rash.

Man, Anna-Lena today, I say.

Jameelah rolls her eyes.

I guarantee that shit about Jessi was a lie, she says.

Not to mention the tampon string, I say, that was just sad.

She actually said the word *panties*, she says, I mean, I just don't get it, who would ever say *panties*? We're not living in some Enid Blyton book.

True, I say, though I have no idea who Enid Blyton is and again I wonder how Jameelah knows this kind of stuff. She always remembers names and all sorts of trivia, like the whole thing with the leaf-miner moths, that they come from the Balkans. It's so German of her, and I want to tell her that, but I'm too hot to bother.

Seriously, says Jameelah, if I'm Stella Stardust and you are Sophia Saturna, then Anna-Lena is Frieda Giga. Frieda Giga, the most frigid cow in the world.

We should ask Amir, I say.

I'd rather not, says Jameelah scratching her upper arm, shit, I got bitten by a mosquito.

Where'd you get that weird scar, I ask pointing at her arm.

I told you before.

No you didn't.

I did so.

Did not.

Really? They're from immunizations I got when I was little, says Jameelah. They shoot it into your arm with this thing that's like a gun, and it leaves a scar. It's not like here, not like the shot they give you for measles or whatever.

Where'd you get that one, she asks pointing at a scar on my neck.

That's from a time I choked on a *wurst* casing and had to get a tracheotomy. My parents were still together then, they didn't

46

understand what was wrong when I started running around the table like a madman. The EMT who responded cut a hole so I could breath. Then I went in an ambulance to the children's hospital. I got to stay overnight. My father left soon after that. I know because when he told us he was leaving I still had the bandages on my neck.

I was in the children's hospital once too, remember, because of this, Jameelah says and lifts her foot and points to a narrow scar on her ankle, I was in the bathtub, leaning my foot on that thing that holds the soap. It broke off and cut open my leg. It bled really bad and they had to give me stitches. The doctor who stitched it up was so nice. I was really sad when I had to go home again.

Me too, I say, I didn't want to leave, I was jealous of the kids who got to live there, even though they were really sick, you know, I didn't care, somehow I thought they had it good there despite that.

Going to the outdoor pool always makes you incredibly tired. We shuffle from the train station to the playground. Like two exhausted pilgrims we let ourselves fall to the ground in the sandbox and bury our feet in the cool sand. The sand sticks to our bare arms and legs like in a magazine photo. I close my eyes but Jameelah says, don't fall asleep, it's not allowed and I shake my head and reach for her hand and we lie there next to each other and let life float by because we have so much time, because the clock has only just struck fourteen minutes past birth, meaning we have nearly another fifty to go, and that's a long time.

Jameelah suddenly stands up.

What is it?

Do you hear that, she asks.

What?

Somebody's crying.

47

I try hard to listen but still don't hear anything.

Seriously, it's coming from the top of the slide, up there in the play fort.

We cross the sandbox, go past our trees, and over to the play fort. Now I can hear it too, someone is quietly sobbing.

Hello, says Jameelah, is someone up there?

Two henna-tattoo covered hands slowly come over the wall of the play fort and then a crying face appears. With her legs pulled up to her chest Jasna is sitting in the fort surrounded by cigarette butts and blue mascara is running down her cheeks in long streaks.

Are you okay, asks Jameelah.

Stupid question, I think to myself.

Do you guys have cigarettes, asks Jasna.

Of course, says Jameelah pulling her tobacco out of her pocket.

I don't know how, says Jasna smiling sheepishly and pointing to the loose tobacco, I don't know how to roll them.

No problem, says Jameelah, I'll do it.

My fiancé always has real cigarettes. I only smoke real cigarettes, that's why I don't know how to roll them.

Where is he, I ask.

He'll be here any minute, we arranged it. I just don't want Tarik to find me. I waited until he had to go to the bathroom and then I ran out.

What an asshole, says Jameelah, at the pool today.

I swear, says Jasna, if he doesn't leave me alone there's going to be real trouble, but I don't want that. Tarik's my brother after all. Without your family you're nothing.

Without your family you're nothing, what an insane sentence, I think to myself, and it's not even true. Everyone always says it but only because other people are always saying it and that certainly doesn't make it so. With her long fingers Jasna reaches for the lit cigarette Jameelah holds out to her and she smokes it in a series of deep tokes, kind of like Dragan. Did she pick it up from him, I wonder, and why do people always become so similar when they're together.

Tarik's just jealous that you're engaged, says Jameelah.

Are you guys really engaged, I ask.

Yeah, says Jasna.

Show us the ring.

Jasna shoves the cigarette into the corner of her mouth, pulls up her right sleeve, and sticks out her henna tattooed hand. I stare at the ring like an idiot, dumbstruck, like when you run into someone you haven't seen in ages. It's narrow, made of gold, with three stones in the middle, two little white ones on either side of a big green one.

Is it real, asks Jameelah.

Jasna nods.

Where'd you get it, I ask.

What do you mean, Dragan gave it to me.

I mean where did Dragan get it?

It's from his mother, and she got it from her mother, it's a family heirloom.

My ass it's a family heirloom, I say grabbing her hand.

What are you doing, says Jasna and yanks her hand away.

That's not his ring, I say, he stole it.

Stole it, what are you talking about? Watch what you say.

That ring never belonged to anyone in Dragan's family, he stole it.

Jameelah looks at me with a questioning look on her face but then Jasna's phone rings.

I'm on my way, she says making a kissing sound and then hanging up.

You can't leave now, I say.

Jasna laughs.

Why?

Because of the ring, it doesn't belong to you!

What's all this shit you're talking, says Jasna, standing up. She flicks the cigarette into the sand, jumps down from the slide, and walks off toward the U-bahn station.

What was that all about, asks Jameelah.

Leave me alone, I say, I need to think.

Think about what?

My mother. Her engagement ring. That was it, that ring on Jasna's finger.

I thought your father took it.

Obviously not, because if he had then Dragan couldn't have put it on Jasna. He stole it, plain and simple.

Jameelah looks at me sceptically.

You're crazy. How is he supposed to have taken it?

I have no idea, but that was the ring.

Are you sure?

Pretty sure.

Pretty sure isn't enough.

Whose side are you on anyway, I say.

Nobody's side. What's wrong with you?

The Sorbs shot off Tarik's leg.

What does that have to do with the ring?

Nothing. But I can understand why Tarik doesn't want Jasna with someone like that.

Serbs, Sorbs, nice O-language switch, says Jameelah.

Fuck O-language, I say, I want the ring back.

Just because that poor Sorb bastard makes too many spit puddles doesn't mean he stole any engagement ring, says Jameelah.

Hello, that poor Sorb bastard is the same guy who threw rocks at our heads, in case you forgot.

50

Nah.

It's true.

You and your childhood memories, says Jameelah looking at me distrustfully, but listen it's too hot out to fight.

When Jameelah and I go shoplifting it usually works like this. We lock ourselves in the girls' bathroom after school and drink Tiger Milk, but not too much, when we're going shoplifting it's not about getting wasted, it's about getting up the nerve. I'm always really anxious about shoplifting, I got caught the very first time I ever tried to steal something. That was a few years ago now, but ever since I can't be the one who actually grabs the stuff. I'm always Jameelah's accomplice, but that's just as important.

We head to the mall a bit tipsy and check our rucksacks at the front of Kaufland. We buy a large Müller milk and dump half of it into the ugly plastic plant next to the escalator, then we go into the Bijou Brigitte shop. I hold the Müller container and whisper that's cheap, real cheap, whenever the saleswoman isn't looking our way. That's the signal that Jameelah can drop something into the milk. If the saleswoman is looking when Jameelah is about to put something into the container I say that's too expensive. You can't believe how much will fit in a wide-mouth container like that, even sunglasses and hair bands.

If Nico is at the planet we let him drink out the milk when we're done stealing, he loves Müller milk, no matter what flavour. He guzzles it down in one go like he's the great sea god of Müller milk draining his own ocean. Sometimes we ourselves can't

52

believe all the treasure lying on the ocean floor of the Müller milk container, the shiny glittering things awaiting us, we feel like real life pirates returning to hoist our buried treasure after many years.

The jewellery we like the best, we keep, the rest of it we give to the others. Sometimes we even take things back, we just leave it on the shelf again, but that's rare I have to admit. I never return any jewellery with green stones, I always take that home even if I know I'll never wear it, if it has a green stone it's coming home with me. I never understood why until recently, but now I get it. I was at a session with Frau Fuhrmeister, the school psychologist, and had to paint pictures of Mama, Rainer, and Jessi as animals and then I had to paint one of Papa. I painted Rainer as a camel and Papa as a dog, I remember because those were the ones we talked about for a long time afterwards. I found it all really annoying, but in the end I realized why I had depicted Rainer as a camel and Papa as a dog, because dogs are my favourite animals and camels, well they are not. We didn't talk that time about Mama's engagement ring or green stones, but it doesn't matter, I'm sure Fuhrmeister would say it's the same as with the animals, it's a psychological tick of mine, because of Papa, and it's as real as the engagement ring and as real as the fact that Dragan, that Sorbian thief, managed to steal the ring somehow.

Today there's something green on the seabed of the Müller milk container, a bellybutton piercing with a green stone, though my bellybutton's not pierced, actually it was but it got infected as soon as it was pierced and then it closed up. I stick the piercing in my mouth and suck off the milk and Jameelah gives the look. It means watch it here comes Lukas. I quickly hide the Müller container in her rucksack. People like Lukas don't think it's cool to steal jewellery in milk containers, seriously, it's the truth, so I understand what Jameelah wants.

53

Hi, he says and touches his hand to his hat as a greeting.

What, is he a soldier now, I think.

We're going to the human rights group meeting at the tea shop, says Lukas, you guys coming?

Human rights group, says Jameelah, of course, and as she says it she digs her fingernails into my hand with joy.

It stinks in the tea shop. It stinks of fruit tea, of the old felt covering the billiard table in the corner, of the old books that are so shit that not even Lukas would read them, of old board games that are all missing a piece or a card so that you can never really play them right, of ancient sofas where grown-ups hang out, grown-ups who act like they know everything but who have fucked up their own lives and are so lonely that they have to jerk off every night. I know exactly what it smells like, it smells of god and his rotten earth.

On the sofa is a scruffy pillow. I don't even want to think about how many tea drinking believers have sat with it in their laps or under their asses, but it certainly looks as if it's seen a lot of laps and asses. I let it get knocked to the floor unnoticed, as if by accident.

Jameelah sits down cross-legged next to me and motions for Lukas to join us and he smiles back awkwardly.

I have a basic idea of what human rights are, why they are important or whatever, but I can't say I understand why Lukas and the rest feel it necessary to meet up here regularly and talk about them. Nadja says something about some document she read online, something about a family in Guatemala. Everyone nods with concern, like they actually know the people. Slowly I begin to realize this all has to do with the fact that they plan to meet up on Saturday in the pedestrian zone to collect money for street kids in Guatemala as part of *engagement week*, to help the kids there, for a better world, that's the slogan painted on bed sheets they must have worked on the week before, *for a better world*. One of the sheets is laid out on the brown floor tiles. I can't help wondering whether they all just took the sheets from home and if they did, what kind of people don't use fitted sheets and also what kind of people can just take sheets, I mean Mama would smack me if I painted a slogan on one of her sheets whether it was fitted or not. Still, I could have found the whole scene amusing if not for the awful head of the group, Herr Kopps-Krüger. He's sitting opposite me, looks like a wolf fish, and has the worst breath in the world. Behind him is a poster, *the field of experience for the expansion of the soul*, it says, it's from some exhibition and I have no desire whatsoever to know what will be expanded and experienced. Everybody is talking about the fundraising campaign on Saturday and how much money they need to bring in so the partner church in Guatemala can buy who knows what for the street kids.

I haven't seen you guys here before, says Kopps-Krüger to us at some stage, would you like to briefly introduce yourselves.

I don't feel like introducing myself but Jameelah says, so this is Nini and I'm Jameelah.

Sometimes Jameelah can be so German, it's embarrassing, but Kopps-Krüger's eyes get wide when he hears the name Jameelah.

It's great that you're here, he says to her, and as he does his head nods like crazy, as if he has that disease the pope had. I can tell that inside his head, in his third world brain, there's thunder and lightning. I count the seconds off, twenty-one, twenty-two, twenty-three, and then it's on.

Nice name, Jameelah, really nice, he says, the Arab people are very poetic, where exactly are you from?

From here, Jameelah says.

Well yes, of course, says Kopps-Krüger smiling placidly, as if Jameelah were a puppy that had just chewed on an old pair of shoes.

But originally, where do you come from originally is what I meant to say. You're not from Germany, surely?

From Iraq.

Aha, says Kopps-Krüger, a beautiful country, the landscape and the people, the Iraqis, unbelievable hospitality, but, he says raising his pointer finger, it's a country where human rights are violated. That's why you came to Germany, am I right?

What a detective, I think.

Jameelah says nothing.

It wouldn't surprise me at all if he had a hard-on right now. It's always the same with these people who pretend to care when all they really want to do is strip you naked and put you up against the wall so they can jerk off about how much better they have it than others. These people with their questions, questions like an interrogation, like Jameelah did something bad. Jameelah and I normally get into trouble together but whenever someone comes and asks these questions I feel like I'm in a cop show on TV, like I'm behind the one-way glass and I can see her but she can't see me.

What's up with all the stupid questions, I say, and why are we even talking about Guatemala or Iraq, I mean how far away are those places?

What would you like to talk about, asks Kopps-Krüger.

There's plenty of injustice right here, I say.

Give me an example, says Kopps-Krüger.

I don't know, like when people are deported. That's not right.

Shut your mouth, says Jameelah looking angrily at me.

Kopps-Krüger raises his eyebrows.

Why, he says, who is going to be deported?

All of a sudden it gets very quiet in the tea shop, Lukas pulls his hat further down over his face and I can see he's no soldier, that's for sure, which is fine, but he shouldn't pretend he is.

Nobody, I say quickly, it was just an example. There are also certainly good things, too, obviously, I mean, Jameelah is about to be naturalized.

I'm pleased to hear it, says Kopps-Krüger.

Yeah then she'll really be German and we're going to throw a potato party, I say looking at Jameelah, right?

Yeah, she says smiling shyly at Lukas. He smiles back.

At nine-thirty on Saturday morning the doorbell rings up a storm, I'm still in bed and when I finally open the door Jameelah is standing there.

We have to go to Wilmersdorfer, it's Saturday.

At first I have no idea what she's talking about.

Hello, street kids of Guatemala, fundraiser, says Jameelah holding up an empty apple sauce jar with a note stuck to it. *For poor street kids* it says.

What, are you crazy? You really want to collect money for Krap-Krüger and his fucking street kids, you can't be serious, I say.

I don't give a shit about the street kids, I want to see Lukas!

Shit, that old Krap-Krüger only wants us to help him so he can congratulate himself for making the world a better place. And the worst part is he gets off on it, I'll bet you anything.

He can jerk himself off until his cock's rubbed raw for all I care, says Jameelah, I want to kiss Lukas and for that I have to help him collect money for the street kids.

I growl something back at her and a few minutes later we're sitting in the U-bahn.

When we get out at Wilmersdorfer station my first thought

57

is that there must be an open-air market going on but then I see it's actually all sorts of stands set up by clubs and activists, and behind one of the tables is Krap-Krüger. Lukas and the rest are already there, unpacking stacks of flyers and booklets from a box and spreading them on the table. I can't believe they bother with all of this, and on a Saturday morning no less, it's all a bit like being a street kid in Guatemala, I think to myself.

Jameelah puts her hands over Lukas's eyes from behind, the same way Anna-Lena did at the planet recently.

Salam, she says to Lukas.

I'm pleased to see you both here, says Krap-Krüger when he spots us.

Jameelah digs around in her rucksack, pulls out her apple sauce jar, and proudly places it on the table.

As far as I'm concerned we can start right now, she says, but Krap-Krüger shakes his head.

Unfortunately that won't work, he says, lifting his pointer finger, the collection boxes have to be sealed.

He pulls a bunch of metal containers out of the box on the ground, but in the end he is one short. Krap-Krüger is having a good day and says, okay you can use the jar. The scent wafting from his mouth smells once again like god's rotten earth.

Lukas stands behind the table.

Aren't you going to collect money, asks Jameelah.

No, I'm staying here to pass out info, he says, but maybe later we can go to the pool?

Sure, says Jameelah nodding like an idiot.

Come on, I say and pull Jameelah with me, her apple sauce jar in her hand, we walk up and down Wilmersdorfer Strasse, up and down, up and down.

We're raising funds for the street kids of Guatemala, perhaps you can make a small donation, that's how it goes the whole time. I'm bored, but I have to admit that Jameelah is good at getting people to part with their money. She makes up stories about Guatemala and the mountains there. The kids sniff glue because they're starving. They get beaten by their fathers and flee into the jungle. I can see it all before my eyes, the mountains and the wild animals in the jungle and the luscious green of the trees.

Everything is greener in Guatemala than here, greener and more luscious, says Jameelah, but also darker and more tragic, and as she says that she shakes the jar as if it's some kind of Guatemalic folk instrument.

Guatemalan, says Jameelah when we're in the bathroom at the ice cream shop taking the bills and large coins out of the jar. We need the money because we want to buy Amir a *Star Wars* towel we saw at Kaufland.

I mean, hey, we're street kids, too, says Jameelah, we're kids and the street is right out there and Krap-Krüger can't prove we took anything, for all he knows we're just bad at drumming up donations.

We go back to the table and when Jameelah sees Lukas she starts shaking the leftover coins in the jar. Just as Krap-Krüger goes to take it from her, the bottom of the jar suddenly breaks and the coins fall to the ground jingling.

Oh boy, says Krap-Krüger, you two are a handful.

Wait, I'll help, says Lukas squatting down beside Jameelah and together they gather up the coins.

So, are we going to the pool now, I ask.

Sure, says Lukas and he smiles and looks at me with his big Bambi eyes. I can see the pool in his eyes, the shimmering green lawn, his green towel and how it's laid out on the lawn, and how he moves little by little toward Jameelah, but then just at the moment when she reaches out to touch his hair and kiss him he jumps up and gallops away, galloping off and disappearing forever in his green life.

I know you can't really see the shimmering green lawn in Bambi eyes, I know that only works with the last unicorn. It's just a Fata Morgana, like a thirsty wanderer staggering across the desert sees.

Oh man, says Jameelah when we're heading home from the pool on the train, Lukas.

What about him, I ask.

Nothing, says Jameelah, he's so sweet. The sweetest.

So?

What?

So what's up with you two, I ask.

No idea, says Jameelah looking at the ground, nothing somehow.

Maybe it's something to do with his school, I say, Laura told me they don't have sex education there until they're fourteen. Maybe he only recently learned how everything works.

No way!

Seriously. They think rape means to ask someone for their phone number.

Shut up, Jameelah says, Lukas isn't that stupid.

Then you just need to get together with him alone, I say, not at the pool or whatever, I mean, getting him to put sunscreen on is okay as a start, but not if that's all that ever happens.

But he likes me, I think.

Of course he likes you, I say, but he's a skittish forest creature, he'll never come to you on his own, he's the type you have to hunt, or better yet lay a trap for.

Yeah, says Jameelah looking out the window, which is why

I'm done.

With what?

I'm done practising.

What are you talking about, I ask.

Come on, you know.

No, I have no idea.

Yes, you do, says Jameelah with a conspiratorial look.

Oh, that.

I don't want to practise anymore, she says, I want to go to bed with someone for real. For the first time, you know, Lukas and me.

Yeah, me too, I say, I just don't know who with.

On the walk home I think about it seriously. What about the sweet guy at Tiergarten? It would probably be nice with him, and maybe everything would smell like Weleda, I try to imagine it but in the end I can't imagine it with anyone except Nico.

At home I notice I have a bad sunburn on my shoulders. I put on my pyjamas even though I'm not tired at all. Jessi is lying on the sofa with Mama watching *Crimewatch*. The sky has darkened and outside it's starting to thunder and lightning as rain begins to smack onto the dry streets. I open the window in my room wide so I can smell the storm. My phone rings.

Thank goodness you answered, says Jameelah sounding agitated, Jasna's on the balcony and she says she's going to jump.

No, I think, this is just another one of Jameelah's stories.

Seriously, she really is standing on the railing of her balcony and unless a miracle happens she's going to jump, there's already an ambulance and a fire truck here.

Quickly I pull a hoodie over my pyjamas and run out and head across the playground. The wet sand squishes beneath my Chucks. The farther I run the louder the sirens get and there's cops and EMTs all over the place, the pavement in front of the building is jammed with people. Jameelah is standing in the street and waves me over to her, the hood of her jumper is pulled down over her face. I look up to the balcony but nobody's there.

She was there until a second ago, says Jameelah, Tarik locked her in their apartment but now she's not letting anyone in. We all had to evacuate to the street because she threatened to blow the place up with the stove if anyone tried to come into the apartment.

I want to answer but just then the door to the balcony opens. Jasna has her long hair pulled into a thick ponytail and it's hanging over her chest all the way down to her hips like in a fairytale, like someone has just shouted for Rapunzel to let down her hair. Her hands claw the balcony handrail covered with henna tattoos, blood-red. All around us are uniformed men in the street, yellow, red, blue uniforms standing around smoking and waiting to see what Jasna's next move will be.

Like on TV, says Jameelah pointing at the firemen who have spread out one of those things you can jump onto and when I see it I get a lump in my throat in the exact spot where the scar from the tracheotomy is and I suck in a deep breath of air like I'm going to have to stay underwater for a long time.

Amir, I say, where is Amir.

Jameelah slowly lifts her arm like she's underwater too and with her lips she starts to form some word but I turn and see Amir and Tarik and Selma and their mother on the pavement not far from us and I go over to them but somehow they're actually really far away even though they are all standing right there nearby and it seems like an eternity before I reach then.

Amir, I say but he doesn't react, he just stares up at the balcony, Tarik, I say, but he doesn't react either. Cautiously I touch his arm and when he turns to me I have to gulp again because I've never seen Tarik crying before, I didn't even know he could.

Kiddo, he says putting his arm around my shoulders, go home, go home as fast as you can but then Tarik's mother throws her hand in front of her mouth and screams. I look up at the balcony and Jasna is sitting on the railing. It's not as bad as it seems, I think breathing deeply, it's just a bad movie, a porno with Rapunzel in the lead role. Now the men on the street, the firemen and EMTs and police, all seem to start to stretch toward the balcony. It's easy to imagine since Jasna's not wearing anything but her yellow bikini.

Dragan where are you, where is my fiancé, Jasna shouts.

Can someone find this Dragan, says a police officer to Tarik, where is this man?

I think he's at the gym, says Amir quietly, I saw him earlier with his duffel bag.

Then you can at least try to talk to her, says one of the firemen to Jasna's mother.

She should get out of here I don't want to talk to her, screams Jasna climbing back down from the railing, get out of here she screams and then she starts throwing all kinds of stuff down from the balcony, rubbish, the rack for drying clothes, Selma's stroller, and everything lands one after the next on the street near us. Jasna's mother sobs more loudly.

Yeah, now you're crying, screams Jasna, but first, first you drag me into this world and then you leave me all alone and now, now when I want to die you cry.

Her mother shelters herself in Tarik's arms and puts her hands on his broad shoulders and makes two fists and in one fist I can see a balled up white tissue. Always the tissues, I think, like tiny stuffed animals but for mothers, for sorrows, sad little stuffed animals made of tears, each with its own story.

A man in a yellow vest shoves me aside. On his back it says Police Psychologist and beneath that a number.

You don't have to die, says the man, there's always another

way out, no matter what the problem.

Jasna laughs.

What do you know about my life doctor psycho?

Suddenly Tarik steps forward.

Then go ahead and jump, he shouts, jump you Serbian Chetnik whore.

You can't tell me what to do, screams Jasna back, you're not my father.

Your father, pah, says Tarik spitting on the ground.

The rain picks up. The firemen tussle and form a circle and one of them opens an umbrella that says Bad Weather on it.

That's enough, says the man in the yellow vest to Tarik, how can you talk to your sister that way, this is not a situation for that sort of talk.

That thing is not my sister, says Tarik looking straight at the man in the vest.

I'll kill all of you, I'll kill all of you, screams Jasna and then she runs back into the apartment.

One of the firemen puts out his arms and says everyone to the other side of the street, please move to the other side of the street and remain calm.

Now the building is going to explode I bet, says Jameelah, she's going to blow it up.

Noura comes down the street toward us, I hear the steady hammering of her heels on the asphalt, I see the white nurse's uniform sticking out from under her jacket.

What's going on here, she asks shaking Jameelah's shoulders, what are you doing outside in the rain?

Jameelah mumbles something but all I can do is stare at the building as muted screams issue from it. The place has trans-formed into a locked music box. The ballerina inside has momen-tarily escaped from the box and is now losing her mind. Somehow

I can understand Jasna, it must be awful to be imprisoned inside a dark box and then every time somebody opens the box you get spun around to some stupid melody. It rains and it rains. The pyjamas under my hoodie are soaked right through to my skin though it dulls the burning pain on my shoulders and when Jasna comes back out onto the balcony and climbs up on the railing again I get goose bumps.

Oh no, says Jameelah, she's really going to do it now.

TODAY IS THE LAST DAY OF SCHOOL AND I PICK UP JAMEELAH and Amir as usual. Amir is in the hallway trying to get rid of another couple of journalists, there have been journalists standing around from morning until night since the whole situation with Jasna.

Is it true that your sister was released from the hospital the day before yesterday, asks one of them. In his hands he has a notebook and he can't wait to write something down in it.

Amir nods glumly. He's had another smacking. Right under his eye is a big round purple blotch that his mother must have put there with her fat gold ring.

Your sister's boyfriend told us that she was transported to a secret location in order to protect her from your family, is that true, asks the journalist.

I don't know, says Amir.

Has she been in contact with you?

No she hasn't.

You are her little brother, she doesn't need to be afraid of you.

Amir looks over at me for help.

She only broke her leg, I say going over to stand next to him.

I mean really, only broke her leg, says the woman standing behind the guy with the notebook, it was a cry for help you need

66

to dig deeper, and when I don't know how to answer her she says, of all people a young woman should. . . but I don't hear what a young woman should because luckily Jameelah comes rumbling down the stairs.

You're annoying, she says to the two journalists, don't you get it.

I'm from the biggest paper in town, says the guy.

Go interview some neo-Nazis, says Jameelah pulling Amir toward the exit.

Amir's eye doesn't look good at all and since we have some time before school we stop at the convenience store and buy a Müller milk and go to the playground. We sit down in the play fort above the slide and smoke a cigarette. Amir holds the cold milk container against his shiner.

In Germany it's a crime to hit a child did you know that, says Jameelah.

I'm not a child, says Amir.

You are in the eyes of the law and if you hit a child in Germany you can be arrested for it.

Even for a smack, I ask.

I don't know, but it's the correct answer in any case.

Correct answer to what, asks Amir.

The German test, that was one of the questions.

Test, I say, do we have a test today?

Oh please no, says Amir.

No, says Jameelah, I mean the test for German citizenship. You have to know everything about Germany, what the duties of the president are and what holiday do you wear a mask for and all sorts of stuff like that.

I have no idea what she's talking about.

Why would you need to know that, says Amir.

For whenever, in case we end up becoming Germans. I'll be

ready for the questions already, it's smart.

It's moronic, says Amir.

Jameelah looks at him angrily.

What's moronic about it?

Nothing, says Amir, what are you trying to tell me? That I should press charges against my own mother or what?

Man, it just popped into my head, says Jameelah, don't get bent out of shape.

Nobody says anything for a while.

I didn't mean it that way, says Jameelah at some point, you know that, right?

It's fine, says Amir.

Come on, I say, we have to get going.

When Frau Struck comes into the classroom with the report cards she looks the way she always does on the last day of school. She's put pink lipstick on her thin lips and rouge on her face. To celebrate the day she also has on a dress, a white summer dress made out of linen, a typical teacher dress. The dress is so flimsy on the sides that you can see her cheap undershirt through it and because she's not wearing a bra her breasts hang there like shrivelled water balloons. Her feet are in sandals and her toenails are painted, but no matter how much nail polish Struck uses her feet still look old, with cracks and scabby skin. Which we get put right in our faces on the last day of school, thanks ever so much.

Frau Struck always smiles on the last day of school because she's looking forward to summer break more than all of us put together and also she thinks we can't figure that out. She puts on a shitty dress, polishes her gnarled feet and acts all friendly, but up front on her lectern next to the report cards are her holiday books – a guidebook to South Africa and a teach-your-self-English crime novel.

So what are you all doing this summer, Struck asks as she distributes the report cards.

Fucking Frau Struck, says someone at the back quietly enough that you can't tell who it was but loud enough for the entire class to hear.

Everyone erupts with laughter. Struck gets red splotches all over and tears well up in her eyes. For a second I feel sorry for her but when she smacks my report card on the table and I see that she's given me Fs in maths and biology that feeling is gone immediately. She should just go and disappear without a trace wherever it is she's heading, abducted like a character in her stupid crime novel, that would be something, Struck abducted by the Taliban and nobody willing to pay the ransom.

The first thing we do at the end of the school day is lock ourselves in the girls' bathroom. We dump the milk out of the Müller container we bought that morning and pour in Mariacron brandy, maracuja juice and the last school cafeteria milk of the year and take turns sipping it and roll a cigarette.

Did I tell you I'm getting my wisdom teeth out at the end of the summer, I say.

Really, says Jameelah looking enviously at me, at the children's hospital? It's so nice there.

Yeah.

So what are we going to do for summer break?

Not fuck Frau Struck, that's for sure.

Jameelah laughs.

No, but how about permitting ourselves to be deflowered, she says, what do you say?

I don't know what she's talking about.

Lose our virginity, we'll lose our virginity. We'll find the nicest

69

boys in the world and go to bed with them. I'm through practising.

Good idea, I say and though I'd kind of forgotten about it, now that Jameelah brings it up it does seem like a good idea and it's about time though she doesn't need to talk in such a sophisticated way about it.

Do you know who you want to do it with, asks Jameelah.

I shrug my shoulders.

I was thinking Nico.

Nico? But you've known him forever.

I know, that's exactly why I was thinking of him.

What do you mean?

Well somebody I've known for a long time might be just the right person. Plus he's so big and strong that it would be easy with him, and it's probably stressful enough doing it the first time that I'd rather do it with somebody I already know well.

But it's supposed to be something special, says Jameelah fidgeting around with the Müller container.

Do you think so? I don't know. I just don't want anything to go wrong.

Jameelah takes a big gulp of Tiger Milk, stares at the floor and continues to fidget with the container, the popping noise it makes puts me on edge.

Now that the time has come we're no more savvy than we were before, she says looking at me with her big eyes, maybe we'd be better off doing it with somebody from Kurfürstenstrasse after all.

Bullshit, I say even though I'm not really sure, she might be right.

Suddenly the door to the girls' bathroom opens. We drop the cigarette in the toilet and stand on the toilet so nobody can see our feet. The door in the next stall opens and then is shut and locked. Jameelah quietly climbs onto the toilet tank.

Salam sisters, she yells.

Laura screams.

Shit you scared me!

Kathi's head appears above the wall of the stall.

How are your report cards, she asks, and do you have anything to drink?

The Müller container makes its way from one stall to the other.

Got an F in gym, says Laura, Herr Wittner's nuts.

It's because you always say you have your period, says Kathi passing the container back.

Wittner started a list so nobody could get out of gym more than once a month.

What do you mean, he writes down who has their period when, I ask.

That's perverse, says Jameelah.

Yeah and he stares at the breasts of all the girls who sit in the front. Last week Anna-Lena wrote Hallo Herr Wittner across her cleavage and he turned bright red when he saw it.

Anna-Lena, says Jameelah, she's frigid.

Yeah, I say, we call her Frieda Giga.

Or Fri-Gid for short, says Jameelah.

I like Wittner. I always help him push the electron gun into the physics lab and he never stares at my chest though I have to admit that with me there's not too much to look at anyway.

You need to be home at eleven, says Mama sternly as I dial Jameelah and hold the phone away from her.

Okay, I say looking impatiently at the clock on the phone, at the latest.

Up until recently it was so easy, on the weekend Jameelah

71

always said she was staying over at my place and I always said I was staying over at hers. Then something stupid happened. We fell asleep at the playground one morning at dawn, completely wasted. We only meant to lie down for five minutes until Noura went off to work at the clinic but then she discovered us there in the sandbox. Jameelah got smacked and wasn't allowed out for ages and always had to go straight home from school.

Ever since then Mama always has to check in with Noura if Jameelah wants to stay at our place. But Noura doesn't realize that Mama buries herself under the sofa blanket at eleven so that nobody can land on her island, Noura doesn't know that Mama stuffs pillows under any part of her body that's not resting evenly and doesn't hear or see a thing until the next morning when Rainer comes home from working his overnight taxi shift and brings her a coffee.

Before I head out I call Amir but he doesn't answer. I go and ring his doorbell but when nobody answers there either I take the bus to the planet. On the way I see that Nico has painted a new *sad* at the Yorckstrasse S-bahn station right where the homeless guys beg for tickets. I'm kind of excited. I know that it stings when I cut my thumb, that it throbs when I stub my toe and that it turns blue, I know that it burns when you fall down and skin your knee, but I don't know what the pain is like when you sleep with somebody or even why it's supposed to hurt. Maybe it's not even true that it hurts and anyway it's pretty unlikely that it will happen today.

Still I did put on my white knee-highs with the little black bows on the them and the underwear Jameelah gave me for my birthday last year, the checkered ones with hearts on them. For a second I feel like stupid Frau Struck in her stupid dress. She must have done it for the first time too, why doesn't she just teach us about it. Actually I can't picture Struck in bed with some guy. It was probably like one of Rainer's pornos with pubic hair all over the place and red lingerie and crumpled sheets and right in the middle a big red stain.

Written in thick sharpie ink on the telephone booth at the planet it says *Party and concert at Viovic's rehearsal studio!*

While I'm reading it I realize that the whole booth is shaking like it's excited about the party and is trying to lift itself off its base so it can come along. I can't see who is moving it around from the inside because it's filled with smoke, but I can guess who it is. I crack the door open and a hand reaches out and grabs me and pulls me inside. I squeal but then Nico whispers close your eyes and shuts the door quickly behind me. It reeks of hash inside.

You could suffocate in here, I say, help.

Nico says that's the way it's supposed to be, I hear Jameelah say next to me.

Yeah that's right, says Nico, this is our opium den, don't worry just close your eyes and breathe deep, you'll get used to it.

I squeeze my eyes shut and inhale deeply. After a few breaths my legs start to feel like jelly, my head feels heavy, and the telephone booth starts to shake again like an old lift that doesn't know which way to go, lurching up and down. Nico keeps blowing fresh puffs of smoke into the air and otherwise it's silent, like we're in a cave.

Somebody coughs.

Who is in here, I whisper.

Me, says Nico.

Me, says Jameelah.

Me, says somebody else and when I squint I see Lukas's closed Bambi eyes through the fog of smoke, he's smiling and his long lashes nestle against his white skin. It must be weird for him to be here with us so far from his wide-open habitat, I think, flying

73

ever farther from his green surroundings travelling through the galaxy in a phone booth and even though I don't feel one way or another about Lukas I think it's pretty cool. Who knows maybe his green habitat isn't so green at all, maybe it's not the way I picture it and maybe ours isn't so hot and sharp-edged either, no idea, when you're fucked up life is soft around the edges and everyone's surroundings are the same colour.

Nico and I sit in the back row for the entire bus ride, totally high, singing *we R who we R*. Nico holds my hand with one of his hands and with the other he scribbles *sad* all over the seatback in front of us. I find it hilarious because Lukas and Jameelah are sitting in front of us playing rock paper scissors and the whole thing with Jameelah and Lukas really is sad though maybe I'm reading too much into it all which I often do when I'm wasted. When we hop out at Grunewald there must be twenty of us. Anna-Lena and Nadja prop up Tobi who felt so ill on the bus that he had to puke under a seat.

What did you do to him, says Anna-Lena to Nico nodding at Tobi.

Nothing, says Nico, why is it always my fault?

You don't have to get so fucked up all the time, says Nadja.

Shut up, says Tobi to her, I'm feeling better.

Nico smacks me on the ass as he walks by.

What's wrong with you, I say.

There was something on you.

Haha very funny, I say even though I do think it's funny.

Did you ever notice, he says putting his arm around my shoulders, that they're all stupid, we're the only ones who aren't he says snorting like a horse grazing in winter. Nico doesn't smell like Weleda, if he smells of anything at all it's Nivea but first and foremost he smells like alcohol and cigarettes. Weird, for some reason all the men I like smell like alcohol and cigarettes. Papa smelled that way too when he came home from work in the evening and drank a beer in the living room while I sat in his lap, my nose buried in his clothes, that's exactly the way he smelled.

Where is Jameelah, I ask.

She's up there with whatshisname.

His name is Lukas.

I have no idea what his name is but he's a poof no matter what Jameelah thinks.

You can't say that. Anyway we'll see, there's something brewing today.

That's not your type right?

What do you care, I say punching him in his side.

As if, says Nico grabbing my leg and throwing me over his shoulder.

I scream like an idiot but Nico doesn't put me down until we reach the door to Viovic's house. There's already a lot going on inside, people everywhere you look, even Apollo and Aslagon are there sitting on a giant leather sofa in the living room. Apollo has a porcelain doll in his lap and is bouncing it on his knee like a little kid.

I had one just like it, he says, I was just a little kid and my mother smashed it.

Why, I ask.

I have no idea.

His lower lip is trembling.

Maybe you deserved it, says Aslagon taking the doll and tossing it into the corner before spreading a big piece of paper across the coffee table.

Give me a hand instead, we have stuff to do.

I'm still pretty high. I squeeze my way through the packed

kitchen to the refrigerator and grab a beer and head to the basement. The rehearsal studio is bursting at the seams. Viovic have a couple of go-go dancers on stage, sweet thin boys who strip while Viovic play. Lukas and Jameelah are jumping around in the front row. I try to fight my way over to Jameelah but there's no chance, zero, and anyway I'd probably just be bothering them if I did make it over there so I stay near the door and take a big gulp of beer. For the first time it occurs to me that Lukas and Jameelah kind of look like each other, the same dark hair, same dark eyes. Lukas reminds me of someone else too.

Whenever my beer is empty I go upstairs to the kitchen and then back down where I stand next to the door and every time I see Jameelah and Lukas again I think it will come to me. But I can't think of who it is he reminds me of, not through the entire concert though it could also have something to do with the fact that now I'm not just high I'm totally drunk.

This is our last song, says Viktoria smacking the go-go dancer next to her on the ass just like Nico did to me before, and you, you get back to my dressing room, she says and everybody shouts.

People clap and howl and shout encore and Viovic bow. I clap and look over toward Lukas and Jameelah but I can't make them out in the crowd. Instead I see Anna-Lena standing against the wall next to the stage. She's glaring at the dance floor with a horrified look and when I follow her gaze I see why. Right in the middle of the crowd Jameelah and Lukas are hooking up. I jump up and down and clap like crazy for Viovic but really only for Jameelah because Viovic played as bad as they always do and as I'm clapping it hits me who it is, Lukas looks exactly like the boy in the black and white picture on the shelf at Noura and Jameelah's place, the photo of Jameelah's brother Youssef, and then I stop clapping because I get a tight feeling in the pit of my stomach but it could just be from all the beer.

The house is absolutely jammed but Viovic just disappear. In the kitchen it looks like a bomb has gone off. Somebody must have tried to bake a cake, the sack of flour has exploded. The entire kitchen is covered in a layer of flour.

Where are Viovic, I ask a guy with green hair sitting at the kitchen table munching on tiramisu out of a tupperware container.

They're cruising around in their father's Jaguar, he says grinning, they're out of their minds but it's pretty funny, eh?

I go into the living room. The first thing I see is the porcelain doll hanging upside down from the chandelier. Its long hair has been cut off and its skirt is dangling down over its face and you can see its underwear. Below the doll Apollo and Aslagon are writhing around on the floor.

You miserable dog, shouts Apollo pointing at the doll, why do you always do this, why do you always destroy anything beautiful?

It's a sign, Aslagon screams back, everything breaks eventually, sooner or later everything rots.

Cut it out, screams Nico opening the door to the terrace. Apollo and Aslagon disappear into the garden. I sit down next to Nico on the sofa. For a second I wonder whether he's just been sitting here in this same spot the whole time on the couch with the bong in front of him and his lunchbox in his lap filled with his magic mixture. I take the bong, stuff a bud in, and when I finish smoking up I roll myself up next to Nico like a ferret and I'm out immediately. At some point, no idea how much later, the room gets loud again.

The transmission's fucked, my father's going to kill us, says somebody, and turn the music down the neighbours are complaining.

I open my eyes, I'm dizzy and nauseous and the shitty beer

is gurgling in my stomach. The first party casualties are lying around the room passed-out and I wonder how long I've been asleep.

Where is Jameelah, I think, and go to stand up but can't manage it. Nico picks me up and carries me upstairs. The next thing I know I land softly on a mattress.

Here, drink this, says Nico holding out a glass of water, and after I do I feel a bit better. I take off my socks and skirt and lie down under the white sheets.

Thanks, I say, and Nico leans down and kisses me. I kiss him back as best I can but I'm still feeling dizzy, I grope for his belt and take off my t-shirt but whenever I close my eyes everything spins.

Shit, I mumble, I have to go to the bathroom.

You need to sleep cutie, says Nico buckling his belt again.

Yeah but first I need to go to the bathroom.

In the hall I feel my way along the wall when somebody suddenly looms toward me.

Do you know where the bathroom is I want to ask but then I realize it's Jameelah in front of me wearing a bathrobe that's way too big for her.

Where's the bathroom I need to get there right away, I say.

Down there, I have to go too, she says looking at me sceptically, is everything okay you look like shit.

Yeah I just need to stick my finger down my throat.

It's cool in the bathroom. I grab the longest eyeliner pencil I can find on the makeup shelf and stick it as deep as possible in my throat and drop to my knees in front of the toilet. The shitty beer and the noodles with ketchup from home shoot into the toilet and I can't remember the last time I felt so relieved.

I have to pee, says Jameelah fidgeting around next to me,

78

hurry up.

Finished, I say filling up a cup with water and sitting down on a big laundry basket.

What's going on with Lukas?

Jameelah gives the thumbs-up as she pees.

He's lying down in the next room.

Where?

In the father's room.

What do you mean, their father has his own bedroom?

Yeah he snores so bad that's why. What about you and Nico?

We kissed but nothing more is going to happen tonight I'm too fucked up.

Jameelah pulls up her underwear and sits down on the toilet seat wrapping her arms around herself.

Do you think it hurts, she asks looking at the floor.

What?

What do you think.

Oh, right. I don't know.

Do you think it'll bleed a lot?

I have no idea, that's the sort of thing you always know better than me.

Half of all women don't bleed at all.

See.

I go to open the door but Jameelah grabs my arm.

Nini, she says, if it really does happen tonight what should I do with the sheets?

What do you mean, I ask.

You know, if I bleed. What should I do with the bloody sheets?

She looks at me like she's being shipped off to a war zone.

We know how it works, I say, we've practised with frogs and corpses, we've practised it all.

Yeah, she says shrugging her shoulders, still it's different now.

79

You don't have to if you don't want to, I say.

Yes I do. And it has to be Lukas, definitely, says Jameelah, he trapped that animal for me.

Maybe it will hurt, maybe it will bleed, but maybe not, I say.

It really is a little like being in a war, I think, and I wonder why nobody else ever thought of it. War hurts and causes blood but Tarik said the bad part about war isn't the pain or the blood but the way war changes people and the fact that nothing is ever the same again after a war. For a second I'm really happy that I'm too fucked up to sleep with Nico tonight.

So?

What?

So what do I do with the sheets?

Oh right, just throw them in the laundry.

The next morning I go to the room where Jameelah and Lukas are sleeping and cautiously open the door. Nobody's there and the sheets are still on the bed. I wander through the entire house, there are party casualties passed-out all over the floor, I have to step over them but none of them is Jameelah. Apollo and Aslagon are asleep in the garden, lying together like spoons. I walk past flower beds and keep going farther into the backyard. In the farthest corner next to a pond with goldfish in it I find her sitting with her bare feet dangling in the water.

So, I say letting my feet plunk into the water next to her, how was it?

It wasn't.

What do you mean?

Nothing happened, says Jameelah, he fell asleep at some point or pretended to and when I woke up just now he was gone.

He must have got scared.

Scared of what, why, I don't get it, says Jameelah, like women are so mysterious.

I want to say something nice but I can't think of anything, like always, so we just sit there next to each other in silence and stare at the pond and the duckweed and water lilies floating in it. The sun shines down on us, it could actually turn out to be a nice day.

I told him I loved him, says Jameelah scaring a goldfish with her foot, I should have let it be.

There's no reason to run away from love, I say but Jameelah doesn't react, she just continues to stare into the dark green pond as if the water has the answer but wants to stay out of it, like the pond is thinking let them learn for themselves. An old lady walks through the garden next door accompanied by a young couple, a couple that looks like they're getting married soon. The way they move, they seem to sway with the anticipation of the future, her in a flowery dress and long flowing hair, him with a jumper draped over his shoulders and tied around his neck like a pair of tennis socks. They look happy but I can see that the woman's hair is thin, right on the border of being too thin to wear down like that.

Listen, I say nudging Jameelah, someday you're going to look like those two over there, walking through a pretty garden feeling happy, with or without Lukas, I'll bet.

Pfff, someday, says Jameelah. Now, right now they are happy but someday they'll split up. People like that think life is like Play-Doh, that you can make anything out of it, but someday life will rip them apart and this morning in their garden will be nothing more than a memory, a memory so painful that they'll wish they never even experienced it. Someday they'll cry the hardest over the moments that made them happiest. Those idiots still believe in the idea of good.

Belief, I say, is wanting things to be true that you know are actually impossible.

Jameelah stares at me.

Where'd you find that quote?

Nowhere, I thought it up myself.

Her mouth begins to crack a smile.

Hermione or something?

Shove it up your Hermione, I say.

You should write a book of, what's it called, a book full of expressions you say.

Haha, no you should, I say though in reality I'm really happy because I was worried Jameelah had forgotten how to smile.

Come on let's get out of here already or else we'll go through another round of garden-depression.

We get our clothes together and step carefully over the passed-out partygoers in the living room. On the sofa directly beneath the porcelain doll that's still hanging from the chandelier Anna-Lena is sleeping with her rucksack next to her. She looks so normal in her sleep, probably because the creases on her forehead are taking a break while she sleeps.

Wait, whispers Jameelah leaning over Anna-Lena's rucksack and rummaging around in it.

Are you nuts, I whisper, her of all people.

I just want to get Lukas's number off her phone, she whispers.

Hurry up, I whisper.

I don't want to think about what Anna-Lena would do if she woke up right now but there's an empty bottle of apple schnapps next to her which puts me at ease.

What the hell is this?

Jameelah stares at a book that she's pulled out of Anna-Lena's rucksack. *The Modern Witch's Spell Book* it says and when Jameelah opens it a photo of Lukas falls out. Jameelah's face goes

82

white and her eyes get dark with jealousy and I take a step back and almost stumble over a body on the floor but only almost because Jameelah grabs my arm and says come on let's get out of here.

The Modern Witch's Spell Book, she screams as we're on the way to the bus stop, see I knew Anna-Lena was a witch. She holds the book up to the sky like the Bible and her thousand bracelets jangle in my face.

It's nothing new, I say.

And Lukas, of course she wants to put a spell on him because she can't get him, that's the way it is, our Frieda Giga always putting spells on nice girls with her fucking *love you my angel* it makes me puke, I've had enough!

The bus is coming, I say pointing at the yellow double-decker monster coming around the corner.

We start running and gasping for air as we try to stay with the bus as it overtakes us. The bus driver takes pity on us probably thinking that we're a couple of the good little kids who live in this neighbourhood and need to get to our piano lesson.

Once we're sitting on the bus we catch our breath and I say give it to me and take the book out of her hand and the photo falls out again.

Be careful, she says and I'd never be able to bend down as quickly as she disappears beneath the seat and I hear her shoes scraping against the floor like sandpaper.

Shit, she says and ouch, where is it but then she reappears with the photo in her hand. She wipes it with her t-shirt over and over again like she's in a trance, and I think who put a spell on Jameelah and is something wrong with me because I'm not like that about Nico but then again maybe I just don't love Nico the same way Jameelah loves Lukas.

Ever since Adam cursed Eve for feeding him the forbidden fruit from the tree of knowledge, leading to the expulsion of both from the Garden of Eden, true love has been a bumpy road filled with disappointment it says on the first page and that as a result you should use magic to help things go more smoothly. It's still not clear to me how taking some dirt from a footprint left by the man you love is supposed to win his love.

Who the hell walks through the dirt with their shoes anyway, I say, we don't live on a farm but Jameelah rips the book out of my hand.

There must be more practical things in there, she says, things we can do. Here look *put a droplet of blood on a used tissue then burn it together with a piece of hair of your beloved and sprinkle the ashes on a salad.* That's tough, where would I get a piece of hair from Lukas? It's easy for you, you can just rip one out of Nico's head he wouldn't care why you did it, he does that kind of crap all the time.

You're good, I say, Nico doesn't eat salad, he won't even eat the pickle on a hamburger, for him vegetables are garbage.

Nico, says Jameelah, typical, then she buries her nose in the book again.

I'm dead tired and lean my head against the cool glass of the bus window. It's talking about salad that makes me realize. Even if Nico did like salad it wouldn't matter, I don't need to sprinkle any stupid ashes on his food because Nico loves me anyway. But I can't just say that to Jameelah because it's so different from what she thinks, it's nothing like she thinks, it's nothing like how it is with her and Lukas, no eggbeater starts churning in my stomach when I see him, no magic. No, it's routine. Nico is just there, he was always there, and he will always be there. Which is nice even if it's not magical. You can't have everything, Rainer

84

always says. Rainer talks an awful load of shit but in this particular case he's right.

I nap the rest of the day, listen to three audiobook mysteries and once in a while grab something out of the fridge. Nico comes by in the evening and kind of acts like nothing happened and I realize I'm happy with that but we don't talk too much anyway because we're so tired that we keep yawning.

Nico says sleep well cutie when I take him to the door and then my phone rings, it's Jameelah.

Nini, she says and I hear that she's sniffling.

At first I think something terrible has happened, the house is on fire or Noura has had an accident.

Terrible. What you consider terrible is all relative, says Jameelah, for me there's nothing worse than the fact that he just disappeared, poof, gone, without saying a word.

I don't understand what she's talking about for a second but then I realize she means that idiot Lukas.

Like I'm a piece of meat you don't feel like finishing, like the last bit of a kebab that you can't choke down so you leave it on the plate together with the dirty napkin and you get up and leave quickly and let kebab man clear it all away.

Bullshit I'm sure there's another explanation, I say and then I think I must sound like that stupid police psychologist telling Jasna that there's always another way out no matter what the problem.

Maybe he had to go somewhere this morning, I say.

Like where?

I have no idea, maybe he plays tennis or squash every Friday or does something with his family. People like Lukas always have big families. Or even if the family is small they all like each other

85

so much that they always have to go to some birthday or funeral or one of those whatever you call them, you know, a baby shower.

Tomorrow he's going to Lake Garda, says Jameelah, with Anna-Lena.

So call him.

I don't have his fucking phone number.

Jameelah sighs.

I wish he would get terminally ill and realize on his deathbed that he loves me. I hope that when he dies they find a box hidden under his bed or someplace that has a photo of me in it, me cut out of that group photo from the ski trip you know, and a letter that he was too scared to give me and that I'm the last person he sees before he dies and he knows that I found the box.

I have to admit that I don't really understand what she means with the box and all that, but I do know there is one thing I just can't take, and that is when Jameelah is distraught. It's hard to explain, but when she's distraught the whole world seems to start trembling like in an earthquake and Jameelah who is like a tower, not just any tower, a famous tower and you know that as long as that tower is standing everything is alright, the other buildings and lesser towers can all crumble as long as that one tower, Jameelah, is still standing, and so I start racking my brain for the right thing to say to her now.

Jameelah says nothing, just sniffles now and again, but I'm so damn tired and my head is so empty and it's so quiet on the other end of the line.

This is going to sound crazy, says Jameelah at some point, but will you cast a love spell with me tomorrow?

Sure, I say.

We have to be naked to do it.

Naked? Why?

Yeah you know there are very few love spells you can cast

without hair or fingernails. But I did find one, it's just that to do it you have to walk naked through a flower garden and throw rose petals, that's it really. Oh, you also have to concentrate on your beloved and keep saying his name too. But no hair or anything weird like that, no ashes in a salad.

Where are we going to find a flower garden, I ask.

I thought we could do it at the playground, there's a few flowers growing there.

Naked?

Yeah, it has to be at midnight anyway. I mean, otherwise it could be a bit difficult.

And what about the rose petals?

In the park, Tiergarten. We don't need too many.

Okay I'll do it with you.

Of course I'll do it. I'll do anything as long as it means Jameelah won't be so distraught.

THE NEXT MORNING I RING THE BELL AT AMIR'S PLACE BUT nobody answers. I ring it again and again until Tarik finally opens the door. He looks tired and it occurs to me that I haven't seen him since the whole incident with Jasna happened.

Is Amir home, I ask.

Yeah but Amir can't come out right now kiddo, Tarik says, Amir has to stay home and help me.

Can I talk to him for a second, it won't take long.

No kiddo, that won't work, says Tarik, really.

Has something happened?

No nothing happened. Go home, go out and enjoy your school break.

What about Amir?

Amir has other things to do right now.

I go back across the playground to our apartment.

What's up, I wonder, why can't Amir come out, it's not really summer break if Amir isn't around. Maybe Tarik is going to start locking Amir in the apartment too, no idea, but wait why would he. Tarik doesn't mean us any harm, he's just trying to keep the family together, that's what Amir said, because Tarik's the oldest and the oldest has to keep the family together, he said, but all I could think was what is there to hold together, honestly, everything's already in tatters, even more so than with me or Jameelah.

88

Jameelah comes over in the evening. Mama phones Noura to tell her that Jameelah is staying over at our place. This time it's actually true, at least halfway. We put on our pyjamas and cart a bunch of food into my room and then the doorbell rings and when I open it Amir is standing there.

Can I come in for a second, he says.

Man, I say, I tried you a thousand times.

I don't have a lot of time, he says.

He looks pale and gaunt, the corners of his mouth are cracked, and the splotch under his eye is still blue. It looks like nothing on him can heal at the moment. He's holding a Reebok shoebox that's taped shut.

I want you to take care of this, he says, in case something happens to me or whatever you have to keep it for me.

What's going to happen to you, come on don't scare me.

It's not about dying or whatever, everything's fine. So you'll take care of it for me?

It's not about dying, what do you mean it's not about dying, what are you talking about?

Settle down, says Amir, it was just an example, man, girls always panic straight away. I just want you to look after the box, don't open it no matter what happens, just look after it. Will you do it?

Sure I'll look after it, I say, but you can still tell me what's up.

No matter what happens don't open it. Promise.

I promise.

Don't worry, says Amir, everything's fine.

Right, everything's fine, the hell it is, I say. But Amir just gets up, mumbles goodbye and leaves me standing there with the stupid shoebox. Jessi comes running out.

Who was it, she asks.

Nobody, get lost.

It was Amir, she says, I'm not stupid. What's up with him, does he have AIDS or something? He looks so messed up.

No but you're going to get AIDS if I hear about you hooking up with random boys at the swimming pool again.

What?

Anna-Lena told me at the pool the other day. I find out about everything, understand?

Oh that, says Jessi, that was just Pepi, she says giggling, I've been kissing him since kindergarten.

She points at the box.

Is that from Amir?

It's none of your business.

Tell me what's in it, Jessi screams throwing one of her puffy slippers at me as I walk away.

Quiet, shouts Mama from the living room, or I'll boil you both in a cauldron.

I slam the door to my room shut.

Where were you, says Jameelah.

Amir, I say shoving the box under the bed, I'm supposed to look after that in case something happens to him.

Jameelah picks up the box and shakes it. Something knocks around inside.

Do you get it?

Nope.

Something's not right, I say, but I can't get a word out of him.

You can't help someone who doesn't want to be helped, says Jameelah.

That's stupid.

No it's an ancient Irani saying.

More like an ancient irony saying.

Jameelah smiles.

You are the true queen of O-language do you know that?

Yeah but that won't help Amir.

Come on you know him, says Jameelah, he loves to be asked. He's just waiting for us to squeeze it out of him. We'll grab him tomorrow and you'll see how much he talks once we plead with him a little.

Yeah, I say shoving the box under my bed again and hoping Jameelah's right.

We watch *Gilmore Girls* and later, once Mama has fallen asleep, we watch one of Rainer's pornos and almost die laughing. Rainer thinks he has them well hidden under a loose floorboard in the kitchen closet. But come on, people stick things under loose floorboards in every single bad movie and it wouldn't even surprise me if Jessi had also discovered them.

When we finally leave the apartment just before eleven-thirty we wear nothing but long tank-tops and flip-flops with no under-wear but that's not really because of the spell, it's because it was so hot all day and barely cooled off after dark. Out of the bushes next to the playground we pull the plastic grocery bag stuffed with the rose petals we nicked from Tiergarten earlier that after-noon and the Müller milk container, the Mariacron, maracuja juice, and milk and climb up the slide to the play fort.

Now we just have to wait for midnight, says Jameelah, pouring the chocolate milk out of the Müller container and mixing the juice, milk, and brandy and stirring it with her long fingers. We take turns drinking Tiger Milk, we look into the sky and say nothing, we just let life float by because we have so much time, because the clock has only just struck fourteen minutes past birth, meaning that we have almost fifty minutes of life to go, and that's a long time. A bird sings off in the distance somewhere, very loud, almost as if it realizes how nicely it sings.

That's a nightingale, says Jameelah, there's a lot of them around here, even more than in Bavaria, and there's supposed to be so much more nature there, pfff, as if.

Is that another question from the citizenship test?

No I read it in the free paper on the U-bahn, says Jameelah blowing cigarette smoke into the sky. I hope it all goes well.

Of course it will, what could go wrong with a love spell, I say.

I mean at the immigration office you idiot, says Jameelah looking at the clock, it's exactly midnight. She lifts her tank-top over her head, grabs the grocery bag and smiles at me.

Here we go.

I have to admit I feel like an idiot running around the playground naked like that, tossing rose petals as I go. Actually the whole rose petal thing isn't so bad, but having to whisper the name is annoying. When you say Nico over and over it doesn't even sound like his name after a while, and it makes me lightheaded, so at some point I just scatter the petals. The grass is sunburned and rustles beneath my feet, and as I watch the rose petals fall past my legs to the ground I suddenly feel tiny. I don't know if it has something to do with the darkness or it's just because I don't have anything on, but for whatever reason, here on this playground, where I learned to walk and to ride a bike and to roller skate, all of a sudden I feel too small for this world, like you could just stick me anywhere, the same way you shove a vacuum cleaner in a dark corner and nobody notices it, like you could just make my naked body disappear because it's so small and unimportant.

Jameelah hops around the playground doing pirouettes and the rose petals flutter around her like confetti. I can't help but smile and I think to myself, come on, don't do it like that, it's too funny. I run back to the middle of the sandbox where the shopping bag is, hoping secretly that we'll run out of rose petals soon, and that's when I see someone coming toward the playground.

Someone's coming I hiss and grab the bag.

Luckily Jameelah understands what's happening immediately and we run as fast as possible up the slide and hide inside the play fort. At first I think the person's just going to pass through the playground but that's not the case, the person comes straight toward us, limping, goes around the sandbox, past our hiding place, and over to the trees, stopping directly under Amir's linden tree.

Jasna, whispers Jameelah.

What's she doing here?

No idea.

Beneath Amir's linden tree a lighter clicks and smoke starts to rise.

Can't we just get out of here I say, we're done with the spell right?

Let's wait to see if the evil Sorb shows up, says Jameelah.

Why, I ask, looking around for my shirt.

So you can throw a rock at his head says Jameelah smiling at me, then you'd finally be even.

I don't want to be naked anymore, it's cold, or maybe it's not but either way I want to put some clothes on right away. But then Jameelah whispers, shhhh, someone's coming, but it's not the evil Sorb, and when I realize who it is I know it's too late. It's Tarik I can tell from his gait, he's the only one who walks like that, with his left leg dragging behind a little. They both limp now, I think, how weird, but then again it's not that weird since they are siblings after all.

Keep your head down, whispers Jameelah.

For a second I think Tarik's seen us but actually he's just checking things out. He lifts an arm and motions around at the rose petals. Jasna shrugs and takes a drag from her cigarette, not really looking at him, staring at the ground, looking past him, fidgeting with her hair or whatever.

Why don't they just make up, I whisper.

Jameelah shrugs her shoulders.

Why can't they just make up, I think, if for no other reason than for Amir and Selma, but also just because, I mean, at the end of the day you always have to make up. Me and Jameelah do all the time no matter how bad a fight we've had and I even make up with Jessi every time. In the end you always have to make up.

Can you hear what they're saying, Jameelah whispers.

Not a single word.

Shit, she says, shhhh I say, and Tarik says something or other.

What, says Jameelah.

Shhhh, I say again, because otherwise you can't get a word of what he's saying.

At one point he says something about family and feet, then something about speaking and helping. Jasna leans her head back and laughs like he's just told a great joke. She sucks on her cigarette and runs a hand along the bark of Amir's linden tree, she stands there and then blows out the smoke as if Tarik is nothing more than the air that she's exhaling. Tarik keeps speaking to her. I can't understand a word of it until Jasna suddenly interrupts him. Her voice gets loud, Tarik flinches, and she says something about in the past and couldn't stick up for myself, but now, says Jasna. But Tarik interrupts her and Jasna flicks her cigarette butt away and blows her last drag of smoke right in Tarik's face. Not your cleaning lady I hear her say and then they switch to Bosnian and it sounds like they are really fighting. Bosnian, Bosnian, Bosnian. It seems like forever until Jasna finally says, I can't do anything about it, but I can't under-

94

stand what Tarik answers. I just see him kick Amir's linden angrily with his bum leg.

Man that must hurt, I think, but then I remember that his leg is made out of metal or something.

You should be ashamed I hear him say, loudly and precisely, like the other day at the pool, only this time it's Jameelah who flinches. Jasna doesn't react at all. She just lights another cigarette and starts talking again, so quietly that we can't catch a single word.

Then, loud enough for us to hear, she says it's not fair, and suddenly everything is silent. I see Tarik take a deep breath, I see how his upper body straightens and then relaxes again. There's a weird calm, though it's not really calm, not when Tarik is standing there perfectly still, with his arms so stiff you'd think he had razor blades in his armpits. We crouch in the wooden play fort and peek through the gaps between the slats. My knees are boring deeper and deeper into the floor planks and it hurts, and even though I know it hurts I barely feel it, especially when Tarik starts doing something really strange. He turns away from Jasna and walks around the sandbox in big, slow steps.

He's completely lost his chador whispers Jameelah.

Jasna leans against Amir's linden tree and smokes, staying very still, just her cigarette hand moving up to her mouth and back down, just her eyes following Tarik like she's watching a wild animal, the kind of animal you're not sure has rabies or not. When Tarik is standing in front of her again he puts his hands up to his eyes and his whole body starts to shake.

Is he crying whispers Jameelah.

Jasna lets her cigarette fall to the ground and stamps it out thoroughly. She goes to hug Tarik but he won't let her. There's no way to hear what he says to her, the words spill out of him half spoken, half moaned. All I catch is fate and goodbye and

95

Jasna nods. It's so quiet that you can hear her fingernails tapping on the bark of Amir's linden and then Tarik steps over to Jasna and pulls her tightly to him.

See, I whisper, in the end you always have to make up, but Jameelah doesn't react. She's staring down at Jasna and Tarik as if she's in a trance. Jasna has her hands on Tarik's back and Tarik has his on hers. They sway slowly to a rhythm only the two of them can hear, back and forth.

Are they dancing?

I think so.

Jameelah giggles softly.

See, he can dance. I mean, it's not the lambada, but still.

Tarik and Jasna dance and they both start to cry, practically groaning, and it's not a happy sound – it's more like they're saying goodbye forever. Who knows, I think, maybe Jasna is leaving and they're never going to see each other again. And even though I'm relieved I suddenly get very sad because all sorts of memories race through my mind, memories of earlier times.

Tarik's entire body is still shaking and he doesn't seem to want to let Jasna go and he keeps stuttering – to be honest it looks really odd and Jasna keeps groaning louder and louder, so loud that I think to myself that's weird, but then again they were all weirdly loud back when their father died, too, the whole family and all the relatives, all sorts of men with strings of beads in their hands and all of them howling like wolves all day and all night so loud that everyone up and down the street could hear them. Frau Stanitzek wanted to call the cops but Jameelah told her that's what they do when someone dies and anyway it would be over soon enough but suddenly Jasna turns to the side and holds her hand to her stomach. I can see that something is dripping from her mouth and then she keels over. She just falls over and not like a person with arms and legs but like a statue, lifeless, like a statue falling off its pedestal. That's the way she hits the ground too, she smacks the ground and lays there as still as a stone.

Tarik looks around in a panic. I want to jump up and tell him we're here and say yeah we'll explain later why we're naked but let us help now but as if she senses it Jameelah puts an ice cold hand on my shoulder and yanks me to the floor and shoves her other hand over my mouth. I want to tear myself away from her and scream but Jameelah just holds me tighter.

His right hand, whispers Jameelah, look at his right hand and then all I hear is her terrified breathing rasping in my ear. Tarik bends down. He stays there for a while squatting next to Jasna, a knife in his right hand. Then he stands up and starts to back away first really slow and then faster and faster until finally he turns around and limps off as fast as he can go. My head, my heart, everything is pulsing like crazy, my mouth is so dry it feels like I've smoked a hundred cigarettes. Jameelah is still holding me down.

Let go of me I whisper.

Slowly she loosens her grip. I stretch out my legs, which have fallen asleep, and push them against the opposite wall of the play fort. In the old days people bit down on a piece of wood to deal with pain, that's what Herr Wittner said one time, and that's what I try to do now with my whole body, wedging myself between the walls of the play fort and pressing until I realize I'm too big to stretch out in here anymore, I can't sit inside the fort and stretch my legs all the way out the way I have for my entire life up here in this fort at the top of the slide. I'm too big now.

Fuck fuck fuck.

Fuck fuck fuck.

I have no idea how long we sit up there. Time and concepts like up and down have ceased to exist, it's like we're in space, the play fort floats through the great beyond with us inside, there's not a sound, no nightingale no nothing, just Jameelah's voice whispering fuck fuck fuck as regularly as if she's counting off a game of rock paper scissors, just that and her breathing and her chest going up and down, just our naked bodies, our skin, and beneath it the fear coursing through our veins like blood.

Fuck fuck fuck.

Fuck fuck fuck.

Jameelah jumps up.

Fuck she says are we fucking crazy? Let's get out of here.

She throws me my tank-top and my fingers are ice cold I realize as I slip it on. We cautiously climb down the slide, everywhere rose petals, rose petals all around. We walk hand in hand across the lawn.

Jasna is laying there. The light from a streetlamp falls on her face. The left side of her body is all red, everything soaked with blood. Something is dripping from her mouth but it's only when we get near her that I can see what it is. Vomit.

Careful whispers Jameelah, don't step in anything.

She's dead I whisper, really dead.

Jameelah nods.

She's dead, you can see it in her eyes. They're not looking anywhere, they're gone, no longer on earth. It's like in that YouTube video where a group of men hunt down a woman and kill her in the street in some hot country, they used a knife, too, and now Jameelah and I are standing in front of Jasna exactly the same as in that video, except we don't have a camera.

The engagement ring is on her finger.

The ring, I say.

Jameelah continues to stare at Jasna's dead body. She's still holding the container of Tiger Milk in her hand. I wonder how she managed to get down the slide holding the Tiger Milk and the bin bag. A nightingale sings up above us somewhere and it sounds horrible.

The ring, I say again.

Shut your mouth says Jameelah and then she bends down and with trembling fingers takes the hairband out of Jasna's hair and drops it into the Tiger Milk.

What are you doing I ask.

Don't ask just help me, she says, then she brushes Jasna's hair back and reaches behind her ears and undoes the giant gold hoop earrings and drops them into the Tiger Milk.

Come on says Jameelah, her watch, her bracelets, her rings, all of it, put it all in the container like we always do, that's cheap, real cheap, got it?

I don't ask. I squat down next to Jameelah and carefully remove a gold bracelet and then another and another, dropping one after the other into the Tiger Milk. We work silently and one piece of jewellery after the next plunks into the Tiger Milk until Jameelah looks away for a second and I take the engagement ring off Jasna's finger. It comes off easily because it's too big for her. But it fits me. It fits me perfectly.

Come on, says Jameelah, let's get out of here.

We stumble down the dirt path to the entrance to the yard, the clip-clop of our flip-flops echoing behind us. Why didn't anyone ever tell us this could happen here I ask myself, why didn't anyone ever tell us it could happen here.

* * *

As I put the key into the lock I noticed how much my hand was shaking. I was so scared that Jessi might hear us – that she'd be standing in the hall with her giant puffy slippers asking us questions – so I stuck in the key and opened the lock as quietly as

I could. Jessi had laid down on the sofa with Mama, all four of her limbs splayed out. She had on her bathrobe and her puffy slippers and Mama was snoring softly.

We went into my room and put on our pyjamas.

I'm cold Jameelah said so I went into the kitchen and warmed up some milk. While I was warming the milk I kept thinking I had dried blood on me but it was just my imagination. It's just that it seemed so real because of the tiny red hearts all over my pyjamas. I went to the bathroom and washed my hands two or three times and then the milk was warm and Jameelah and I drank it in bed.

I didn't sleep I just pretended I was asleep and Jameelah didn't really sleep either, I know because she laid there too still and too compact, different from the way she normally slept. I did it to try to calm Jameelah and I don't know but I bet she probably did it for the same reason.

At one point I went to the bathroom even though I didn't need to go. I sat on the edge of the bathtub and stared at the ring. The green stone in the middle wasn't really green it was dark-green, almost black, though I guess it could just be its age – maybe gems were like people and if you hadn't seen them for a long time you didn't recognize them at first glance. I wanted to take the ring off and put it in the little basket on the shelf so Mama could find it but it wouldn't come off so I ran my finger under the tap and used soap to pull it off. But then I put it back on.

I couldn't fall asleep forever and all I could think about was how often Jasna had given me cigarettes or gum, how she gave me a henna tattoo once, how we dunked our hands into the warm red liquid and it squished up between our fingers. I laid in bed and wondered again why nobody had told us that it could happen here, and how it would have been easier to bear if Jasna had screamed. Then I would have known that it was Jasna and that her scream could shatter the world like so much glass. There were people who could do that, I'd seen it on TV, but Jasna hadn't screamed she'd just moaned a little. I realized that ever since I was a little kid I'd thought that death was something loud, like in the movies, blood spraying, screams, pieces of flesh flying, but none of that is true. Death is silent, it doesn't make any noise at all, and it smells of rose petals. Death takes you in its arms and softly moans goodbye.

Jameelah fell asleep at some stage but not me, because every time I thought of Jasna I also thought of Tarik. A thousand things popped into my head all at once, even more things than when I thought of Jasna, and not just the lambada and the way he always mimicked MC Hammer. No, also the way he sometimes played with me and Amir, the way he played made-up games with us like plane crash in the Carpathians or left for dead in prison, the way he told us how to lick the moisture off the walls of the prison so we wouldn't die of thirst, or how you could eat the flesh of dead passengers to survive, how that was okay in a situation like a plane crash. And then I remembered how he gave me a belt for my birthday once, a pink leather belt with rivets. He'd added the rivets himself he said, ten rivets, each with a big glittering stone on it, a happy birthday for each year, Nini, he said, and as all of this flooded into my head I realized it wasn't just Jasna who was dead but Tarik, and that because Tarik had killed Jasna he was even more dead to me than Jasna and then I ran to the bathroom again even though I didn't need to pee, I just needed to cry.

I didn't fall asleep until it was light outside and even then I kept waking up, once because the room smelled so weird, like blood and milk. You're imagining it again, I thought, just like the hearts on my pyjamas, but then I noticed that the Tiger Milk container was sitting on the nightstand and that the smell of blood and milk was coming from there, from the metal jewellery, so I shoved it under the bed next to Amir's box and when I saw Amir's box I thought for a second I should just open it.

I wake up at one. I go to Kaufland and buy cornflakes. Back home Jameelah and I eat cornflakes in bed. Jameelah just stares at the wall and shovels cornflakes into her mouth and she reminds me of Mama with her blank hazy look, and just like with Mama I'm afraid to ask what she's thinking about and I just rub my eyes and figure she'll say something at some stage, probably something about the jewellery or whatever, but she doesn't and there's just the murmuring sound of cornflakes crunching.

What are we going to do now, I ask at some point.

Just wait, says Jameelah, believe me I know how to act in a situation like this.

I don't really understand but Jameelah calmly drinks the milk out of her cereal bowl and then says you can't rush into anything, you can't make a move without considering it carefully do you understand, she says, normal thinking doesn't apply anymore, one thing following from another, waiting to see what happens, no way. Now you have to stay out ahead, your thoughts galloping out in front of events, always a step ahead.

I nod and keep eating my cornflakes.

Time ticks away and we lie in bed without saying a word. At some point I lean down and pull the Tiger Milk out from under the bed and put it on the nightstand.

What's the story with this stuff, I say, do we go to the cops with it?

No. We have to get rid of it, all of it.

Get rid of it why, I ask, why did we even take it?

102

I don't know.

What do you mean you don't know, you had a plan for the jewellery.

No I didn't.

Yes you did.

No, I did not. It was just an impulse.

Impulse, I shout jumping up from bed, you had an impulse? You've lost your chador I shout. Why did we take the fucking jewellery, tell me right this second why we took it!

I don't know says Jameelah quietly, burying her face in her hands, and anyway you did it too.

No I only did it because you did, because I thought you had a plan.

What the hell kind of plan was I supposed to have had?

I have no idea, maybe something to do with your beliefs or whatever, or maybe to take the stuff to the police to prove something or other.

What fucking beliefs screams Jameelah, since when do I have beliefs and why am I always supposed to know everything and have a plan?

It feels like my skull is vibrating.

Jameelah gets up, drinks the Tiger Milk in one gulp and dumps the jewellery into the grocery bag with the bottles.

What do we do with it now, I ask.

We'll deal with it later, Jameelah says, I have to go home.

I put the grocery bag on my dresser. We slowly get dressed and I double-knot the laces on my Chucks. Mama and Jessi are watching TV and fortunately don't pay any attention to us. We head out but the playground is all cordoned off. There's a tarp ringing Amir's linden tree and a bunch of men in black jackets are standing around drinking coffee while one of them picks up all the rose petals with a litter picker like the one we use in

103

Tiergarten.

Great now we have to go all the way around, what a bunch of shit, says Jameelah but all I can do is look up at the play fort and the slide and at the cloudy sky above and that's when I see it as clearly as the digits that Rainer's alarm clock projects onto the ceiling above the bed, I see our clock which yesterday had only just struck fourteen minutes past birth, meaning we had about another fifty to go, is now at twenty-past, meaning we've only got another forty minutes of life left. That's not possible I think but then again maybe it is, what do I know.

The pavement in front of the building is full of journalists. They've brought their cameras and are leaning on their gangly legs against the building's façade drinking coffee, the crap coffee Frau Stanitzek sells, and talking, smoking, laughing. I'd love to know what there is to laugh about here.

Should we really go over there?

Of course, says Jameelah, I know how to act in a situation like this. We'll do it just like Hollywood actors. Hold your backpack to your chest like it's as precious as a Louis Vuitton and then we'll shove our way through them all slick and cool and if they get pushy we just say no comment like Angelina, you know. Sunglasses would be helpful but who cares we can do it without them, okay?

Okay I say, got it.

It's not so bad that we don't have sunglasses with us because they don't actually pay any attention to us. They just stand there staring blankly as we push our way through them to the entryway, which is lit up by the cameras like they're shooting a movie here. Sure enough there's Frau Stanitzek with her mangy pooch in her arms standing in the doorway telling her life story to some creep from the tabloids, talking about her dead husband and her shop and all her fucking health problems and whatever else.

I could tell you things, says Stanitzek, but I won't because I'd just get threatened again. If I said what I really think I might as well close my shop.

Just as we're about to go up the steps and inside a journalist comes up to me, the same woman who was here the time before, when Jasna jumped off the balcony.

Just a broken leg, she says looking at me scornfully, is that still your story?

No comment, I say and press my backpack to my chest.

Jameelah is trying to pull me up the steps when a police car drives down the street with its siren blasting and blue lights flashing. The tabloid reporter leaves Frau Stanitzek standing in front of the doorway.

We go back into the street and I get hot flashes as the door of the police car opens and Tarik gets out. He has Selma in his arms. Together with a police officer Tarik helps his mother out of the car. She hides her face behind a big white handkerchief, a rag so completely soaked with tears that it's see-through and you can see her face shimmering through it like a ghost. Another cop gets out and slams the car door shut and hands Selma a chocolate and tickles her tummy but she just throws the candy on the floor.

Majka, she screams and starts to cry again.

There's your mummy, says the officer pointing at Tarik's mother but Selma just screams louder and squirms in Tarik's arms.

Majka, she screams, Majka.

Tarik puts an arm around his mother. A few journalists shout questions. Tarik answers gallantly as if nothing has happened. That he can be standing on the street here with Selma in his arms like that, it's just not right. God's earth is rotten. It must be. Because if there were any such thing as god or justice then there's no way Tarik could stand there with Selma. If there were then you know what would happen, at this very instant fire would rain down or at the very least frogs would rain down or maybe a giant bolt of lightning would strike Tarik. But it's not raining at all, not even the tiniest spark or most pathetic frog is falling from the sky and the only blitzes of lightning are coming from the cameras.

Have they arrested anyone, the tabloid reporter asks the police officer.

No comment says the officer.

The cameras are glued to Tarik and his mother. Maybe this is all just a movie I think, like one of those gala premieres you see on TV except that we're not the famous actors, Tarik is. The only thing missing is the red carpet and for Tarik to start signing autographs. There's one other thing missing, too. Amir.

Where's Amir I whisper.

Jameelah shrugs her shoulders and at that moment Dragan comes around the corner. When he sees Tarik he stops in his tracks as if he's grown roots then suddenly starts running directly toward Tarik.

Uh oh, I think, and just as I do I also realize I'm scared of Tarik.

I'm going to kill you, you fucking cripple, screams Dragan, you better start praying to your Allah right now!

The two cops try to wrestle Dragan to the ground but it takes a while before they can subdue him even though there are two of them. I can see he has tears in his eyes, tears of rage and tears of grief. Tarik's mother screams, Selma cries even louder, and the journalists stand there with their cameras trained on the scene. All of a sudden I hear someone shout from above.

Get up here this instant!

It's Noura standing in the window staring angrily down at us.

You have no business being down there, says Noura, no business you hear me!

It was by accident, says Jameelah upstairs, we couldn't avoid it, and anyway what happened?

Take your shoes off, there's food.

The table is set in the living room. Noura gently shoves me into a chair and grabs a third plate from the kitchen.

I'm not hungry, says Jameelah.

It's lunchtime and we're going to eat.

But I'm not hungry, Jameelah says again crossing her arms.

Then don't eat, I don't care. But you shouldn't be hanging around downstairs, says Noura.

What happened, asks Jameelah again.

That poor girl, dead, Noura says, they murdered her, little Jasna.

Really, says Jameelah with a look of disbelief on her face, why, or, I mean, who?

There's no reason why, says Noura passing me the bowl of parsley salad, it's just the evil in the world.

I'm not hungry either but I don't want her to notice so I take some salad. I guess this is what Jameelah means by staying a few steps ahead, ask questions first so you know what everyone else knows, your thoughts always galloping out in front of events, but I don't think I can make my brain get out ahead, it's like with maths and science, I just can't do it, it makes me dizzy trying and so I stare at a piece of tomato in the salad. That's what you do if you don't want to lose your balance, you keep your eyes on a fixed point.

Do they know who did it, asks Jameelah.

They took the entire family to the police station, says Noura.

Amir too, I ask.

Yeah him also, says Noura.

But Amir's not an evil person, I say.

I know but sometimes, not always, but sometimes, how do you say it the apple doesn't fall far from the tree. These people don't know any other way. All they know is war and sorrow, they're used to it. But we didn't come to Germany to witness this kind of thing, she says putting her hand on Jameelah's shoulder.

Enough Mama, says Jameelah.

No it's true and it scares me.

It's annoying Mama, says Jameelah.

Noura looks at her angrily.

It's annoying that a girl in our building is murdered?

Stop it, screams Jameelah jumping up and running into the kitchen.

Jameelah, calls Noura, then she says something in Arabic and follows her into the kitchen.

I sit alone at the lunch table, just like in the old days when Mama and Papa used to fight. I stare at the cabinet on the opposite wall of the room. In it are black and white photos of Jameelah's father and brother. I stare at the luminescent green parsley salad in front of me, back to the photos in the cabinet, at the salad, at the photos. Stupid Lukas and his stupid green life, I think, if it wasn't for him we'd never have been scattering rose petals at the playground.

They should go back where they came from and all kill each other, I hear Noura say in the kitchen and then she switches to Arabic again and I can't understand. Eventually the voices from the kitchen get softer and softer until they fall silent and there's nothing to hear but faint sobbing, which I understand because crying sounds the same in every language.

I don't want any more and set down the fork and shove the plate with salad on it away from me. I fidget back and forth in my seat as tragedy slinks around beneath the table and brushes my leg. I want to get up and leave, I want to go home. But home, is that where Rainer and Jessi live, where Mama and her sofa are? I don't know. I have no idea where I want to go. I want to climb to the very top of Amir's linden tree so the leaves hide me and nobody can find me. I want to find the ends of the threads sticking out of the branches and hold onto one like an ape, just hang there until somebody puts the world below back to together.

I stand up and go to the window. I brace myself on the windowsill because everything is starting to shake like during an earthquake and I quickly fix my eyes on the street below. The police are still in front of the entryway and Stanitzek is there in her bathrobe with her dog in her arms and I see Tarik standing off to the side with Selma and how she nuzzles him and he gives her a kiss on the forehead.

Enough with staying a few steps ahead. I walk down the hall and bend down to tie my Chucks. That's when Jameelah comes out of the kitchen.

What are you doing, she says.

I'm going downstairs and I'm going to tell them everything.

You can't do that, whispers Jameelah.

Yes I can, I say quickly, but as I move toward the door she grabs me by the arm just as firmly as she did last night.

Let go of me, I say.

I pull my arm but the harder I pull the tighter she holds me, let me go I shout, let me go, but Jameelah's eyes fill with tears which swell over her lower lids and drip down to the corners of her mouth.

Why are you crying I want to say, goddamn it why are you crying, but suddenly I hear a strange noise getting louder and louder, vibrating and wheezing like a train and I think, huh, a train's coming, but there are no tracks near here. It takes a minute before I realize that it's not a train at all but the kettle, just the tea kettle boiling in the kitchen, and then Noura comes into the hall and says we're going to have a nice hot cup of tea together. Jameelah says I'm not thirsty and pulls me into her room.

That's your Tarik, your Teddy Dragon who looks out for everyone, says Jameelah. See what happens to people who don't do what he wants.

We have to go to the police, I say.

Right, so I'll get dragged into the whole thing, says Jameelah looking at me incredulously. No way. I told you already, I know what to do.

So what is it?

For one thing not go to the police.

But we have to tell them who did it.

No we don't. They'll figure it out themselves. Why should we get involved?

Because Tarik is just walking around with Selma in his arms.

Just give them a little time to investigate things.

So we're supposed to just do nothing?

No, but we'll let the police do their job first, there must be evidence or something, says Jameelah letting herself drop onto her bed.

What if there isn't?

We're going to wait. We can always go to the police later. First we have to get rid of this jewellery.

110

Why did we take the jewellery, I say.

We had to do something, says Jameelah, better to do something wrong than to do nothing at all.

Why did we take it, I say, why did we take the fucking jewellery, but there's no answer.

Hanging on the wall behind Jameelah is the padded clothes hanger that we used to play shopkeeper with. Noura had hung half an orange peel from each side, look, she said putting nuts in each orange peel half, it's like a scale. I have no idea why it's still hanging here or why we were able to spend hours and hours playing with it.

Jameelah raises her nose.

Do you have a tissue?

I shake my head. You can hear the TV from the apartment below, someone is jumping from channel to channel.

Do you hear that, I say.

No, says Jameelah even though for sure she hears it because she always complains that Tarik turns the TV up so loud. Tarik in front of the TV with the remote in his hand, his bad leg stretched out, his eyes half closed – that's exactly how he's sitting down there now just a few metres below us with nothing but a thin ceiling separating us from him.

I stand up and say I have to get out of here, I have to do something or I'm going to go crazy.

Me too says Jameelah, let's go do something.

What?

No idea, something nice.

Something cross.

Yeah, something fucking cross.

Come on, I say, let's go to Kurfürsten.

We buy a Müller milk container at Frau Stanitzek's shop and then stop at my place and grab the shopping bag and then walk to the station.

We should get rid of it, says Jameelah grabbing the bottle of brandy, the milk, the maracuja juice and the jewellery and then stuffing the empty bag in a rubbish bin.

Let's throw that out too, I say pointing at the jewellery.

You're an idiot we have to throw it out farther away, says Jameelah. She puts the various containers on a bench and stuffs the jewellery into her backpack. Rose petals are still stuck to the containers.

Hurry the train's coming in three minutes, I say.

We dump the Müller milk out onto the tracks, mix up a batch of Tiger Milk and pour it down our throats.

When the train pulls into the station I can see our reflection in the windows and realize we look messed up. Jameelah's eyes still look like she's been crying and I look a bit like Amir did that time he rang my doorbell and dropped off that box. That time, I think, man, that was only yesterday, which seems impossible, but anyway, looking messed up like this is perfect, it's exactly what the guys on Kurfürstenstrasse are into.

Here, says Jameelah handing me the empty container.

I mix another batch and we drink. The train jerks slowly along the heavy tracks carrying us from station to station, carrying us to the other side of the city, farther and farther away, away from the playground, from Tarik and Noura, from the black and white photos in the cabinet. I wish Jameelah would tell a story like she always does, something completely ridiculous she's just thought up, something hilarious that makes me laugh, something insane that makes me shake my head and say you're nuts, or something only a drunk would think up and I say you're wasted. Just imagine, she should be saying, picture it in your mind, we're at the playground in flip-flops and tank-tops and then Tarik shows up and kills Jasna right in front of our eyes, just like that.

Shut up, I would say, that's too morbid.

My god, Jameelah would say, it's just a story you baby, like having Tiger Milk come out of your breasts or like the thing about the animal Lukas caught for me, it's just a dream. Except it feels like reality and Jameelah doesn't say hey it's just a story she says these fucking rose petals are driving me crazy and she fidgets with her elbow where there are rose petals stuck and with her skirt where there are petals stuck, and she picks them all off and then gathers the ones on the floor and opens the window and throws them out of the train. They flutter away so quickly that you can't even see them go.

Someone has left a smudge on the window with their greasy hair. There's nothing more disgusting than smudges left by greasy hair on the bus or the train. As far as I'm concerned it's another form of shitting on something, all that people leave behind is the foul stuff. The greasy smudge is so disgusting that I can't look away. It's round and the swirl of fine hair in the middle shows where the forehead smacked the window surrounded by the chin, cheek, and tiredness. When you die you have to leave something good behind on earth, that's only clear to me now for the first time and all because of this greasy hair smudge. You have to leave

113

something good behind and it has to be something you can't touch, something clear, something invisible, so that grease and blood and shit aren't the only things left behind. I'm so tired that my eyes keep drooping shut but I make sure that my head doesn't fall against the window. I'm not going to leave a greasy smudge.

Do you think it still worked, asks Jameelah all of a sudden.

What?

The magic. Do you think it will still work even though, well, you know.

You're good I think to myself but what I say is yeah I think so, the one has nothing to do with the other.

I wonder what Lukas is doing right now, says Jameelah looking at me with her big eyes.

Probably swimming. That must be what you do at Lake Garda, right?

Yeah, says Jameelah, probably swimming.

I saw a picture of Lake Garda once at the dentist's office. Everything was green and right in the middle was the blue lake, just the way a holiday is supposed to look.

Yeah and he's swimming in it right now, says Jameelah.

Yeah, I say taking the Tiger Milk out of her hand, he's got it good.

I'm pretty sure I'm drunk but it has never felt as good as it does today. Sometimes alcohol is like medicine, especially when it tastes as good as Tiger Milk, so sweet and fruity, so healthy. I guess that's why there's alcohol in almost every medicine, it makes sense, so clear and invisible. You can wash everything away with it, grease, blood, and shit. You can wipe away the whole of god's rotten earth with alcohol. And then all that would be left behind would be a clean, empty bottle.

* * *

114

I completely forgot that today is Sunday. There's never anything happening on Kurfürsten on Sunday. The guys would rather drive around in the green countryside with their families or go to the movies or whatever it is they do, in any event they don't come here. Not even the woman with the dog and the liquorice skirt is here. The sky is totally overcast. We pull the striped thigh-high stockings out of our backpacks, hop up on our usual electrical box, sit down, pull on the stockings and let our legs dangle.

Nobody's going to come by anyway, I say, and if someone does it'll be someone who's desperate for it.

No, says Jameelah, if someone comes by it'll be a nice guy who has just had a fight with his wife. It'll be someone who drives once around the block and then goes home and makes up.

Or else an old lonely bastard, all the days are the same to them.

Or somebody we know, says Jameelah giggling, just imagine, Herr Wittner or whatever.

He would never do it, I say.

You're so naïve.

I can picture Krap-Krüger, imagine if he turned up here all of a sudden, I say.

Jameelah laughs out loud, jumps down from the electrical box and starts talking in his voice.

Lovely sense of hospitality, the Iraqis, but, she says raising her pointer finger, they violate human rights.

I laugh so hard I nearly keel over.

Jameelah hops back up next to me on the electrical box and we let our legs dangle and look at the empty street.

What did he mean anyway, I ask.

Who, mean with what?

Krap-Krüger about human rights in Iraq.

Yeah, well, it's still a war zone, says Jameelah, not officially. It's not as bad as it was before but life is still grim there, it's like a mini-war all the time. That's what Krap-Krüger meant. And it's true. But what's it to him, he should take care of his own shit.

That's why you came here.

Exactly, says Jameelah.

But your father and Youssef, I say cautiously, they died there.

Jameelah nods.

Did it have something to do with human rights?

They died because my father got involved. But also because of human rights, because a lot of people in Iraq still go by an eye for an eye, says Jameelah taking another swig. Everyone has to get involved, wherever you go. But it just makes things worse.

Is that why you cried like that, I ask softly.

Jameelah doesn't say anything. She grabs her tobacco out of her rucksack along with the filters, the rolling papers, her zippo. I look at her hands and her black polished fingernails, her tongue as she licks the paper.

When something bad happens my mother always fears for us, says Jameelah, it's from before. She flicks the zippo.

What did your father do that was so bad?

Listen do you not want to understand or are you really that stupid or both, she says looking at me angrily. If there's no human rights then you don't die because you did something bad but because nobody protects you, even Krap-Krüger understands that.

Sorry, I say.

Sorry my ass, says Jameelah.

For a while neither of us says anything.

Sorry, Jameelah says at some point, but you know I really don't want to think about it or talk about it or anything else.

116

Not now, understand, not when everything is so uncertain. I just don't get it, I mean, they can't just send us away.

Stop saying that, I say, they're not going to send you away, you're crazy.

Jameelah frowns.

My mother, she says, I think she must have done something wrong.

Done something wrong, how?

No, not done something wrong, just said something stupid at the immigration office, something they shouldn't know or something they didn't need to know.

Like what?

Nothing bad, says Jameelah, nothing illegal or whatever if that's what you're thinking.

I'm not thinking anything.

It's nothing like that, it's just that my mother always wants to be so correct about things you know, always wants to be totally honest.

I know, I would never think she'd done anything bad, it's more that I think you're getting worried over nothing, I say and take her hand. But she pulls her hand away and jumps down from the electrical box and walks over toward a car that's cruising past very slowly. The window is rolled down. The guy at the wheel of the car is bald, he looks old, he has to be over forty, and he's not the best looking guy either.

So, says the guy, got any plans for the day?

It'll cost a hundred euros, says Jameelah leaning down to the open window all slick and cool.

The guy rummages around in his glove box and then hands her two fifty euro notes and she tucks the money into the top of one of her stockings. I have to smile because it always looks so real, as if we're real hookers, only this time with the whole leaning-into-the-car-window thing it looks almost like *Pretty Woman*.

Just a second, says the guy as we are about to get into his car. He points at a baby seat secured to the backseat, I have to put that in the trunk, he says.

When he's done with that he says step right up, like at the circus. I have to laugh. The interior of the car smells like the pine tree air freshener hanging from the rearview mirror and there are cookie crumbs all over the backseat. At my feet is a ten-pack of Capri Sun juice packs that must be for his kid.

I'm Stella Stardust by the way, says Jameelah, and this is my friend Sophia Saturna.

Can I have one, I ask holding up a Capri Sun.

Sure says the guy stepping on the accelerator.

We wouldn't even have needed to go in the car since the guy drives only a couple of blocks and then stops in front of a Thai bar at Nollendorfplatz. Thai bars all look the same with pink neon out front and the windows full of little Buddhas and those golden cats with the left arms that wave nonstop. Those cats scare me. Inside everything is sparkling clean, the bar, the little tables with the plastic flowers and candles in the middle, the floor, the windowsills. Everything looks as if it's constantly mopped and wiped down, even the fruit machine that's sitting in the corner next to the little dance floor.

Have you ever seen a place so clean I whisper to Jameelah.

I think it has to be, she says, like at a slaughterhouse or some-thing, you know, wherever dirty work is done they have to pay extra attention to cleanliness.

Behind the bar is a little Thai woman. She smiles. The TV above her head is showing a news programme on mute.

Something to drink?

Tiger Milk says Jameelah grinning and as she tries to explain to the woman behind the bar how to make it I look over the guy. He has a three-day beard and is wearing a leather jacket with cuffs, jeans, and New Balance trainers. There's a long blond hair tangled around his ear, probably from his wife or daughter. Maybe his wife or daughter hugged him right before he drove off to Kurfürsten and the hair got caught, I think, and maybe I should become a detective except for that you must need a degree.

How old is your kid and what's his or her name, I ask.

I don't have a kid, says the guy, the car belongs to a buddy of mine who'll be here any minute.

Your buddy, says Jameelah turning to us, we never agreed on that.

No worries, says the guy putting down another pair of fifty euro notes on the table. You don't need to worry about him he's a half-pint.

I don't understand, says Jameelah tucking the money into her stocking.

You'll see in a minute and as if on cue the door opens, but not all the way, instead it kind of opens and closes part way as if a dog is trying to push its way through. The little Thai woman hurries to the door and holds it open smiling as a man in a wheelchair comes in. I can't make out his face at first because he's wearing a cowboy hat. It's only after he comes closer and hugs baby-seat-guy and takes off his hat that I can see how messed up he looks. Rainer would say he shows the wear and tear of life. Because even though he's younger than baby-seat-guy everything about him looks old and burned out, his thin blond hair, his gaunt smoker's face. The worst part is his legs – he doesn't have any. One is completely missing and the other is cut off at the knee.

This is my buddy and you're going to sit on his lap, it's his birthday today, says baby-seat-guy pushing me into the wheel-chair.

Upsy-daisy, says the guy in the wheelchair smiling at me. I land on his lone leg and there's no lap for me to sit on and for a second I'm worried it's going to hurt him. He smells of booze, must have knocked back a few belts of schnapps before he rolled in. Baby-seat-guy hands us glasses and we sing him happy birthday. Then I raise my glass with him and toast to brother-hood which he finds incredibly funny. When I put my arm around him he grabs my thigh and his fingernails keep getting caught in my stockings which is annoying so I take his hand and kiss him. Baby-seat-guy and Jameelah are kissing too and he has his hand under her shirt already.

Let me go, squeals Jameelah trying to squirm out of his arms, smiling, I want to dance.

Me too, I say.

We go over to the little dance floor.

Can you turn the music up, I ask the woman behind the bar.

She nods and smiles and turns around and fiddles with the audio equipment behind the bar, though I have the feeling that the music doesn't actually get louder.

Louder, I call.

It's already loud, says the woman, but it doesn't seem like it to me. Maybe it has something to do with yesterday, maybe it's like when you go to a concert, I think, and the next day your ears ring. Sometimes the music just has to be loud even if your ears ring for days afterwards, sometimes the music can't be loud enough to drown out the sound of your life and today I want to drown out the sound of my life.

The guys look at us and smile as we dance. It's always the same when you go off with someone from Kurfürsten, that's what's good about it. You notice you have something they don't have, you're doing lots of things for the first time, you have a real life that you're fully involved with. I get the impression that adults don't really live, that they look at everything from outside like they're at an aquarium. But when they put their hands on our stockings and kiss us something starts to flow inside them, they dive into the water for a little while, and sometimes they even light up like neon fish and we're the ones who light them up, we light up and when we touch someone he lights up too because we have enough light for two.

My body feels numb and I bet it's because of the dancing, I bet I could lift up an entire horse right now I feel so strong, I bet it's because we saw a murder, I bet it makes you strong to witness death, we're strong, we're real hookers, we saw a real murder, we light up.

When the song is over the guys clap, we bow comically and this time Jameelah sits on the lap of the guy in the wheelchair.

Do you feel anything there she asks poking his half-leg with her pointer finger.

No says the guy in the wheelchair.

How did it happen?

In Afghanistan, he says.

Really, I say, are you a soldier?

I was.

So how did it happen, asks Jameelah.

It was friendly fire.

That's when you accidentally shoot the good guys instead of the bad guys, right, asks Jameelah.

Exactly, says the guy.

And did you know him?

Know who, asks the guy.

The guy who did it, says Jameelah.

Yeah we all know each other well, says the guy putting his

hands on Jameelah's hips.

That's terrible.

Better that it was one of us than one of them, he says.

Why, says Jameelah.

Well, it's not the pain that's so bad or the missing leg. The bad part is when some nutjob wants to hurt you. Violence is when somebody wants to inflict pain on you, not the pain itself but the intent.

Aha.

I have no idea what they're talking about so I say war is shit, which usually goes over well, but the guy in the wheelchair says, what the hell do you know.

Come on, no sad stories, says baby-seat-guy slapping him on the back, it's your birthday.

Leave me alone, says the guy in the wheelchair staring at the floor.

It gets very quiet, nobody says anything. I look at Jameelah, baby-seat-guy looks at us, and wheelchair guy stares at the spot where his legs should be. Suddenly Jameelah starts laughing.

What's so funny, says baby-seat-guy glaring at her.

Nothing, squeaks Jameelah, nothing, but it's too late, she looks at me with her hand over her mouth and her eyes squinting then throws her head back and laughs so loud that I can see right down her throat past the tonsils and it looks so weird that I can't help laughing too.

Stop it, says baby-seat-guy.

Don't be so hard on them, says the guy in the wheelchair grabbing Jameelah's breasts. She is still on his lap. He'd probably bounce her on his knee if he could, I think, and that makes me laugh out loud again even though it's not even funny. I don't know myself why we laugh so hard, no idea, it's all just so fucked up, I mean, we just wanted to cast a love spell, and we scattered rose petals over the entire playground, I could die laughing.

Alright, now we drink up, says baby-seat-guy shoving the glasses in our faces.

Why, says Jameelah.

Because we're going someplace else.

Nobody knows about the whole thing with me and Jameelah and Kurfürsten, nobody except us two. There's all sorts of reasons for that. People would just worry, I mean if Nico knew he'd probably smack me. But basically nothing can happen to us, we have our dogs, the Grims. Two huge black dogs both named Grim, Jameelah got it out of some book. They're not real but in our imagination they are always with us like a pair of body-guards. I don't really think of them much, only when I get a strange feeling. That's when they pop up and run around us in circles so nobody can get at us. I'm not an idiot or something, these dogs do protect us and they have for a while. There are some horrible guys in the world, the types who grab your crotch as they walk past you and that kind of thing, we've seen it all. But since we got the dogs nothing like that has happened, seri-ously, if I concentrate really hard on the Grims men who I would be afraid of actually cross to the other side of the street. It's a question of concentration. That's why I don't get scared anymore.

We've never been to a hotel room with anyone. The guy in the wheelchair is already completely drunk, I guess he can't hold his liquor though I'm not sure if it has something to do with his legs or whether it's just because he's so skinny. Baby-seat-guy is also pretty well oiled, and obviously we are too. The lift opens and we stagger down the hall to the last room.

Sophia Saturna, whispers Jameelah, I think this time we have to sleep with them.

Could be, I say.

Maybe it's not all that bad, maybe it's even better this way, I think, at least we'll have it behind us, this whole stupid first time thing. And who knows, maybe today is the perfect day first and foremost because if there's going to be blood it would fit the day to a tee, it would almost be poetic. Noura always says you should live your life so it reads like a poem. She never said it had to be a happy poem, just a poem.

Baby-seat-guy unlocks the door, puts his black bag down next to the desk facing the window and lowers the shades. Under the desk is a little refrigerator that the guy in the wheelchair opens.

Can you help me onto the bed, he says, his lap full of mini-bar schnapps bottles that tinkle onto the white sheets like marbles when we drop him onto one of the two beds. He pulls me to him and fumbles around with my breasts then lifts my t-shirt over my head and the sheets rustle, they're stiff from being cleaned so often. But my bra, the one with the little bow that Jameelah gave me for my birthday, he can't unhook.

Baby-seat-guy turns on the TV and ARD is showing a *Terra X* nature documentary. He zaps from one channel to the next, god dammit isn't there a music channel, he says, but then he finds music videos on VIVA.

Now you're going to dance real nice for us, says baby-seat-guy, I know you two love to dance, he laughs taking off his trousers and opening a beer.

Right, take your clothes off, says the guy in the wheelchair grinning like an idiot from the bed.

Jameelah smiles and takes off her top and starts shaking her hips to the rhythm of the music. I've never done a striptease before but like Rainer always says there's a first time for everything so I strip, meaning I dance and while I'm dancing I undo my bra

124

and toss it onto the bed and then at some point I take off my underwear and do the same thing, toss them on the bed. I just do it the way I imagine it's supposed to be done. My hands, arms, knees, everything is in motion and my naked feet twist around on the carpeting until they start to get warm from the friction.

Keep cool, whispers Jameelah putting a hand on my shoulder, just keep dancing.

When I was younger, before Jessi arrived, I used to dance to Mama's favourite music in the living room all the time. Sometimes I was allowed to put on Mama's red leather skirt and she did up my hair with hairspray and put makeup on me and we got in the car and drove around to her friends' places like a pair of vacuum cleaner salesmen and I sang '99 Red Balloons' in front of them. She's going to be a singer they said to Mama and laughed until they cried, I'm telling you she's going to be on TV one day, but I just wanted to sing, I didn't want to go on TV because Tarik told me the singers on TV don't even sing they just move their mouths to the music and moving your mouth to your own music is shit.

When I think about it, sad poems are way better than happy poems anyway. And who knows, maybe it's just the first verse of my life that's not so happy, I mean nobody said it was impossible, I'm sure there are poems that start out not so happy but are happy by the end. Anything is possible and why should it be that nobody on earth ever hit on the idea, who knows maybe my life will even turn out to be a proper fairytale and fairytales always begin disastrously and end up happy.

Look, says the guy in the wheelchair pointing at me, she's crying.

Everything okay, asks Jameelah looking at me with shock.

Yeah I say quietly, it's just the song, it makes me sad.

Baby-seat-guy knocks back another miniature schnapps bottle.

125

What are you crying for, he says.

I'm not crying, I say, I have something in my eye.

Baby-seat-guy looks at me searchingly.

With you women you never know if you're really crying or just acting.

Ah let her cry, says the guy in the wheelchair.

No, you're going to go wash your face, says baby-seat-guy switching the channel back to the nature show, *Terra X*.

When I come out of the bathroom I see Jameelah lying in bed with baby-seat-guy. The guy in the wheelchair is waiting for me, his cowboy hat is sitting on the nightstand and he's taken off his trousers and t-shirt. With his pale skin and long blond hair he looks like an albino slug. As I crawl toward him in bed I wonder if he can even get a hard-on. He presses me down onto the bed and starts to lick me all over and it leaves me cold. When he lets me go for a second I reach into Jameelah's rucksack which is between the beds and search for a condom. I find a red one and put it in my mouth with the tip facing in. Wheelchair guy is ready, I can see his thing didn't catch any friendly fire so I put the condom on it and he moans. *Terra X* is still on in the background, they're talking about glaciers and perpetual ice. Polar bears don't bury themselves in winter they lay down on icebergs and wait for the snow drifts to cover them and once they are totally covered they give birth to their offspring, says the man on TV.

It's actually good that the guy in the wheelchair doesn't have any legs because at least that way he can't get on top of me, in fact he can barely move around at all, which is good. I close my eyes and imagine someone nice is sitting next to me on the edge of the bed and says go ahead you know how it works it's not so bad and you know it's just practice no different from frogs or corpses, listen that's not a real person it's just practice, I think

126

to myself, this is all just a form of practice. I do it slowly so it doesn't hurt but somehow it doesn't hurt at all, even if I go faster it still doesn't hurt, it just feels like something is wedged in there but maybe it's because I'm drunk. I move back and forth and the guy thrusts as best he can using his upper body and the overall effect is kind of like when Mama used to let me ride that mechanical horse at Kaufland, the one you can ride for fifty cents a minute, though I have no idea whether that's what it feels like to ride a real horse because I've never ridden a real horse and maybe I'm making this association only because people always talk about riding when they talk about fucking, Rainer does anyway, and Rainer is like everybody.

I take the cowboy hat from the nightstand and put it on. Wheelchair guy has his eyes closed, he moans, and in the background *Terra X*. They're still talking about the North Pole and it occurs to me that I used to watch *Terra X* with Papa sometimes, I remember one episode about the rainforest where aboriginal boys about the same age as me and Jameelah had to wait in line. They had their hands in front of their balls like in a soccer game when there's a free kick, except that they were all naked and instead of standing in front of a goal they were outside a little tent. Crying boys kept emerging from the tent with blood on their cocks.

Wheelchair guy moans again.

It wasn't about soccer, it was about becoming an adult, at least that's what the man on TV said. You could see the boys were scared shitless but the man on TV said boys waited their entire lives for this day because afterwards they'd finally be accepted as adults and as a result they weren't scared, they were excited and proud. I'm not scared, excited or proud but when I close my eyes I see a purple spiral staircase. I'll have to ask Jameelah what that means later, I think, she's good at interpreting dreams.

127

Wheelchair guy moans some more but then thankfully he stops and lets his head fall to the pillow as if he's dead. I slowly disconnect myself. My thighs hurt a little like after gym. For a little while I lay there next to the guy and then he starts to snore quietly which makes me think of Nico, I wonder what he's doing right now, probably working off the books somewhere, painting at a hotel or whatever. That's what he usually does on Sunday, work off the books, because he can't live on the money he makes from his apprenticeship.

I look over at the other bed. Jameelah is sitting on the edge of the bed in her tank-top smoking. She doesn't look at me, she's looking toward the window. Baby-seat-guy throws his legs out of bed and stands up. I gather my clothes as quickly as I can. Jameelah stubs out her cigarette and just as she reaches for her rucksack baby-seat-guy puts his foot on her passport, which must have fallen out when I was rummaging in her bag for a condom.

What's this, he says picking up the passport with his toes. His nails are yellow like Frau Struck's but even worse because he's a guy.

Give it back, says Jameelah grabbing for the passport. As she wrestles for it her residency permit falls out. The guy looks at it calmly.

Your residency permit is about to expire, he says.

I'm aware, says Jameelah, grabbing the permit and stuffing it together with her passport into her rucksack.

Did you know Jameelah means beauty in Arabic, says baby-seat-guy. When she doesn't answer he laughs loudly and says, why didn't you say anything, we could have done it in the ass and you'd still be a virgin when you get married.

I look him up and down.

What the hell are you looking at, he says.

His cock is dangling between his hairy thighs, long and thin

128

and red like a sick worm, so ugly I have to look away. Still laughing he disappears into the bathroom.

Jameelah quickly puts on the rest of her clothes and crouches down on the carpet in front of the black bag. Inside, baby-seat-guy's wallet has at least five hundred euros in it. I turn and look over at wheelchair guy. He's still asleep.

It's cheap, I whisper.

From the bathroom comes that noise that only men make, hacking up yellow mucus and spitting it in the sink, hacking up from deep inside, again and again like an Olympic sport. As I get dressed Jameelah shoves the money into her Chucks. Then we rummage around in the bag some more.

Look, I whisper grabbing a bottle of Tabac cologne, Amir loves this stuff.

The nearly full bottle finds its way into my rucksack.

Jameelah smiles and shoves a pack of gum, an expensive organic lip balm and a nail grooming kit into her rucksack.

What a little girl, she says, come on let's get out of here.

Did it make you bleed asks Jameelah when we're back out on Nollendorfplatz.

No, I say, you?

No, me neither, there was just a weird feeling between my legs.

Me too. Like a muscle ache.

Now what?

No idea, just not home.

Planet?

Planet.

We get a currywurst on the corner and then we get the train to Wilmersdorfer Strasse. Apollo and Aslagon are sitting at the planet and Aslagon is cleaning his fingernails with a toothpick.

Here, says Jameelah pulling out the nail grooming kit, it's a gift from me.

Is it made out of silver, asks Aslagon suspiciously.

No, I don't think so.

Then no thanks.

Why not?

I'm only allowed to accept gifts of silver. All other metals let evil in.

Bullshit, says Jameelah, there's no way that nail clipper you had the other day was made of silver.

Do you see a nail clipper anywhere around here, asks Aslagon holding up his toothpick.

We sit down at the planet and stare at the dry cement basin. I'm itchy all over, I hope the guy in the wheelchair didn't have some kind of disease, I think. Apollo and Aslagon start whispering to each other.

Lies are told in whispers, I say.

We're not lying, says Apollo.

No, says Aslagon, we're not telling lies, we're talking about you guys, about your wings.

What about them, says Jameelah.

They're gone, says Apollo, where did your wings go?

We sold them at the flea market.

Then you're no longer wing-children, just so you know.

I think we can live with that.

Somebody came by looking for you by the way, says Aslagon looking at me.

Who?

The big guy who always has pot in his bag, says Apollo with his gravedigger's grin, he wrote something on the phone booth.

I hop up and go have a look.

Nini call me right away, Nico it says and next to it is today's date.

Come on I have to buy minutes for my phone.

Wait a second, says Jameelah, we have to take care of something first.

What?

The jewellery she whispers.

Oh yeah, I say, that's right.

We walk over toward the S-bahn together. Right where the road goes under the tracks is a bin.

Anybody looking, asks Jameelah.

No, I say, take it easy.

We rummage around for Jasna's jewellery among the lip balm, condoms, tampons, and pens.

One piece after the next goes into the bin. Then Jameelah's eyes light on my hand and she stares angrily at the ring.

Are you completely fucking crazy, she says grabbing at my finger.

What, I say, I've had it on the whole time.

Are you planning to keep it?

Of course, it's mine after all, or my mother's I mean.

You have completely lost your chador.

What do you mean, I say but Jameelah starts trying to rip it off my finger.

Leave it alone, I say, I want to keep it.

Bullshit, give it to me.

It won't come off anyway, it's too tight. You can only get it off with soap and water.

Jameelah raises her eyebrows and looks at me for a while then she grabs my wrist faster than a crocodile and shoves my finger in her mouth.

I scream.

131

Jameelah starts sucking like mad on my finger.

Let go, I say but Jameelah just keeps sucking.

I feel her tongue swirling around my finger and her sucking and sucking and then I feel the ring working its way off my finger. Like a piece of bone she's just choked on she spits the ring onto the street.

You can't do that, I shout.

Yes I can, you saw for yourself, she says picking up the ring and tossing it into the bin.

I stare at her stunned.

That's my mother's ring!

No it isn't and even if it is, says Jameelah, it was on Jasna's finger and if somebody sees you with it you'll either be dead or under arrest for murder. I'm protecting you, try looking at it that way.

I lean over the bin and stick my arm in as deep as I can just as Nico comes speeding up on his BMX bike.

Why aren't you answering your phone, he says screeching to a halt, I tried calling you a thousand times. What are you doing anyway? Have you joined the ranks of the deposit bottle collectors?

Haha, I say straightening myself, what's up?

What's up? Jasna is dead.

We know, says Jameelah.

Nico stares at us, first at Jameelah and then at me. He looks really angry and Nico hardly ever gets angry.

Aha, he says, and did you know that the cops have arrested Amir?

What?

Nico looks at me chidingly.

Are you drunk, he asks me but Jameelah grabs him by the arm and shakes him.

132

Tell us everything, start from the beginning!

Like I said I tried to call you and then I went over to your place and rang the bell but nobody answered, says Nico. So then I went to Amir's and there were cops and television crews everywhere and the old lady on the ground floor told me everything, that Jasna was dead and that they took Amir in.

Frau Stanitzek is always running her mouth, says Jameelah.

No, says Nico, everyone said the same thing, and also that Amir had confessed.

What do you mean confessed?

What do you think, he said he did it.

All of a sudden I feel like I'm going to be sick. Amir. I see his face before my eyes. Jameelah wasn't even there yet when he stood on the playground and looked over at me and we touched hands inside the tunnel we'd dug in the sandbox, I see his fingers, the ones he played marbles with, and how when Santa Claus came to our school Amir told him Allah is great, much greater than Jesus, his nimble legs and the way he scurried up the linden tree, the way he sat up in the tree shouting Allah is great but I'm Leonardo DiCaprio and I'm the king of the world.

Nini, says Nico reaching out to me at the last minute, then I throw up right in front of the bin. My knees hurt, my head hurts, my legs, between my legs, my arms, hands, feet, everything hurts, the whole world is hurting me.

Here, says Nico handing me a tissue.

I wipe the puke from around my mouth.

He didn't do it, I say.

Of course he didn't do it, says Nico. Amir of all people, he won't even burn an ant with a magnifying glass, but you'll have to prove it.

There's proof, I say.

Jameelah looks at me threateningly.

Nini are you okay, she says putting a hand on my forehead, you're burning up, she says like she's some kind of nurse, you need to drink something right away, let's go.

She grabs my arm and pulls me to the mall, angrily shoves open one of the glass doors and then pushes me onto an escalator and up to Tiziano ice cream shop and into the bathroom there. She never lets go of my arm, vice grip, just like the night before at the playground. She pushes open one of the toilet stalls and shoves me inside.

What the hell is wrong with you, I say ripping my arm free.

No, she shouts, what the hell is wrong with you. You're crazy. We had an understanding!

What kind of understanding?

That we'd keep our mouths shut about Tarik and let the police handle it.

But we didn't know they would arrest Amir!

It doesn't matter, a deal is a deal. You can't just go telling Nico everything without getting my approval first.

Understanding, approval. You're so German. Amir is innocent and we have to help him.

I'm so German, she says, you're so German! You're so naïve you have no idea what that was on the playground, do you?

Of course I do, I say, it was a murder.

It wasn't just a murder, says Jameelah getting right in my face. Her breath smells of Tiger Milk and used condoms.

What do you mean? What else could it be?

Jasna, says Jameelah, always off at the clubs drinking with her Sorb. You have no clue. They all planned it and Amir is in on it if he told the cops he did it. But of course I'm the evil Nazi, by all means!

Stop it! Amir would never plan something like that!

Then why did he say he did it?

134

No idea, maybe Tarik threatened him.

No idea, yeah? I'm going to tell you something. If you're the sister of a guy like Tarik and you fall in love with a Serb and go dancing and drink rum and cokes with him all night you are living dangerously. But you wouldn't understand. You can't possibly imagine that because you're so German – you are the one who is a typical German.

I am not! It might be true that I'm not the smartest but you don't have to have read as many books as your beloved Lukas to understand what a murder is and what you should do when you witness one. It's Lukas's damn fault that we're mixed up in this shit in the first place.

Oh right, now it's Lukas who's guilty is it?

No! But Tarik should be punished not Amir. You can't just let this stand. I mean, first you take the jewellery then you throw away my ring and now this, it's not on.

Have you ever stopped to think about all the questions they'll ask, says Jameelah, we stole from a corpse! They'll end up thinking we did it.

We just have to explain it to them. Come on help me find the ring in the garbage and then we'll go to the cops.

No fucking way am I going to the cops, says Jameelah pressing herself against the wall of the stall. Her lower lip starts to tremble, her eyelids flutter like two tiny butterflies.

I swallow.

You have no idea what all of this could mean, says Jameelah, all you can think of is that stupid ring that you don't even know is your mother's or not, which makes sense because you have no need to worry that you'll be deported to someplace where they make their houses out of camel shit.

What does that have to do with this, I say.

Everything. This shit with Jasna will bring nothing but trouble, nothing but bumps in the road and right now the road needs to be smooth until everything is settled with the immigration department. And Tarik is dangerous, really dangerous. An eye for an eye, that's the way they think. Just imagine if more shit happens.

I grab Jameelah.

What else could possibly happen, I say but Jameelah throws my hand off her shoulder and says, Do you think I don't know what I'm talking about? Just imagine coming home and finding cops all over your living room and seeing your mother and Jessi lying dead on the sofa, imagine that.

Someone enters the bathroom and goes into the next stall and starts taking off their clothes. I hear the rustle of a tampon package. Jameelah is still leaning against the stall divider which is covered with scrawled notes. *Hey sweetie lets fuck but only if you're blonde* says a note written in fat sharpie right next to her head, and I wonder what that is doing in the women's bathroom.

You still don't get it do you, whispers Jameelah looking at me with a triumphant look.

I shrug my shoulders.

I think you're exaggerating.

Then go ahead and talk to the cops, whispers Jameelah, you can talk to them for all I care, just keep me out of it. I don't know anything about it and I was nowhere near there whatever you say, understand? And don't ever bother calling me again because if you go to the cops we're done being friends.

You don't care about me anyway, I say.

That's not true, it's the opposite.

And what about Amir? Why don't you care about him?

What a load of shit that I don't care about you guys. Man, don't you get it, I'm trying to protect you.

That's not true, I say, you're only thinking of yourself. Amir

136

doesn't matter to you. And you say you don't want to go to the police because you know I won't go on my own.

Listen to me, says Jameelah taking my hand, we will go to the cops, just not yet. First we'll talk to Amir. He has to tell the truth. We'll try to convince him to tell the truth. It's the only way I'll consider doing it. Until that happens we can't tell anyone, nobody can know that we saw it. He has to say it first, then everything will work out.

And what about the ring, I ask.

Jameelah rolls her eyes.

Fine we'll go get the ring, she says, but first you have to swear. Swear that you won't say anything to anyone.

I swear, I say.

Pinky swear, whispers Jameelah holding out her pinky finger.

Okay, I say, pinky swear. I hook my pinky into her pinky and kiss my thumb.

ON TV PEOPLE WHO'VE SEEN SOMETHING BAD ALWAYS WAKE UP drenched in sweat. They dream about the bad thing night after night and each time they wake up they're happy that this time it was just a dream and they fall back to sleep exhausted and everything is alright again. It's in scenes like those that you can tell they are actors, you notice it especially with the whole bathed-in-sweat thing. I mean, what would have to happen for someone to wake up drenched in sweat? You only ever see people bathed in sweat on TV, there's no such thing in real life, which is how you can tell that very few people have ever really been through something bad, because I know how fake that is now that something bad has happened to me.

In reality it's the other way around. Everything is dark and quiet at night but when the light comes through my window in the morning that's when everything comes back, Jasna's bloody clothes, the smell of blood and jewellery and Tiger Milk, and anything unpleasant takes on huge proportions, way bigger than it should, like Jessi's crying or Mama's sofa and pillows, and anything nice seems insignificant, like the sun, the food at the pool, the planet, the summer school holidays. Some things also look different or sound different, for instance I'll think I see the moon but it is just the light atop a crane, or I'll see a face sighing at me in the sauce warming up on the stove even though it's just

138

crap spaghetti from a can. The whole world is warped and distorted like you're cross-eyed all the time. It's only when it gets dark again that it stops and everything is quiet, though in summer it gets dark so late, which is why I wish it was winter.

Rose petals were strewn around the scene of the crime it says in the tabloid. And next to that caption is a photo of Amir from our class ski trip last year. Jameelah is standing right next to him but they've put a black bar across her eyes, so stupid, a bar like that doesn't do anything you can still easily recognize Jameelah, she's smiling and like in every class photo she's making a V with her fingers behind Amir's head so he looks ridiculous. The photo should be enough for anyone to tell he couldn't be a murderer but because of the caption it has the opposite effect – the clowning around makes it all seem creepy.

The newspaper is still sitting next to my bed in my room but today I'm going to finally throw it out, today is the right day for it because today we're finally going to visit Amir. It's really the only thing I've been looking forward to, that and when I'll go to the children's hospital to get my wisdom teeth pulled.

Actually Jameelah and I went to visit Amir more than two weeks ago but we had to turn around immediately.

You can't just pop in, the man at the gate had said. He gave us a telephone number and Amir's case number and we had to call the number and set up a visit. Since we're underage we can only visit Amir accompanied by an adult but Nico changed the 1996 on his ID to 1988, his was the easiest to change because all he had to do was add a half circle to the bottom of the nine and the top of the six with a pen he got at the shop where he buys his spray cans. Nico can pull it off, he looks a lot older than he really is. When we called the number we were given another number that Nico called to get an application for a visitation permit, without a visitation permit you can't talk to Amir. We had to go to the middle of nowhere to pick up the visitation permit and once we got there we had to wait an eternity before they gave it to us.

The visitation permit is tucked into the *The Modern Witch's Spell Book* along with Lukas's photo. It's a good place for it, won't get lost there, Jameelah said, and I take Jameelah at her word that she would never lose a visitation permit that is stored alongside a photo of Lukas.

Before Jameelah and I head to the prison we go to the mall, down to the lower floor where there's a shop that sells gift baskets. I think gift baskets are the best present in the world, they're big, they fill you up, and they all have names, like good, warm-hearted people. I've always wanted to receive a gift basket but since that will probably never happen I'd at least like to give one once, and this is the perfect occasion. When the salesclerk asks us what occasion the basket is for we're suddenly not sure what exactly to say.

It's for our best friend, says Jameelah, we want to cheer him up.

He's in a bad place at the moment, I say, and he can't really get out of it.

He's in a kind of hospital, says Jameelah, in the woods, a forest hospital. We think it's a bad hospital with bad food so we want to take him something good to eat.

Forest, food, hospital, says the woman, I think I have something for you.

She leads us down a long aisle with various gift baskets and I read the names as we go past, Sinful Sweetie, Lil' Stinker, the Cheese Champ, one is called Bachelor Party and is full of tampons and condoms and miniature schnapps bottles. Maybe it should be called Kurfürstenstrasse, I think, and who gave the baskets all these names and I'd love to have that job but of course that's not going to happen. Mama applied for a job here a few years ago but they told her she wasn't qualified enough and didn't give her the job.

Here we are, says the salesclerk standing in front of a green basket called Hunter's Heil.

Aha, says Jameelah, and what sorts of goodies are in there?

Jagdwurst, wild mushroom soup, hunter's stew, Jägermeister, lingonberry juice, woodland fruit compote, crackers, and shortbread.

Jameelah looks at me.

What do you think?

Sounds good to me, I say, except it might not be big enough. Maybe if there was twice as much of everything, you know Amir, he eats like a horse.

Would that be possible, says Jameelah taking out the tin of hunter's stew and reading the ingredients.

No problem, says the salesclerk.

Great, Hunter's Heil it is, but with double everything.

And this has to go in, I say holding up the bottle of Tabac cologne we took from baby-seat-guy.

Right, and this has to come out, says Jameelah pointing to the jagdwurst and the Jägermeister, it has to be halal.

What do you mean, asks the salesclerk.

No pork and no alcohol, says Jameelah, that stuff isn't halal and we'll have to replace it with other stuff. He'll like the theme of Germany and the German woodlands, but we have to make Hunter's Heil into Hunter's Halal. Is that possible?

I have to smile, Hunter's Halal, that's typical Jameelah. The woman from the shop goes into the back and returns with a huge basket that has all the things from the small basket already in it.

To that she adds the stuff from the small basket and takes out the jagdwurst and Jägermeister and replaces them with a kilo of black tea and a jumbo package of chicken sausages. She puts the basket on a wooden table and rips off a bunch of cellophane wrapping paper and starts to wrap it up. The paper rustles and the noise the scissors make as she curls the ribbons sounds like Christmas and birthday all wrapped up in one. Jameelah puts a fifty euro note on the table and I put down another fifty. The saleswoman smiles and we smile back though we're smiling for different things. She's smiling because she thinks we're nice girls who have saved up our pocket money to get something for a dear friend and we are smiling because we're thinking well at least the whole thing with baby-seat-guy and the guy in the wheelchair was worthwhile since now we're able to buy this gift basket for Amir.

Hunter's Halal is ridiculously heavy. Carrying it to the train was bearable but by the time we've made it halfway down the forest path between the station and the jail I'm totally exhausted. My arms hurt like hell and I try not to think about it, looking up at the sky and all around at the green trees. What kind of trees they are I have no idea but the little twigs all over the path look like the skeletons of small animals.

Forests kind of drag me down, I say.

Me too, says Jameelah looking up at the tops of the trees, what's the story with the Germans and their weird obsession with the forest, can you explain it to me.

How should I know, I say dropping the basket to the ground without warning.

I can't carry it any further.

Me neither, says Jameelah, man my tongue is already hanging out, do you have anything to drink?

No.

We both look longingly at the lingonberry juice beneath the cellophane in the basket.

I'm going to die of thirst.

Me too.

Do you think Amir would be pissed off if we drank his juice?

No way, I say.

That's exactly what I wanted to hear, says Jameelah picking at the knot in the ribbon, shoving aside the cellophane, and grabbing greedily at the juice bottle.

Hunter's Heil, cheers.

Hunter's Halal, guten Appetit.

Damn I've never tasted something so good, says Jameelah handing me the bottle, her teeth all purple.

I look at the bottle and then drink.

You're right, I say, it's almost as good as Tiger Milk.

Nico is standing near the entrance to the prison smoking. His BMX bike is leaning against the wall and he has his lunchbox in his hand.

Finally, he says, what took you so long?

We stopped to get something for Amir.

That, says Nico pointing at the basket, you'll never be allowed to take that in.

Why not?

Because this isn't a youth hostel, it's a prison even if it doesn't look like one at first glance.

Now that we brought it all this way we'll get it inside somehow, I say.

Nico takes a drag off his cigarette and grins.

I can't wait to see how you pull that off.

Oh yeah, says Jameelah, well I can't wait to see how you manage to get your stupid lunchbox in.

We lug the basket to the gate. The same guy is there who gave us the telephone number and the information packet last time.

Identification and visitation permit, he says.

We take the permit out of the *The Modern Witch's Spell Book* and put it along with our school IDs on top of Nico's ID, which is already sitting on the desk. We shove it all under the window and the gatekeeper barely looks at the IDs before saying, everything looks in order. As we start to go in he points to the basket.

You can't take that in, he says.

It's not for us, I say, it's a present for a friend.

I know, says the gatekeeper, which is exactly why you're not permitted to take it in.

You can search it if you'd like, we didn't put a file in a cake or anything, says Jameelah fluttering her eyelashes. But the gatekeeper shakes his head.

It's not allowed.

Are we not allowed to bring our friend anything at all?

Prisoners are permitted to receive packages three times per year but they have to be declared in advance and sent by mail, normally at Christmas, Easter, and on the inmate's birthday. The prisoners look forward to it that way. There's no point in sending them without an occasion.

He kicks open the door to his gatekeeper's booth.

You can leave it here and pick up on the way out.

I knew it, says Nico grinning as we walk across a yard toward the main entrance.

Shut the fuck up, says Jameelah.

This isn't a normal prison, there are no adults here, only youth offenders awaiting trial or sentencing, I read that in the information packet we got last time we tried to come here. Nico is right that it doesn't look like a prison from the outside, more like a cross between a youth hostel and a nuthouse, what with the metal grates over the windows. But when you get to the main entrance it looks just the way you picture a prison looking. Behind glass is a man in uniform who shoves little plastic baskets through a special trapdoor, baskets like the ones Noura uses to collect dirty clothes. We have to put everything that we have with us into the baskets, including the stuff in our pockets, loose cigarettes, gum, I even have to hand over a couple of tampons.

The case, says the officer pointing to Nico's lunchbox, that's got to stay here.

Jameelah grins.

Can't we take our friend anything, asks Nico handing his lunchbox over reluctantly.

When we are finished here you can use up to fifteen euros in coins to buy things from the vending machines and turn those items over to the prisoner.

It's like a prison here, says Nico.

Nobody laughs.

The noise it makes when the steel doors open and close, the heavy jingle of the keys on the hips of the officers, the serious look on their faces, it all makes me jittery, though the thing that makes me squirm the most is the fact that Amir is waiting for us somewhere in here. This must be how it feels for people to see each other after a long time, I think, just like on TV, on those reality shows about long-lost lovers.

When the uniformed guy finally escorts us into the visitors room Amir isn't there yet. Our steps echo, that's how bleak and empty the room is. It smells of Febreze. The windows are covered with pigeon shit and the sunbeams that shine through the shit illuminate the dust dancing in the air. I have to sneeze. The uniformed guy stays next to the door like a tin soldier – the only

145

thing missing is one of those stupid bearskin hats.

Are those the vending machines, asks Nico pointing toward the far wall.

The guy in uniform nods.

Next to a soda machine is a machine that looks like the animal food dispenser at the old East Berlin zoo. We went there once with our school, Amir, Jameelah, and me. I still remember how cute the deer were as they ate the food out of our hands from behind their barred cages, how warm and soft it felt on my hand, how peaceful the noise was that they made while eating, that strange sideways motion they made when they chewed, and if that machine hadn't have been here I wouldn't have thought of the deer in the old East Berlin zoo, and how one of us was like the deer in the cage now, just as innocent as those deer, and how we were supposed to feed him now with food from the same type of machine.

Do you want something to drink, asks Nico, they have tea, coffee, and orange juice.

The orange juice tastes disgusting, like the East Berlin zoo, like youth hostels, like nuthouses, like prison. It's bright orange and way too sweet, it must have all sorts of stuff in it, just no oranges. Nico drums his fingers on the table. Next to him are a packet of cheap chocolates, a sack of fruit, and a pack of gum, all from the vending machine. Jameelah blows on her steaming plastic cup, the tag on the teabag says Healthy Happy Yoga Tea but Jameelah barely sips it as if she's frightened she's going to scald herself on all the health and happiness. I drink my juice and think to myself that it would taste much better with brandy and a dash of milk. That's when the door opens.

*　*　*

I see Amir's hands first. They're in handcuffs, steel loops clamped

146

around his wrists until the uniformed guy unlocks them. Amir smiles. He looks tired but somebody has smeared skin cream on the corner of his mouth and the blue bruise below his eye is gone. He's not wearing a striped outfit the way I imagined, he has on the Picaldi shirt he always used to wear for gym class. I want to run up to him but the guy in uniform says halt, no bodily contact.

We're allowed to shake his hand right, says Nico going up to Amir.

Yo, he says, good to see you.

Amir slaps him five.

I reach out my hand, Amir takes it and squeezes it.

Hi, he says smiling.

Jameelah stands up, wipes her hands on her jeans and then extends a hand to Amir.

Salam, brother.

Stupid question but how are you, asks Nico.

Amir smiles again.

Alright.

This is for you, says Nico handing him the chocolates, gum, and fruit.

Thanks, says Amir, how are you guys?

How do you think with you sitting in here, says Jameelah.

Do you have a good lawyer, asks Nico.

There was some woman here, says Amir, I have no idea if she's good but she said she would defend me free of charge because my case was so unusual. Not sure but I think she's doing it as a career move. But it's good anyway because we don't have any money for a lawyer.

And the trial, when does it start, asks Nico.

Soon. It's something to do with the juvenile justice system, it's faster than normal adult cases because I'm not supposed to

147

stay in pre-trial custody for too long.

What did the lawyer say?

If I'm lucky I'll only get five years and then I'll be deported directly from prison to the airport and then back to Sarajevo.

Nico shakes his head.

What the hell?

What, says Amir.

This whole thing, says Jameelah, do you think we're stupid or something?

We know that you're innocent, I say softly.

You don't know anything, says Amir.

Man, says Nico, we know you could never do something like this and so does anybody else who knows you even a little.

Guilty, innocent, says Amir looking out the window, there's no difference.

Bullshit, I say.

You're throwing your whole life away, says Nico, in four years you'll be eighteen and you'll have a serious police record. What can you do after that? Plus you'll be deported.

It's not so bad. I don't want to live in Germany anymore anyway. Did you know I can do my middle school equivalency right here in jail? The teacher is nice, not like that witch Frau Struck. I might even be able to finish my high school degree and start college. I've been thinking I might want to be a doctor. Or maybe I can do something related to soccer, I don't really know.

Doctor or soccer, says Jameelah tapping her forehead, you're crazy, you're in jail, don't you get it, you're going to be sentenced for a crime you didn't commit, that's insane.

Leave me alone, says Amir.

Did Tarik tell you some bullshit, asks Jameelah, did he say that you'd be the hero of the family if you took all the blame on yourself, that all the doors would be open to you, is that what he said, yeah?

Just go over to that guy and tell him the truth, I whisper nodding toward the guy in uniform.

Cut it out, says Amir, I thought you wanted to visit me.

We do but are we supposed to just sit by and watch you throw your life away?

What I do with my life is none of your business, it's only to do with me, with me and my family.

You're a coward, says Jameelah, saviour of the family my ass. You know what you are? You're a little girl exactly like Tarik always said.

Shut up shouts Amir, you always know everything, you always tell us what we're supposed to do. Jameelah says it's like this and that's the way it is, like you have a clue about life! Believe me, there are things that you don't understand at all, things that aren't logical but are still right, but you'll never get it because you don't have a family, you don't know what it's like to think of anyone but yourself!

Jameelah jumps up and her chair falls over.

You can kiss my ass, she shouts turning toward the door.

You kiss my ass, says Amir.

Cut it out, says Nico grabbing Jameelah's arm.

The fuck I'm going to sit back down, she says, what the fuck do you know anyway you fucking kraut. You act as if you have a clue about what's happening here. It's pathetic.

Settle down, calls the guy in uniform, otherwise the visitation permit will be immediately revoked.

Nico makes a fist. I look pleadingly at Jameelah. She hesitates, looking at the door, then sits back down on her chair shaking her head.

Listen, says Nico looking at Amir, we just want you to think long and hard about what you're doing. Family is important but

Jasna was family too. You're innocent I know it, even if I can't prove it. But if you protect the person who really did it you open yourself up to other charges.

With his arms folded on his chest Amir looks out the window.

She wasn't my real sister anyway.

What?

Only half.

What do mean only half?

She had a different father, says Amir, it happened during the war.

Aha, says Nico.

The sun streams through the window and the tiny dust particles float in the air like in outer space, weightless, without a care in the world, they've got nothing else to do in life other than fly around and then gather into a dirty pile. From the perspective of the universe, like Herr Wittner always says, the earth is no different than a speck of dust. Who knows, I think, maybe the particles here in this room are planets and we're just too big and stupid to see the life living there and all the stuff happening there, bad stuff and beautiful stuff, who knows, that's the way it is with earth after all which is nothing more than a speck of dust, a rotten speck of dust full of blood and shit.

What's up with you says Nico.

Jameelah rummages around in her trouser pocket but Amir is faster and pulls a huge checkered handkerchief out of his pocket, the kind only old men carry around.

Don't cry he says holding it out to me.

I blow my nose. I don't know if it's the grandfather handkerchief or what, no idea, but I've never blown my nose so loudly in my entire life, it sounds like the old men who sit in the park and blow their noses and the only thing missing is for me to hold one nostril closed and shoot snot from the other one onto

150

the path. For as long as I can remember Jameelah and I have tried to protect Amir, from the boys who tried to throw his book bag in puddles and said things like what's the point of all the books and folders you can't read anyway you can't write anyway, from the girls who opened shaken up soda bottles in his face and said you stink take a shower, and most of all from Tarik who would smack him on the back of the head and say stop crying you're not a little girl but now I realize that Amir's not little at all, no smaller than us, he's just as big, bigger even, and much bigger and adult and older than all of us combined. I never had a grandfather but this is how I'd imagine him, like Amir, giving me his handkerchief and saying don't cry like he'd become fifty years older from one day to the next. Maybe that's how it is, maybe we all get old all of a sudden. Can that be true I wonder, is it possible that it's not the passage of time that makes us old but the things that happen to us, that make us despair, but that we have to go through whether we want to or not because they are bigger and stronger than we are because life is bigger and stronger than any one person, that maybe it's these things that make us old.

I didn't want her to die you have to believe me, says Amir, you have to believe me, I didn't want her to die.

I hand the handkerchief back to him.

We believe you, I say and look at Jameelah.

She's sitting with her arms crossed looking at the toes of her Chucks then she looks up at Amir, at me, out the window and then back at Amir.

Of course we believe you otherwise we wouldn't be here, she says reaching for Amir's hand.

Slowly I reach out my hand and put it on the table on top of Amir and Jameelah's hands then Amir puts his other hand on top of mine and then Jameelah does the same and then I pull out my other hand and put it on top of hers and Amir smiles and pulls his hand out from under ours and puts it on top of the pile of hands, Jameelah, me, Amir, just like when we were kids, one for all and all for one Jameelah always used to say, she got it out of some book but now, I think, it's not like in a book, nothing is like it used to be no matter how many games we play with our hands.

The uniformed guy clears his throat loudly.

Time's up.

Dig in man, says Nico nodding at the food and shaking Amir's hand, and think it over, take some time to really think it all over.

Salam brother, says Jameelah.

See you soon, I say.

See you soon, says Amir handing back the handkerchief, here, take it, consider it a gift, you can wash it and keep using it. Not bad, eh? They've got tons of them here.

Thanks, I say putting it in my pocket.

Do you still have the box, Amir whispers when Nico and Jameelah have moved off to the door.

Of course, what do you think?

Get rid of it.

Why?

Get rid of it. Don't open it just throw it away, okay?

Fine.

I'm not a bad person Nini.

I know, I say, I know who you are. We're going to help you, it's a promise.

No, says Amir, it's too late and now that it's too late I'd rather bleed than break.

* * *

Totally sad, says Nico when we're back outside the exit. He takes a sketchbook and a pen out of his lunchbox and walks off along the prison wall. The gift basket is between me and Jameelah and we open the cellophane and take turns drinking from the second bottle of lingonberry juice.

What are you doing, I ask but Nico doesn't answer he just stands in front of the wall and doodles in his sketchbook. The sun beats down on us.

Jameelah rolls her eyes.

The master artist at work.

I'm already finished anyway, says Nico stuffing the pad and pen back in his lunchbox.

What's the story, says Jamelah.

This place needs to be tagged, he says, right there on the wall it needs to say sad.

Jameelah looks at him in disbelief.

Aerosol really kills brain cells, eh?

Oh shut your mouth.

Nico this is seriously stupid, I say, there must be cameras all over the place.

Nope I saw it when we went in, they can't see the bit right up close to the wall just around the corner here, he says bending down to the gift basket. He pulls out a can of hunter's stew, rips open the pull tab, and gulps it down cold.

You're an animal, says Jameelah turning away in disgust.

What's the problem, says Nico with his mouth full, it's the perfect dish for this weather.

How can you eat right now, says Jameelah, especially that stuff that was supposed to be for Amir.

Sorry, I'm hungry, says Nico, what am I supposed to fast? That won't get Amir out.

His calm face and his hands which he keeps wiping on his stained trousers are somehow settling to me. Things will go on. Everything will go on. The trains will continue to run chugging from station to station and the sun will continue to cross the sky, no matter what happens the earth just keeps spinning and us with it, no matter how sad or hopeless you feel, everybody has to eat and drink and shit sooner or later and not just us, Amir too, whatever it is he gets to eat.

Nico gets off the train at Wilmersdorfer.

I have to hit the art supply store, see you later, he says kissing me on the cheek but nearly on the mouth.

What was that, asks Jameelah as the train pulls out of the station, are you guys a couple?

Don't be silly, I say, he wishes.

And you? Don't you wish it too?

No idea.

Come on don't pretend, says Jameelah smiling at me slyly.

Cut it out, I say looking out the window.

I'm not pretending, I can't possibly think about something like me and Nico at a moment like this. Amir's handkerchief is in my pocket and I pull it out and make a knot in it, for Jasna, and then another, for Amir, and then I tie another one, for Tarik, one for each dead person, for Jasna because she's really dead and Amir because he'll never really have a life again and for Tarik because he's the most dead of all of them because when you kill someone you kill yourself.

What are we going to do now, I ask.

I'm going to the tea shop, says Jameelah, Lukas is back and he might be there. Want to come?

You said we'd go to the police once we'd visited Amir.

No I didn't.

Yes you did, you promised even.

I did not, says Jameelah, I promised to help you fish the damn ring out of the bin and I kept that promise. I'm sorry we didn't find it but I've already said that about a thousand times. But

154

other than that I didn't promise anything.

You did so.

No you promised something or have you forgotten, says Jameelah, you promised you wouldn't go to the police until we spoke to Amir, you even pinky swore it.

I look at the floor and fidget around with Amir's handkerchief and tie more knots in it.

I kept my word, I say, and now we have to go to the police.

Nini it won't help him for us to talk.

Of course it will help him if we talk.

Right because Amir said to go straight to the cops, I rescind my confession, says Jameelah looking at me like I'm mentally disabled, I must have misheard all of that somehow.

No, I say, but he did say he didn't want her to die. He was sad.

Because of Jasna, says Jameelah.

No, also because he's innocent.

He said it's none of our business what he does with his life.

That's just bullshit you know how he is, I say.

Bullshit? Have you already forgot the way he shouted at me? You provoked him!

Yeah because I tried to press the truth out of him! So we wouldn't have to get mixed up in this shit and find ourselves at the cemetery just like Jasna.

That's crazy talk.

No it isn't. Ever heard of the witness protection programme? You get a totally new identity, a new name, you go to another city, it's James Bond shit. You're not allowed to have contact with anyone from your previous life. Is that what you want?

You watch too much TV.

Says you of all people! For god's sake, they're deciding at this very moment whether I'm allowed to stay in Germany, do you have any idea what that means? One little thing, one false word, and I'm fucked.

You're exaggerating, I say, I mean we're not street kids in Guatemala.

Jameelah sighs.

Then go ahead. Go to the cops and tell them everything. But keep me out of it. I wasn't with you and didn't see anything, she says standing up, I have to get out.

Why?

I'm meeting Nadja at the tea shop I already told you.

Krap-Krüger tea shop?

Yep, you coming?

Nah.

Fine then don't.

Bye.

Bye. Amir will be so thankful to you. And Tarik most of all.

I don't go to the cops I go home, into my room, finally stuff the tabloid paper into the bin and take it down to the yard. I empty the bin into an overflowing skip and the tabloid stays lying there on top, Amir and Jameelah, suspect written above Amir's head. Up to now I always thought some things were forever, they never changed, never disappeared, like the fossils of animals in biology that are apparently millions of years old. But it's not true, things aren't fossilized, Jameelah is right, things always change whether you want them to or not.

I shove a frozen pizza into the oven and sit down with it in front of the TV but when I go to start eating I notice there are mushrooms on the pizza. I hate mushrooms so I take them all off and burn my fingers doing it and then I realize I don't feel like eating salami either or ham. At some point there's nothing left on the pizza but cheese and tomatoes and the cheese and tomatoes are good but when I bite into the pizza I realize it's still frozen in the middle. I run downstairs to the dumpster again with the plate in my hand. The pizza lands right on Amir's face.

My phone rings, it's Nico.

How's it going cutie, he says.

Like shit. How about you?

I went to the art supply store and got spray cans. Should I stop by?

I don't know, I say.

Is Jameelah there?

No she went to the tea shop.

And you?

Fuck human rights, I say.

What's up?

Nothing, just Lukas, I say, he gets on my nerves.

Like I always say he's a poof.

Cut it out.

Okay, okay. Is my brother with you?

They all went to the cinema.

Send him over when they're back, yeah?

I will. Are you going to head out tonight?

Yeah, says Nico, I feel like it's the only thing I can do.

Can I come?

No, better not, it's dangerous.

That's why I want to. I can be the lookout.

Fine, says Nico after a long pause, but it'll be really late. Take a nap and I'll call you, then you come down and meet me at the playground.

Not the playground.

Fine how about in front of our door. But be quiet, got it?

Got it.

157

See you then cutie.

I hang up and want to go back to my room but just then the apartment door opens and Mama, Rainer, Jessi, and Pepi come in. Jessi has vampire teeth in her mouth and she jumps into my arms, her hands smell like popcorn and bananas.

We went to see *Twilight Eclipse*, they say.

In addition to the smell of popcorn and bananas there's also the smell of french fries and suddenly I realize I'm starving. Rainer has two big paper bags in his hand and he goes into the kitchen and unpacks four gyro platters.

So, now it's time to eat, says Mama.

Can Pepi stay to eat, asks Jessi.

Nico called, I say, and Pepi's supposed to go home.

My crown, shouts Pepi and pulls a crumpled Burger King crown out of one of the bags.

Bye, he says putting on his crown.

Mama's hair is down and she has something on her lips, she seems to be in a really good mood. She gets plates out of the cabinet, sets them on the table and puts utensils next to each plate and places napkins from the takeaway bag under each set of utensils. I wonder for a second if I've forgotten someone's birthday but I haven't.

Is there ketchup, asks Jessi.

No, says Rainer pointing first at the meat and then at the tzatziki sauce, you eat it with the white sauce there.

Sit down sweetie, says Mama to me as she puts a bottle of Lambrusco and a bottle of coke on the table.

Can I have some of that, asks Jessi pointing at the wine.

Rainer laughs darkly.

Now listen up my daughters.

He pours wine for Mama and himself and we get cola.

To family, he says lifting his glass.

We clink our glasses together, I pull my hair back and start to eat. The tzatziki has no flavour, just yoghurt and salt, so I go into the kitchen and grab the ketchup bottle out of the fridge.

Thanks ever so much, says Rainer glaring at me reproachfully.

What, I say squirting ketchup onto my plate in a pattern of small red dots.

Give it to me, says Jessi but Rainer rips the bottle out of my hand and puts it down on the floor next to him.

You eat it with the white sauce there I already told you.

Don't be ridiculous, says Mama to Rainer picking up the ketchup and putting it back on the table. Jessi reaches for it and drowns her entire plate in a sea of red with just a few islands of white tzatziki.

Goddamn it, says Rainer, this isn't America.

That's enough Jessi, says Mama taking the bottle from her.

I'm just playing environmental protection, says Jessi with a full mouth, this is the ocean in Japan when they are slaughtering the whales, we learned about it in school.

And what about you, says Rainer looking at me, what are you learning about in school?

Papa, says Jessi bursting into laughter, school's out for summer.

Something is beeping. It's pitch dark, I look sleepily at my phone and it says Nico, it's just after twelve-thirty. I drink the rest of a glass of coke that's sitting on my nightstand, get dressed, take my Chucks in my hand and creep past Mama's bedroom.

The door is open and Rainer is snoring, it sounds like too much Lambrusco. As quietly as possible I close the door behind me and walk downstairs barefoot. Nico is sitting on his BMX bike, smoke is rising above him. He smiles when he sees me and runs his hand along his clean-shaven skull which is gleaming in the light of a streetlamp.

Hey, says Nico taking me in his arms.

I press my nose to his throat. He smells like the stuff in the spray cans, that stuff that Jameelah meant when she said it kills your brain cells. Nico's not stupid, Nico's clever, more clever than all of us together, he just doesn't make a point of showing it like Lukas.

Hop on, says Nico putting his feet on the pedals.

I get on behind him, standing on the stunt pegs attached to his rear axle, and he pedals off.

There's barely anybody on the streets in the middle of the night, the city drifts past us, buildings, trees, traffic lights. We ride down the length of Yorckstrasse to Kleist and then Ku'damm, we barely speak, just the sound of the spray cans rattling quietly in Nico's rucksack. I've never gone so far on a bike before, I never ride bikes at all, but standing behind Nico on the pegs I like it, and I also like the way Nico never looks left or right when we cross an intersection. Theoretically we could get run over at every single intersection and it feels like we're playing a game of rock paper scissors with our lives, but when I see that he's turning onto the autobahn it seems a little weird to me.

Are you crazy, I shout.

Nico laughs and races down the emergency lane as cars honk like mad as they whizz past.

We'll be off again in a second, it's a shortcut.

He leans into a curve and turns off at the next exit ramp. We go under an S-bahn bridge, straight ahead until the lights become smaller and less frequent. The noise of the autobahn gets softer and softer and at some point you can't hear anything at all anymore, just the swaying of the tree tops in the forest. The BMX bike bucks like a young horse over the tree roots. Nico brakes.

You've lost your mind, I say.

The opposite of living is being bored, says Nico grinning.

What the hell kind of bullshit saying is that?

Don't be like that, it all went just fine.

My eyes slowly get used to the dark. It seems like an eternity since Jameelah and I carried Amir's gift basket along this very same trail even though it was only this afternoon. Twigs snap beneath our feet and something chirps not far away.

Do you hear that, I say. It's a nightingale. Did you know there are more of them here than in Bavaria? Jameelah told me.

This is the animal capital of Germany after all, says Nico lighting up the joint that he's had tucked behind his ear up to this point.

Animal capital of Germany, what does that mean?

No idea, people just say it. Probably because there are so many dogs. It's just like the cows in India except here it's dogs.

I like dogs, I say.

Me too. I like all animals, says Nico.

Most men hate animals, I say.

Bullshit, says Nico.

It's true. They rip off their wings or burn them with magnifying glasses or shove straws up their asses to blow them up until they explode. It's true that's what boys always do.

I don't know, says Nico.

They do, I say, that's the way it is and do you know what they do with the most beautiful animals of all? The most beautiful animals are captured and stuffed. Or they spear them, like with Jasna.

You're crazy, says Nico.

In front of us you can make out the prison in the distance. There's a bright light above the wall, it rotates like the beacon in a lighthouse and shines over the tops of the trees. We stop at the edge of the woods and Nico hides his bike in some bushes.

161

Listen, he says putting his hand on my shoulder, you stay here and watch the road for people or cars coming past. It doesn't matter what kind of car you yell, okay?

Okay.

Have you ever seen *Forrest Gump*?

Yeah, why?

If I say run then you run as far and as fast as you can, got it?

Okay.

Nico grabs a mask from his rucksack.

Why is it a crime to paint walls anyway, I ask.

Painting walls isn't a crime, putting an innocent person in prison is a crime, says Nico putting on his mask.

I must have fallen asleep somehow.

Sleepyhead, whispers Nico shaking me gently.

Sorry, I murmur.

Do you want to have a look?

Yeah, I say getting slowly to my feet. My legs have fallen asleep and they tingle as I cross the street. I can already make it out from far away. I want to go closer but Nico shakes his head. We stand silently in the bushes with the freshly painted wall in front of us. Sad it says in big blue letters on the wall, dark blue outlines, light blue inside, and all around the prison wall, the letters are round and soft and funny. The rotating beacon lights up Nico's face at regular intervals.

Blue is Amir's favourite colour, I say.

Blue also means sad, says Nico.

Somewhere behind there he's sleeping, I say.

Maybe he's not sleeping at all, says Nico, maybe he's lying awake thinking about what we said to him today, maybe he's shitting himself about throwing his future away and is finally coming to his senses.

Yeah, I say, I hope so.

But the other guy, says Nico, I'll bet he's sleeping nice and sound.

What other guy?

The real murderer of course, says Nico looking at me.

He puts the empty spray cans back in his bag and pulls his bike out of the bushes.

Come on let's get out of here.

We walk silently along the path through the woods. I keep turning around because I think somebody is following us.

There's nobody there believe me I'll never get caught, says Nico, but I keep turning back anyway. I'm worried that there will be cops there, I'm afraid of the shadows that look like a giant black horse. If only this had all never happened, I think, if only Jameelah and I hadn't seen anything, if we'd not gone out to the playground, if only Lukas had just fallen in love with Jameelah straight away, then that giant black horse wouldn't be following me, that giant black horse is the whole experience but I don't want it to follow me I want to bury it, bury it and then stomp on the dirt on top of it, but how am I going to bury a giant black horse all by myself.

Nico stops and takes my hand.

Is everything okay, he asks.

Yeah I'm just sad. This isn't the way I pictured summer break.

Yeah, says Nico, I know, then he puts his arm around my waist and kisses me. His mouth tastes of cigarettes and menthol, the menthol is from a piece of gum he's chewing, a normal white piece of gum, not red, not green, not strawberry or Waldmeister, just plain old white, plain old menthol, grown up. Arm in arm we walk through the woods and he pushes his bike along beside him all slick and cool.

Have I ever told you about the engagement ring, I ask, my mother's ring that my dad apparently took with him when he left? Mama always claimed he gave it to his new wife.

No. What made you think of that?

Jasna had a ring just like it on her finger, it looked just like Mama's ring, that's why.

Have you ever asked your father?

What?

If he took the ring.

No. I haven't heard from him in ages. The last time was when he sent me something for one of my birthdays. Five euros and a stupid card. I don't even know where he lives now and don't know if Chico is still with him or if Chico's even alive anymore.

Don't worry, dogs live pretty long, says Nico.

In the distance I can make out the S-bahn bridge. Nico gets on his bike and I stand on the stunt pegs.

It's okay if you want to go on the autobahn again, I say.

Nah, we don't have to.

I want to now, I say, come on.

We ride under the bridge and shoot onto the autobahn. The cars honk right in my ear, I close my eyes and let the wind buffet my face as we ride, I let my hair flutter in the wind and I bet the people driving by in their cars think it looks like a motorcycle advert.

You can tell your kids about this, Nico shouts pedalling even faster.

Yeah, I shout back, but will my kids even know what a BMX bike is I wonder, maybe to them they'll see a BMX bike the way we look at those bikes with the giant front wheel like they rode around on before the war, the kind in those pictures in that U-bahn station in the Hansaviertel, and anyway, kids, having kids sounds so strange like some exotic country, Guatemala,

164

street kids don't have kids, they never get old enough for that and if they do they're not kids anymore, kids who have kids, that's impossible, and me I'm no better than a street kid, I think, and then suddenly I'm shitting myself with fear the way I'm standing on the stunt pegs behind Nico, shitting myself about the idea of having kids and being lonely and getting old and dying young and that something bad could happen to Nico before all of that, something really bad.

Shit, I think, this is love and I quickly open my eyes. Standing on the pedals in front of me Nico looks like a tall black tower, all around him the glittering city lit up.

THE BIRTHDAY CARD WITH PAPA'S ADDRESS ON THE ENVELOPE is gone. I turn over my entire room and even find the blue piggy bank I thought Jessi had stolen behind my desk along with two old donald duck paperbacks, but the birthday card is gone and I'm not even sure I didn't throw it away myself along with the CD of *The Bodyguard* soundtrack that Papa sent along with the card. Obviously I didn't tell Nico about the *Bodyguard* soundtrack, I'm not stupid. I go out into the hallway and look in a drawer of the cabinet there for the key to the basement but there's no basement key anywhere, just crap like an empty lighter, all sorts of stuff nobody would ever need.

Mama, I call, where's the key to the basement but Mama isn't home, just Jessi, I can hear shuffling around in the living room. When I hear the click of the glass-front cabinet I throw open the door to the living room and find Jessi in front of the cabinet with her skinny legs sticking out of her short pyjama bottoms. She looks at me startled.

What are you doing?

Nothing.

Keep your hands off the Eier liqueur, I say.

I was just going into the goodie cabinet, just wanted something sweet, she says.

You weren't opening the goodie cabinet you were opening the

166

glass-front cabinet. I heard it. And if I catch you again I'll tell Mama, got it?

I'm hungry, says Jessi and then the doorbell rings.

I ram into the open drawer in the entry hall cabinet. It's Jameelah. In one hand she has a thick folder with a German flag on it and in the other a package of strawberry-filled Turkish cookies.

You didn't go to the police, asks Jameelah, right?

No, I say rubbing my bruised hip.

Are you still pissed off?

I never was, I say and then point to the folder, what's that?

The questions for the German test. Can you quiz me?

Have you already started studying for next year's classes? You're crazy.

No it's for the test you have to take if you want to become German.

Ah right. Do you have to know them all?

Not yet but I might soon so I'm studying during break while I have time, understand?

To be honest I can't say I really understand but before I can say that Jessi comes into the hall. She looks longingly at the package of cookies.

Can I have one, she asks with her eyes bulging.

Cut it out, I say.

But I'm so hungry.

Come on I'll make you a sandwich, I say but Jessi says, there's no bread. Jameelah opens the cookies.

Here, she says handing Jessi a stack of cookies.

Thanks, says Jessi walking back into the living room with her arms loaded with cookies and then the TV starts blaring.

Where's your mother, asks Jameelah.

No idea.

167

I look at the jumble of stuff in the open drawer, old batteries and lighters, tangled thread, dried up bottles of nail polish, and in between all sorts of action figures, smurfs, kung-fu pandas and donald duckies lying in a coma on the bottom of the drawer with their arms wrapped around binder clips and old West German pennies. At the very back is a beginner's knitting set with a half-unravelled strip of knitting trailing away from it. This is exactly why Papa left, I think, because of Mama and her sofa and the fridge, the beds, the air in this place, everything just like the stuff in this drawer, dirty, tangled up, and useless, I know it now and I knew it then when Papa was still here but I could never say anything.

Nothing but shit, I say and rip the drawer right out and let everything crash out onto the floor, it sounds like a thunderstorm, the kind you wait for all day.

What's up with you, asks Jameelah putting the cookies and folder down on the entry hall cabinet and squatting next to me.

Nothing I'm just looking for the key to the basement, it has to be in here.

You mean this, asks Jameelah pointing to something shiny.

Come with me, I say grabbing the key, you have to help me. I'll quiz you afterwards.

I don't like going into the basement, I mean, nobody likes going into the basement but our basement is particularly spooky because the light only lights up the first part and it's pitch black back by our storage space.

Give me your phone.

I unlock the gate and shine the light from Jameelah's phone into the space. It smells of foul water from the heating system and musty clothes and in the front right corner there's a pile of old coal from years ago, we've had central heating for ages now. Stacked against the walls are soggy moving boxes with Mama's old clothes hanging out of them and next to the boxes is Rainer's collection of useless electrical devices. No wonder that they keep piling up here, a waffle iron, a nacho heater, like we ever had homemade waffles or nachos. As above so it is below, didn't Jesus or somebody say that, anyway that's the way it is, our mouldy basement space looks like the drawer of shit in the hall cabinet, I think, and then I stumble over my old ride-on car past a broken kiddie pool and back to the Barbie dollhouse. The Barbie doll sitting in the living room is the one that lifted up that piece of chewing gum years ago, somehow it's calming to see her, like there's someone guarding the basement, like she's the Hausmeister and probably the only Hausmeister in the world wearing nothing more than a metallic gold swimsuit.

Are we looking for something in particular, asks Jameelah. She coughs.

Yeah, that's it there, I say pointing at an old guitar case sitting behind the Barbie house and covered by a thick layer of dust.

I didn't know any of you could play guitar.

None of us can, I say pulling the thing out of the corner, my father played and he took his guitar with him, I say knocking on the case, but he forgot this.

Together we carry the case upstairs.

Jameelah moans.

What on earth is in there, she asks.

Anything I don't want anymore but can't throw away.

We drag the guitar case into my room. It's filled to the brim with stuff and looks no better than the drawer in the hall cabinet. And there at the very bottom between a folder of old school essays and my autograph book is a bundle of postcards and

169

tucked in there is the birthday card and underneath it is the CD.

The Bodyguard, says Jameelah giggling, let me see it.

She goes over to the CD player and puts it in. There are balloons on the front of the birthday card and mice are sitting atop the balloons, not cartoon mice, normal mice with four paws. The mice are watching butterflies and ladybirds and the tails of the mice form the letters *Happy Birthday*.

Is that the card?

Yeah, I say, but there's no address on it, Mama must have thrown out the envelope.

Why do you want an address, asks Jameelah, you want to write to him?

I was thinking about it.

Have you searched him online?

Yeah but there was nothing. There were so many people with the same name, over 900,000 results.

Give me the card, says Jameelah stuffing a cookie in her mouth. Whitney Houston is singing 'I Will Always Love You' in the background. Just don't cry, I think and swallow hard.

Watch it with your strawberry fingers, I say.

It's fine.

Jameelah opens the card and frowns.

This is impossible to read, she says, the writing how can you read that writing?

I don't know, I always asked Mama to read it to me but she didn't want to, she refused, I say looking at the scrawl, typical adult writing, you really can't make out a single word. Jameelah squints and leans over the card tracing the scrawled writing with her finger.

Wake? No that can't be it, doesn't make sense. *Make* maybe? That's it, *make like* and then the next bit is illegible again.

I take the card out of her hand.

Sandal or something like that, I say, *make like a sandal*? No that's stupid.

Sun something, sundial, *make like a sundial*, says Jameelah, if that's it then I know what it says.

What?

It says *make like a sundial and count only the hours when the world is bright.* It's some kind of saying, I read it somewhere. See, look, it also would fit with the words, says Jameelah pointing to the second line of scrawled letters.

True, I say, and then *with love, Papa.* That was the only part I could ever read before.

Why would somebody write that on a birthday card, says Jameelah.

What?

You know, make like a sundial.

Who knows, it's just a saying.

Just a saying my ass, abandoning your family like that and then telling your daughter to make like a sundial. That's fucked up.

You think so?

Yeah I do. Do you have a photo of him?

I get up and go to get my photo box out from under the bed and then I see it, Amir's shoebox is there and I'm supposed to get rid of it and I've forgotten to and I'll have to take care of that later, I think, once Jameelah's gone because if she catches wind of it she'll definitely want to open the box or whatever, that's just the way she is.

I pull the box of photos out from under the bed, here I say, handing a photo to Jameelah.

Papa has me on his lap and is playing chess with the person who shot the photo. I know for a fact that Mama took the photo.

171

If I didn't know it for a fact it would never occur to me that Mama had ever played chess. Mama and chess are about as far apart as I don't know, whatever the farthest apart two things can be is.

Never seen him, says Jameelah staring at the photo.

Of course not, how would you?

I don't know, on Kurfürstenstrasse maybe.

That's enough, I say ripping the photo out of her hand.

Just imagine, says Jameelah, picture us on Kurfürsten sitting on our usual electrical box and then all of a sudden your father comes past, that would be something.

That would not be something, I say, shut up.

Take it easy, says Jameelah.

Take it easy my ass.

Gingerly she takes the photo from me again and looks at it for a long time.

Be happy, she says, at least you still have a father. Mine can't ever pop up somewhere, not even on Kurfürsten.

It doesn't do me any good. If you don't hear from somebody they might as well be dead.

Bullshit, says Jameelah, if you really wanted to you could see him. Or at least write to him.

I wanted to, I say, because of the ring.

Then do it. Just call him. That's what I'd do. I'd tell him off. Just up and leaving his family like that.

Call him, I don't know. I'm not sure I have the nerve.

Does you mother have an address book?

Yeah.

I'll bet your mother has his number in it.

Why would she? They don't have anything to do with each other.

Parents have that sort of information, especially when they're

172

enemies. Believe me parents who are fighting with each other are more tightly bound together than parents who get along.

Jameelah stands up and swats the cookie crumbs off herself.

Come on, show me the address book.

When we're in front of Mama and Rainer's bedroom I knock before I open the door just to be safe but there's nobody there and the bed is freshly made, the decorative quilt is even on top, that must have been Rainer. There's a table next to the window with a small TV on it and beneath the TV is a drawer where Mama keeps the remote and the TV magazine. Underneath the magazine is her address book.

Here, I say handing Jameelah the book with my heart pounding.

What's his name, she asks.

Jameelah sits cross-legged on the bed, wets her pointer finger and starts leafing through the book. I watch over her shoulder as she goes through G, H, I, the quilt is all rumpled, hopefully nobody comes home, I think, Mama doesn't like it when we go into her room.

There he is, Joachim, right below my number. Funny, eh, that we're right next to each other, says Jameelah grinning, come on you're going to call him now.

My head starts to throb.

You're nuts, I say.

Why?

I haven't spoken to him in forever.

All the more reason, says Jameelah.

I can't.

Come on, at the end of the day he's just your dad!

No, I say, there is no chance.

Fine, says Jameelah grabbing the pen on the table and writing the number on her arm, then I'll call him

Together we smooth out the quilt and go back into my room. I carefully close the door.

Like the old days, says Jameelah changing the settings on her phone so the number is anonymous.

What do you mean like the old days?

Prank calls. Good afternoon we just wanted to notify you that you won the lottery. Your house will be demolished today. Remember?

It's not like the old days, I say, and what do you want to say to him anyway?

Not sure yet, says Jameelah typing the number and turning up the volume. I sway nervously back and forth on my bed. I hear it ringing.

Hello?

He's there on the line, from one second to the next suddenly there on the phone, but somebody must have stuffed an insane amount of cotton in my ears because all of a sudden I can barely hear anything and the blood rushes at the speed of light into my head and then back down to my legs, everything pulses and whooshes and jumps, heart and lungs and stomach. As if from very far away I hear Jameelah talking to Papa.

Hello Joachim, so, how's it going?

Who is this, I hear Papa say.

Come on, says Jameelah acting surprised, don't you recognize me anymore?

I don't believe so, says Papa and laughs.

It's been years, says Jameelah.

It's been a light year since the last time I heard Papa laugh, exactly one light year, the living room was dark, I was on his lap, pretzel crumbs everywhere, the TV flickering in front of us

174

showing a movie where Bud Spencer is punching everybody. I can still hear the sounds distinctly, Bud Spencer's fists landing and Papa laughing.

I'll give you three guesses, says Jameelah.

Papa laughs again and this time he sounds unsettled.

I really don't know, I hear him say, there's a rustling sound on the line as if the wind has just blown into the mic on his phone.

I'm sorry, says Papa, I'm afraid you must have dialled the wrong number.

No, I definitely have not.

Hang up, I whisper but Jameelah doesn't listen.

Make like a sundial and count only the hours when the world is bright.

Excuse me, asks Papa.

Make like a sundial, says Jameelah again, and count only the hours when the world is bright. What kind of stupid expression is that anyway?

It's dead quiet on the other end of the phone. My head and heart pound.

Nini is that you, asks Papa.

Before Jameelah can answer I grab the phone.

Papa?

Nini, he says again, is that you?

Yeah Papa, it's me.

Suddenly I have a horrible squeaky voice.

My God has something happened, where is your mother?

No idea.

Is everything okay?

Yes, I say.

What a scare you gave me dear child, says Papa, I thought it was something serious.

To be honest I don't really understand what he's talking about with a scare and something serious. I would love to ask that and a thousand other things. I close my eyes and try to form a sentence but my mind is completely empty and just like that loose thread and the action figures in the drawer the words get all tangled up in my lungs, in my throat, in the air.

There's a rustling on the line again.

I'm on a train, says Papa, I can't hear you very well.

I can't hear you well either, I say.

He answers something but his voice and some of the words break up into unintelligible snippets and at some point the call is dropped and there's nothing more than the radio silence of a dead zone. Papa is gone. There's a beep and I hold the warm phone in my hands for a while longer, it feels a bit like a warm hand, I think, like the still-warm hand of someone who's just died, since hanging up is a bit like dying, hanging up is a little death.

Fucking dead zones, says Jameelah, come on call back.

No, I say and I realize that my voice is back to normal.

A thousand things go through my head, all the things and questions I wanted to ask, all the tangled up words are suddenly lined up like toy soldiers, perfectly straight lines, rifles aligned with their feet, standing at attention forming perfect sentences. I wonder if he still has the key chain I made for him out of bottle caps in kindergarten, whether Chico is still around and Grandma Muelsig, why he sent me the *Bodyguard* soundtrack, whether it was supposed to be a sign, you know, like I'll protect you even if only from a distance, and why he didn't just take me with him instead of protecting me from a distance. At least he could have asked me. But then again maybe he didn't want me to go with him, maybe I was little and irritating and useless, dirty and tangled up like the stuff in the drawer of junk, like Mama's clothes in the basement or Rainer's useless electrical devices, the kind of stuff you weed out when you move because you don't want it at a new apartment.

You okay, asks Jameelah.

I don't know. Strange situation. It's been so long since I spoke to him. And it was all so sudden.

At least you have his number now, says Jameelah, you can call him whenever you want. It's great.

Yeah, I say, that's true, even though I know I never will. I'll never call Papa again and then it occurs to me that the reason I wanted to talk to him was the ring. Fuck that ring, what business is it of mine, Mama's whining about the ring, why should I care whether Papa took the thing or not and then I catch myself wishing that I really had met Papa on Kurfürsten. Sure, there would have been trouble, Mama and Rainer would have found out and the school principal, and Papa would be incredibly disappointed in me, all of that is true. But at least he would have to have thought about me and the fact that he had a daughter out there somewhere, one who got herself into a lot of shit, and then he'd have to worry about me like it or not. At least for one single moment he'd have to worry about me.

Noura always says you should do something nice once in a while, something that belongs just to you and you alone. Today I'm going to do something nice, and all by myself. Mama and Jessi aren't home, they said goodbye this morning and Mama gave me twenty euros before they took off and another twenty for the taxi.

My rolling suitcase, the one I got for the school ski trip, is packed and waiting in the hall. I look at the time, I can only eat and drink for exactly one more hour and then not until tomorrow when everything's all done, but I'm so worked up that I haven't been able to eat since breakfast anyway. I take my suitcase and go down to the street and wave down a taxi. I've never been in a taxi by myself, the best I ever did was once together with Rainer but luckily Rainer has the late shift today.

When I'm in front of the hospital I fish around in my trouser pocket for the doctor's referral. A girl is sitting at the entrance, she's not much older than me, maybe sixteen or so, but she looks like a real nurse, she's wearing a white smock with a white cardigan over it. She hands me a clipboard and I have to fill out all sorts of forms. Once I'm done with that another nurse comes over to me, an older one.

You're far too early, she says taking my suitcase and putting her arm around my shoulders. We walk down the hall together. The walls are painted from floor to ceiling but not the way Nico does it, the way sick children would, sick kids who are bored. There's a pink rhino, a yellow crocodile, a smiling crab with huge pincers, a colourful clown and next to that a black guy saying to the clown, I don't have anything against people of colour. It's the worst joke I've heard in I don't know how long, but as I'm walking by and read the speech bubble I find it somehow funny, it's so harmless.

The nurse opens the door next to the clown and there are two beds in the room. The one in the back, by the window, is empty but there's someone in the closer bed, I don't know if it's a boy or girl, I mean I could probably tell if I looked but all I can do is stare at the legs in the bed, they distract me from anything else. The legs are charred, born to a crisp you could say in O-language, it would be a bit of an exaggeration but you're allowed to exaggerate in O-language, in fact O-language is made for exaggerating because you use it either for a laugh or because things are way too cross and mossed up and regular language just can't express how cross and mossed up things are, but anyway the legs are burned.

This is your bed here, says the nurse pointing to the empty bed. She pulls up the shade and opens the window, sun streams in, I have to squint. Outside is a big park with lots of trees and in between the trees are bushes with white flowers, the only thing missing is a lake, then it would be like it is in Italy.

So, says the nurse walking around the bed and fluffing the covers, we'll see if the anaesthesiologist has time to meet with you.

I look over at the other bed again.

What happened, I ask.

The nurse sighs.

Nylons. Matches and nylons. She's still very weak. She was in intensive care until yesterday.

She goes to the door and her nurse shoes clop on the floor like my flip-flops, just healthier. As I unpack my things and stow them in the drawer of the nightstand I feel pretty grown-up, in a different way from on Kurfürsten. I look over at the girl. Her wounds are yellow and red, the scabs are spiky and saw-toothed and in between are big black spots. Hospitals are something serious, you don't mess around, and that's good because everyone here knows not to mess around. I stretch out on the bed and wonder to myself whether anyone has ever died in this room or even right here in this bed. It wouldn't be so bad, with a view of the park, the sun shining in your face, there are worse ways to die. People who say hospitals are creepy places really don't have a clue, it's such a throwaway thing to say. I mean sure, this isn't a playground, but anyone who seriously thinks it would be nicer to die at a playground than here must have lost their chador.

There's a knock at the door.

Come in, I say.

It's Jameelah.

Salam! What is this the Four Seasons, she says letting herself drop onto the bed next to me, couldn't wait to check in, could you?

I put my arms behind my head and smile.

It's almost as nice as Italy, I say.

Wait until you see the food, it's usually crap, says Jameelah and then she looks over at the other bed.

What happened to her, she whispers.

Nylons, I say, and matches.

Really?

There's another knock at the door. Three doctors in white lab coats come into the room. You can tell which one is the boss right away. He's the tallest, looks great, and he walks ahead of the others.

Guten Tag, he says smiling, I'm Doctor Berkenkamp, I'll make sure that you are fast asleep before the operation tomorrow. We'll give you a shot and then send you off to a beautiful island, what do you think?

Sounds good, I say.

He sits down on the bed next to me. His eyes are deep blue like Tarik's.

Can I come to the island too, asks Jameelah flopping into the wicker chair next to the window.

The lead doctor laughs. He gently feels my neck with his cool fingers. He taps on my cheekbones and asks if it hurts and then he looks down my throat.

Which would you prefer, Greece or Italy, he asks tossing the tongue depressor into the bin next to my nightstand.

Italy.

Good, in that case we will send you to a beautiful island off the cost of Italy.

Fine with me, I say, but the important thing is the anaesthesia.

Don't want to have to wake you like Sleeping Beauty, says the lead doctor pinching my cheek, his hands smell like expensive cologne and I think that it wouldn't be so bad if he woke me like Sleeping Beauty.

The next morning a nurse wakes me. She rolls me down the hall in my bed to the lift. We go down to the basement, past fluorescent lights and through some thick glass doors that swing open and then the lead doctor is there. I recognize his blue eyes even though the rest of his face is covered.

We're off to Capri, he says putting a needle in my arm and attaching it to a long hose but after that there's nothing, no Capri, nothing at all.

181

I wake up slowly. Mama and Jessi are sitting at the table next to the window. Jessi is playing with her rubber hand clackers and Mama is looking out at the park and the first thing that comes into my head is what Mama would have answered, Italy or Greece.

Nini, calls Jessi jumping up and sitting at the end of the bed, you look like a Chinese mental patient.

So do you, I say. It hurts a lot to talk. The stitches in my jaw hurt.

How do you feel, asks Mama.

Okay.

Mama looks at the time.

We have to go, she says and kisses me goodbye on my forehead, you slept for such a long time.

It's fine, I say and fall back to sleep.

I only wake up again when a nurse pushes a trolley in with two trays on it. On one is normal food, on the other one, the one the nurse puts down on my nightstand with a smile, is a plastic container filled with puree, it looks like diarrhoea with a straw in it. I start grumpily slurping.

Come on another bite, says the nurse to the burned girl holding a piece of bratwurst under her nose, but when she turns her head away again the nurse gives up. As she goes to the door Jameelah comes in.

She grins at my container of diarrhoea.

Tasty?

Ha ha.

I told you.

She gets a great meal and doesn't even touch it, I whisper nodding at the burned girl.

She must have private health insurance.

I'm hungry.

Go ahead and take hers, says Jameelah.

Very funny.

What, are you scared, she says walking over to the other bed.

Hello, she says, your food is getting cold, hello, she repeats waving her hands in front of the burned girl's face. I can't help giggling.

Well then, as long as you don't give a shot, Jameelah says grabbing the tray and sitting back down next to me.

Give me some, I say but Jameelah shakes her head and shoves another delicious looking piece of wurst into her gullet.

You were too scared to take it, so enjoy your diarrhoea.

Come on just a piece of bratwurst.

Man you're not supposed to eat any solid food with those stitches in your mouth, they'll pop and then it'll be a huge mess.

Then mosh up a piece for me.

Mosh for mash, that's good. But don't give a shot wasn't bad either, eh?

Give me a piece.

I'm going to call the nurse if you take any, says Jameelah putting her hand on the red call button next to my bed.

Blackmailer, I say.

The squeaking sound of the food trolley wakes me. A sweet guy in white clothes walks in.

Sorry for the delay, he says picking up a tray with another container of diarrhoea. He looks at me, uncertain.

That's for her, I say pointing at the burned girl.

Sorry I'm just filling in today, he says putting down a tray with a plate of spaghetti on it next to my bed. With the fork I cut up the spaghetti as small as possible and carefully start to eat it. It doesn't hurt, or barely hurts, only when the stitches

183

stretch. I go into the bathroom and look in the mirror. I'm slowly starting to look less and less like a Chinese mental patient, more like a hamster with a fat lip, or somebody with two super balls in their mouth who refuses to spit them out. When I return to the room Nico is sitting on my bed.

Hi cutie, he says.

I can feel my face flush with happiness.

Don't say anything, I say, I already know that I look like a Chinese mental patient.

Why Chinese?

That's what Jessi said because the swelling went all the way up to my eyes. But it's a bit better now.

Nico stands up.

Are you allowed to be kissed, he asks and kisses me on the mouth before waiting for an answer.

Careful, I say, everything's still swollen.

I'm being careful, he says and kisses me again.

Do you have any smokes, I ask.

Are you allowed to smoke already?

Don't give me that.

He hands me a cigarette begrudgingly.

We go downstairs and out to the park. The cigarette gives me a rush and my eyes go black for a second but I like it when you get dizzy from smoking, the curtain comes down, the curtain goes back up again and in a few seconds it's all over, like a passing cloud casting a shadow.

I wanted to come yesterday, says Nico, but I wasn't sure when the visiting hours were, whether it was too late to stop by in the evening.

No problem, I say taking a drag.

So are you bored?

I shake my head.

Somebody died here today.

Crazy.

Yeah but luckily I didn't see anything, I say, I just heard about it. Morbid. Have you ever seen a dead person?

Just my grandmother, says Nico.

And?

Wasn't so bad. It was sad, but not disgusting. She was really old.

Death is weird, I say, don't you think?

Yeah, says Nico, but at the end of the day death is something totally normal.

I don't know, I say, that's sounds like bullshit.

Why, says Nico, death is part of life.

See, that's the same kind of bullshit. Everybody says shit like that. People talk about death like they talk about the weather but only because they're scared shitless about it. That doesn't fly with me.

Nico thinks for a minute.

But we all have to die sooner or later.

I ram my elbow into his ribs.

Yet another cliché.

Well there you go, in that case I'll get in bed with you right now, says Nico grabbing my legs and slinging me over his shoulder. I squeal. Hanging upside-down on Nico's back I see a nurse coming across the park toward us.

Visiting hours are over, she says tapping on her watch and looking at us sternly.

I was just about to leave, says Nico.

You were not, I say when the nurse leaves again.

What?

Leaving.

No?

No, I say taking his hand. Like thieves we slink through the park to the entrance and then up the stairs one floor after the next. I cautiously open the door to my room and pull Nico to the bed.

You're crazy, he whispers nodding at the burned girl, what about her?

We'll have to be quiet, I say and kiss him. We creep our way to the bed, kissing like our mouths are fused together, it's nice but my cheeks hurt. I realize I'm dead tired but then I hear the clink of Nico's belt and in the next instant his baggy trousers fall to his knees.

Carefully, as if it would make noise, Nico takes my t-shirt off, I don't have a bra on so I quickly get under the covers even though it's almost dark outside and it's dark in the room already. His hard-on is sticking to my thigh.

Sorry, says Nico.

It's okay, I say pulling down his boxers and then my underwear which rolls up as I push it down my legs, that would normally never happen, it's just because I'm rushing, and why really, I wonder, and then as if Nico can read my thoughts he lies down next to me all calm and looks at me.

Don't say anything like are you sure you really want this, I whisper.

I wasn't going to say that, Nico whispers back.

I stand up, grab my wallet and disappear into the bathroom and rummage around for the condom that I've been carrying around all this time for just this moment, the same way other people carry a treasured family photo in their wallet all the time. All the condoms Jameelah and I have ripped open, at first by ourselves in her room and then taking them to the bathroom to fill with water and dropping them on people from the window, then later unrolling condoms over cucumbers and Barbie dolls, and then all the stuff on Kurfürsten started. I look at the expiration date and then toss the condom in the toilet. Even if it wasn't already expired, I think, condoms are for kids and hookers and I'm neither one of those.

I creep back into bed with Nico. I lie down on my back so Nico can get on top of me, I don't think we're going to try it any other way on our first time.

Quietly, I whisper before he starts.

This time I'm aware of everything because I'm not as fucked up as last time. This time it hurts bad, like getting poked but at the same time also like when you pinch yourself in a door or something. The purple spiral staircase is there again, I forgot to ask Jameelah why I see that when I sleep with someone. Maybe it's the staircase that leads out of childhood. The real world is up there, or the fake one, or the rotten one, it hurts in any event. Without wanting to, I bite down and press my teeth together and the pain from below mixes with the pain in my mouth, somehow it's nice though, no idea why, it sounds stupid but it's true. Maybe it's the kind of pain Rainer's always gabbing on about when he shows us his pitiful tattoo for the hundredth time, and I have to think of the guy in the wheelchair and what he said about violence, only now do I really understand what it was he was trying to tell us. The guy in the wheelchair is right. Violence isn't about the pain itself but the intent to cause pain, it's when somebody wants to inflict pain on you. The guy in the wheelchair wasn't so stupid after all, and the fact that he wasn't so stupid is a comforting thought to me.

I bleed, this time I bleed so much that I completely mess up the sheets. Nico is appalled.

It's normal, I say.

I know, he says, but still.

Give me a hand, I say.

Together we strip the bed and I stuff the sheets into the bottom

187

drawer of the cabinet. We creep back into bed. Nico snuggles up to me. I hear a siren outside as a fire truck drives past on Argentinischen Allee.

I'm supposed to say hello to you from Amir by the way, says Nico.

What, I say sitting up, you went there again?

No I called him.

Called him? How did you get his number? I want to call him too.

You can.

I jump out of bed.

Not right now, says Nico, it's already too late.

Why, I'm sure Amir's not asleep yet.

Get back in here, whispers Nico pulling me gently back onto the bed, you can only call during certain times. We can call tomorrow. Besides, I have something for you.

For me? What is it?

Only if you settle down.

Fine, I say letting myself fall back onto the pillow.

Nico gets up and looks in his trouser pocket and then hides something in his hand. I can't help smiling.

I saw it, I say.

No you didn't, says Nico.

You're right, I didn't.

Close your eyes, he says fumbling around with my fingers.

Out of nowhere my heart starts beating like crazy.

Now, he says.

I open my eyes and look at my hand. On it is the ring, Jasna's ring, Mama's ring, Papa's ring, three stones, two little white ones and a green one between them.

I know, maybe it's a bit over the top, says Nico, but do you like it anyway?

I look at Nico and at the ring and at Nico again.

Where, I whisper, how did you get it?

I found it, says Nico, under the S-bahn, does that bother you? I took it to the lost and found office but when nobody picked it up after two weeks I was allowed to take it. I went to a jewellery store, it's real.

I know, I say looking at the ring again.

My hand slowly starts to tremble, only a little bit at first but it keeps getting stronger and then the trembling crawls up my arms and into my shoulders and down through my guts to my hips and legs until my entire body is shaking, I can't do anything, I can't stop, it's like in an earthquake or a storm, some kind of natural disaster.

What's wrong, asks Nico, his voice sounds very distant.

I shake my head and look at the ring, all I can see are the small stones, Mama and I are the small white stones and Papa the big green one, I think, then everything goes blurry and something warm starts running down my legs but luckily the warm stuff running down my legs is just sperm.

What's wrong, Nico keeps saying.

Nothing, I say trying to get myself together, go get me some toilet paper please.

Nico goes into the bathroom. The burned girl has woken up, at least she's moving around in her bed. Nico comes back with a roll of toilet paper.

Will you please tell me what's up, he asks.

I wipe my nose.

Tell me.

Quiet, I whisper. My jaw, the wounds, everything is throbbing, the toilet paper is grey and so hard it hurts when you wipe your eyes and makes you cry even more. I take a deep breath, I look over at the burned girl, she's not moving around anymore, maybe she's trying to fall back to sleep, maybe she'd like to say something, like we need to stop screwing and crying I want to sleep, cut it out she'd probably like to say but maybe she can't talk, I think, and then that if she can't sleep we have something in common she and I, but we don't have anything in common because I can talk and I can say something right now and I want to. I take a deep breath.

We saw it, I whisper.

Saw what?

How he stabbed her at the playground.

Nico looks at me incredulously.

What?

There's no what about it goddamn it, we were sitting at the top of the slide and we saw the whole thing. How he took her in his arms and then how he executed her with his knife, how Jasna laid there in her own blood and puke.

You can't be serious, says Nico.

You don't know a thing about death, oh it's natural and a part of life, you don't have a clue.

Nico is silent and stares at the bedding.

Who, he asks at some point.

I shred the rough toilet paper between my fingers.

Tarik, I say, it was Tarik.

You have to go to the police, Nico says for about the hundredth time since we woke up.

I jump out of bed and pull up the shades.

Leave me alone, I say, I don't want to talk about it anymore.

You can't act like nothing has happened. Like I said I'll go with you if you want, you don't have to get through it alone.

Get through it, I can't hear it anymore. The fuck you'll help me get through it, you have nothing to do with it, I say.

I do now, says Nico.

I throw him his clothes.

Here, I've got a visitor coming, you have to leave.

Looking hurt, Nico gets dressed. We take the lift down to the ground floor together without saying a word. When we're at the exit Nico looks at me for a long time.

What, I say.

I really don't want to say this but if you don't do it I'm going to.

What are you going to do if I don't do it?

Go to the cops, says Nico, you open yourself up to being charged as an accomplice if you don't say anything. And so do I.

Do you really think I didn't think about that?

Think it over, otherwise I'll see it through myself, seriously, says Nico then he turns and leaves.

I stagger to the lift and then back to my room like I've drunk too much Tiger Milk, that's exactly how I feel. The burned girl is sitting upright in her bed slurping from my plastic container, she looks at me reproachfully. I crawl back in bed, her breakfast is on my side table, muesli with yoghurt, I dip my spoon into it hiding the muesli beneath the yoghurt like the polar bear on *Terra X* burying itself in the snow, I bury the flakes of grain under the cold yoghurt but the muesli sticks to my teeth and I try to chew it up anyway.

Jameelah and I need to talk, but even the thought of that is out of the question, game over, might as well leave the playing field and hit the showers. Amir, I think, I need to talk to Amir, I have to tell him everything, maybe that will make him come to his senses, I should have done it ages ago, why on earth haven't I done that, I think.

The burned girl clears her throat.

191

You're bleeding, she says.

I turn to her.

There, she says pointing to her mouth.

Shit, thanks.

In the bathroom I look in the mirror. Everything is bright red back by the stitches inside my mouth, blood is trickling out of one of the wounds. I shove toilet paper into my mouth and bite down on it.

Thanks, I say again.

I'm being transferred, says the burned girl as if it's any of my business.

Nice, I say pulling my phone out of a drawer. I go out into the hallway but I don't have any minutes left so I go down to the information desk.

I desperately need to make a call, I say putting a piece of paper with Amir's number on it on the counter in front of the nurse, Nico wrote it down for me just this morning.

She dials the number and hands me the receiver, it rings a few times until finally some bureaucrat answers.

I would like to talk to Amir, I say, Amir Begovic.

That's not possible, says the bureaucrat, the inmates can only use the phone from six until eight.

When I get back to my room the burned girl is gone. I still have the taste of blood in my mouth so I go into the bathroom and rinse it out. There's blood and bits of muesli when I spit out, everything hurts like I've just gargled lemon juice. I open my mouth as best I can and see that both sets of stitches on my lower jaw have popped out. I sit down on the toilet, close my eyes, and try to think of jokes instead of the pain, it's something Jameelah and I came up with and it usually helps but this time it doesn't so I shred toilet paper and sit there on the toilet seat trying to deal with the pain. Then somebody knocks on the door.

Where are you, I hear Jameelah call, I have to tell you something. I really have to tell you something!

When I walk back into the room I see Jameelah jumping around on my bed. Her hair has grown over the summer and now goes down past her ears almost to her chin, the way she laughs and her hair flies around while she hops up and down, it looks beautiful.

I have to tell you something, she shouts, I really need to tell you something!

What is it, I say.

It begins with L and ends with S!

Tell me!

Guess, says Jameelah letting herself plop down on the end of the bed with her legs crossed and looking at me expectantly.

Just tell me, you idiot.

Okay, what did we talk about at the beginning of the summer? In the bathroom? About what we wanted to do during summer break?

You slept with Lukas?

Bongo, Jameelah shouts and starts hopping on the bed again, bongo bingo bongo!

Cross coincidence, I say.

Why?

Why do you think?

What, you too, says Jameelah, no way!

Yes way, I say and to prove it I pull the bloody sheets out of the drawer. Jameelah shields her face with her hands.

Here in the hospital? Cross.

I smile.

Did you bleed real bad too, I ask.

Nope not at all, says Jameelah.

Are you guys a proper couple now, you and Lukas?

193

No idea, maybe. What about you and Nico?

No idea, I say, and even if we were what does that mean these days.

You sound like a grandmother. Like a forty-year-old, says Jameelah.

No seriously. Actually I don't even know if I want to be together with him.

Don't overthink it, says Jameelah, anyway it's crazy, right? So we're like cosmic-virgins or virgin-soulmates except more like the opposite, deflower-mates, what would you call that connection?

Deflower like deforest?

No, deflower like devirginize, says Jameelah, but the point is we need to think up a word for friends who lose their virginity on the same day.

Oh right, I say, yeah.

Jameelah stops jumping and lets herself drop onto the bed and looks at me with worry in her eyes.

What's wrong with you, she asks.

Nothing, I say.

Something's definitely wrong.

I dab toilet paper around my mouth.

Nothing, I say, my mouth just hurts. I think you were right.

The stitches came out?

No idea but it's definitely bleeding, but don't worry somebody's coming to have a look in a little while. Have you heard anything from Amir, I ask.

No, says Jameelah.

I called him, I say.

Really? I didn't know you could call him.

Me either but Nico told me.

So?

He wasn't there, he's only allowed to go to the phone at certain times.

Aha.

I look out the window.

What is it, says Jameelah.

Maybe we should go to the cops after all, I say.

Don't start that again.

What happens, I ask, if it turns out that somebody saw us?

Who could have seen us?

I don't know but it's possible. If somebody did we're accomplices to murder, you can go to jail for that.

Where did you hear that?

Nowhere, it just occurred to me last night.

Last night?

Jameelah looks at me suspiciously.

You didn't tell Nico did you?

Bullshit what do you think, I say and fidget with the bedclothes making lots of small folds and looking out the window, at the bed, out the window, at the bed, out the window, in the reflection I can see Jameelah chewing on her nails and spitting chips of nail polish out on the hospital floor, then she pulls out her keychain and works at her nails with a key and then suddenly she looks over at me and there's a smile across her entire face.

I've got it, she says.

What?

Shaglings.

What?

Shaglings. That's what you call two friends who lose their virginity on the same day.

Sounds stupid to me, I say.

No it doesn't, you're just saying that.

No I'm not.

Yes you are.

Kiss my ass.

I go over to the window and look out at the park.

The playground's open again, says Jameelah.

Really?

Yeah, the day before yesterday they took away the barriers.

Cross.

Jameelah looks at the clock.

I have to go, I'm meeting Lukas. Just wanted to tell you the news.

Sure, have fun.

I stay at the window. A few minutes later I watch Jameelah run off through the park, jogging between the trees until she's just a tiny black hopping dot. I lie down under the covers and try to sleep but I can't. I pretend I'm sleeping, lying there like the burned girl, like Mama when she's on the sofa, on her island, like Papa when he says the connection is bad, I'm on the train and then hangs up, that's exactly the same as pretending to be asleep, I can do it too, if Mama and Papa are so good at it maybe it's genetic and I have the gene too. You can wake up a sleeping person but you can never wake somebody who's just pretending to be asleep, I think but I don't think it in a normal way I just keep thinking the same sentence over and over again like the Catholics with that one poem they keep repeating and call it praying, or like those Indians in the orange robes who lie on a bed of nails or on glowing coals, they always repeat some phrase, that's why they don't need to eat or drink because it's like some kind of magic spell that protects you, it's like saying abracadabra and managing to do something that's actually impossible in the normal world.

I open my eyes suddenly and gasp for breath like after a bad dream.

196

I need to get out of here, I need to do something, I can't wait for the doctor to come, I grab my suitcase out from under the bed and pack up my stuff as fast as I can then I creep down the staircase and out through the park.

MAMA, I CALL WHEN I UNLOCK THE DOOR TO THE APARTMENT, but Mama isn't there and instead I hear 'Mr Boombastic' coming from the TV at deafening volume. Jessi and Pepi are in the living room in their underwear jumping up and down on Mama's sofa. Jessi has stuck something into the front of her underwear but I can't tell what it is.

Mister Boombastic, sings Pepi jumping from the sofa to Rainer's comfy chair, Mister Boombastic, he has a carrot in his underwear and the orange tip is sticking out. Next to the TV is Amir's box, open.

What's going on here, I shout.

Watch, screams Pepi pointing to the TV.

Only now do I realize that the music is coming out of Rainer's stereo and that the TV is on mute. I look at the TV but the whole screen is the colour of flesh, what kind of movie is this I wonder, and then at second glance I realize what I'm looking at is a close-up of naked flesh. A naked woman is lying on a lounge chair and having her upper body smeared with oil by a hairy man while she shoves a hairbrush up her ass. I notice my jaw is hanging wide open as the woman with the brush moans.

Oh my god, Jessi yells bouncing on the sofa like a rubber ball, oh my god, and then I see that Jessi has a courgette stuck into the front of her underwear. The woman on the lounge chair moans, the man has his hands on the brush now and he's moving it faster and faster.

Stop, I shout, both of you.

Jessi squeals, Pepi jumps off the sofa and runs to the door and the carrot falls out of his underwear.

Go straight home do you hear, I call after him.

Jessi starts to cry.

I pull the TV plug out of the wall, jump onto Mama's sofa and smack Jessi, I grab the courgette and throw it to the other end of the apartment.

What are you thinking messing around with my things, I shout while shaking her.

Pepi isn't allowed to go home, Jessi screams, Mama said so.

Why not, I ask.

They said we had to stay here, I hear Pepi say, he's in the doorway standing with one foot on top of the other and his toes curled up.

Who said?

Nico.

And Mama, says Jessi.

They went to the police, Nico said, right away, and then, says Pepi, and then they said we have to stay here and not open the door for anyone.

The police?

Yeah, the police.

Get dressed right away, I say.

I go to the stereo and turn off the music and then take the DVD out of the DVD player and take Amir's box under my arm into my room. I grab the ashtray that's sitting outside on the windowsill and crumble apart old cigarette butts and collect the dregs until I have enough leftover tobacco to roll a new one. I inhale deeply on the dregarette and the old tobacco burns down fast, I take another drag straight away, smoking like Dragan, inhaling so hard that it can't keep up, and then with my fingers trembling I open Amir's box. There's a pile of DVDs inside with naked people on the covers, mostly women, the one on top shows a woman blowing a guy. I take the DVDs out of the box and lay them cover-down on the floor in front of me like I'm playing memory, like this will somehow help me figure out why Amir gave all of this to me. One after the next I turn the covers right-side-up. I still can't figure it out.

I put the DVDs back in the box. On the last one there's actually a cute guy on the cover. He's reaching with one hand into his underwear and grinning, he has the same blue eyes as Tarik and the same dark curly hair, but I've never seen Tarik so happily grinning like that, Tarik only smiled sadly and unlike the guy on the DVD Tarik's hair never looked cute because whenever it started to look cute Tarik cut it immediately. Tarik never wanted to be cute even though he could have, but then again that's exactly what I liked about him. I take another deep drag on the cigarette as if it will help fend off the sadness and then I see that there's blood on the filter. I go to the bathroom, shove toilet paper into the back of my mouth and look in the mirror.

Noura said one time that brave people are the ones who do things they are afraid of, that is, when someone does something they're not really afraid of anyway, like diving off the ten-metre platform, then no matter how brave it looks it has nothing to do with bravery.

I put the DVDs and the box into a rubbish bag. Jessi and Pepi are sitting on the sofa watching TV, they're in normal clothes. I go to the goodie cabinet and grab a packet of cookies and put it on the coffee table in front of them.

Listen up, I say, you stay here just like Mama and Nico said, eat cookies and watch TV, I'll be right back, don't open the door for anybody, not even someone you know, understand.

Yes, says Jessi and nods.

I sprint down the street like an idiot, I run as fast as I can, like the red-haired girl in that one movie, I saw it on TV, she ran through the entire city and was just as out of breath as I am now, and just like me she had a plastic bag in her hand though hers had 100,000 euros in it instead of pornos. I run panting across intersections, cars beep their horns, up on top of the minaret of a mosque a muezzin howls, a flock of black birds that Jameelah would say were rooks not ravens takes off fluttering totally directionless around the minaret, swarming, they look like a giant Palestinian scarf floating in the wind.

On the pavement in front of the police station I brace my hands on my knees and pant for breath. The children's hospital, the lead doctor, the green park, Nico's kisses, it all seems impossibly far away, like I was never there, I must have dreamed the whole thing. This, this is real life, side stitches, pornos, and the taste of blood. I pull the wad of blood-soaked toilet paper out of my mouth, toss it into the plastic bag with the rest of the crap, and go inside.

The station smells like file cabinets and coffee and like rooms where you're not allowed to smoke anymore. I run down the hall but I don't have to go far because I can already see them all sitting there, Nico and Mama, Noura and Jameelah, and two police officers with serious looks on their faces. Nico looks away when I show up. What a coward.

Mama comes up to me.

What have you got yourself into again this time, she says as if this kind of thing happens to me all the time, as if I might as well live up there in the play fort at the playground and constantly

201

watch as girls are stabbed to death by their brothers next to Amir's linden tree.

Is this the other witness, asks one of the policemen.

Yes, I say, but the thing with the jewellery, I can explain that, I wanted to take it, not her, I say pointing at Jameelah, she had nothing to do with it. At first we threw it all away but then we went back but the bin men had already taken it.

It's alright, he says, your friend already told us everything.

So, I say, are we going to get in trouble?

No, he says laughing but then he frowns.

You're bleeding, he says.

Yeah, it's my wisdom teeth, I say, the stitches popped out.

And that on top of it all, says Mama.

The policeman hands me a tissue as a young female officer comes down the hall.

We got him, she says, he was apprehended at home.

And, asks the policeman, any drama?

Not really, he barricaded himself in and we suspected he was planning to harm himself, but the team got in and was able to subdue him. No corporal damage.

Corporal damage. I let the phrase float past me. I know what it means, everyone around here does because they always say it on the train when somebody jumps in front of an S-bahn and you have to wait until they've scraped the corporal damage off the tracks before the train can continue. Sometimes it's better to die than to live with whatever has happened, which is probably what Tarik was thinking. I'm sure that it's true.

Mama pulls me to her.

How do you get yourself into these things, she says stroking my hair.

I shrug my shoulders.

No idea, I say, no idea what I'm supposed to say, I didn't get myself into anything, I didn't do anything at all. Mama doesn't get it, she's forgotten everything off on her island though I'm really only realizing it now. I try to look past Mama to Jameelah but she looks away, off in the other direction, though Nico does look at me and I give him the dirtiest look of all time, at least I hope that's the way it comes across.

Sorry, says Noura, what has happened with little Selma and her mother?

They've been taken to an undisclosed location, says the policewoman, because of the press.

And the boy?

He'll be released from custody as soon as everything is verified, says the policeman.

And then what? Where will he live?

I don't know, to begin with he'll probably be put in a home of some sort.

Can't he live with us for a while, asks Noura.

Yes, theoretically, says the policewoman, you'll just have to clear it with the department of youth services.

They'll certainly allow it, says the male officer putting a hand on Noura's shoulder, and don't you worry about the immigration department. There is absolutely no downside to coming forward as a witness like this for you or for your daughter. It would be crazy if it was permitted to have a negative effect.

Mama stands up.

Can we go now? I have two little kids at home.

Sorry, says the policewoman, we still have to take your daughter's statement, but the rest can go.

Nico gets up. He comes over to me and starts to open his mouth.

Leave me alone, I say and turn to Jameelah.

Noura stands up.

Come on, she says to Jameelah, but Jameelah doesn't move, she just sits on her chair with her arms crossed and a blank look on her face. Cautiously I sit down next to her.

Did you hear that, I say, you don't have anything to worry about. Everything's going to be fine.

Like in slow motion Jameelah turns her head in my direction. I wince.

Traitor, she whispers while glaring at me. If looks could kill.

Ramadan has arrived. I actually like Ramadan, the men sit zonked out on the benches in front of convenience stores and do nothing but fiddle with their strings of beads with their eyes closed and wait for the sun to finally go down.

It's funny in school. Half the class is hungry and does stupid shit. Orkhan and Tayfun keep having short outbursts. Today Orkhan tipped his chair over backwards and smashed into the wooden map of Germany the class has been working on and it fell to the floor with a huge crash and when the entire class started laughing Frau Struck was so irate that I thought for a second she was going to keel over.

Everyone is agitated the way only Jessi is normally but then it gets dark and the lights go on all over the city and it's absolutely silent in the streets, all you hear is the faint sound of laughter and clinking dishes wafting out of windows. Then people start streaming out of the buildings, the women carrying Tupperware containers, people wishing each other happy holidays and the best part is that the children are allowed to stay awake as long as they want. Ramadan is like a month of New Year's Eves, just with no fireworks. Normally I like it. Normally Jameelah comes by in the evening and brings a plate of rice with raisins and roasted carrots. We sit on the balcony and stuff ourselves, drink Tiger Milk out of a chocolate Müller milk container so Mama doesn't notice, and think up A-words. Ramadan is an A-word so when it's Ramadan we take a Ramadan from O-words and switch to A-words, which is tougher, but it's alright, steering becomes staring not storing and Anna-Lena is Frieda Gaga instead of Frieda Giga, which suits her better anyway and I think Jameelah would agree but this year she and I can't agree on a single thing because this year we don't spend a single evening on the balcony together speaking in A-words, Jameelah and I don't speak to each other at all anymore.

I'm standing in front of Frau Stanitzek's store with my swim things in a bag smoking a Pall Mall I stole from Rainer. The sun is shining. I don't like standing here, I look over at the entrance to the building. Where is Amir, I don't want Jameelah to turn up and see me standing here, I think, making circles in the dirt on the pavement with my flip-flops, but on the other hand if she did turn up I could try one last time to speak to her normally, though the note she left, that was bad, what are you supposed to say to somebody like that.

Don't ring my doorbell you backstabbing Schwein, I've already left is what she wrote on the note she taped to her door on the first day of school. And then at school, with the new seating chart, it was the same thing. Ever since we could read and write Jameelah and I have sat next to each other, me on the right and Jameelah on the left so that our writing hands wouldn't knock into each other. Frau Struck tried to separate us now and then but it never lasted, we always ended up sitting next to each other again in the end, first in Wittner's class then in all the other classes and then finally in Struck's class too but not this year, this year when we all pushed the desks together into pairs during the first period after summer break and Struck said you two up here to me and Jameelah so I can keep an eye on you, Jameelah just shook her head and said I don't want to be next to her.

206

The school year is starting well, said Frau Struck smiling a broad smile, she was suddenly in a great mood. She put Jameelah in the last row and me all the way up front.

And did you have nice summer holidays, Struck asked once we were all seated, she was tanned from her holiday in Africa. I just stared straight ahead. The seat next to me was empty.

Where is Amir, Frau Struck asked, is he going to be late already on the first day of school?

Nobody said a word. Frau Struck didn't know anything, the whole thing had passed her by while she was down in South Africa and she hadn't had enough time in the teachers' lounge yet to hear the news. Jameelah raised her hand at some point.

He won't be here until tomorrow, she said.

All of a sudden somebody shoves me. Jameelah's standing in front of me on the pavement and staring at me with an evil look.

What are you doing here?

Waiting for Amir, I say.

Wait someplace else if you don't mind.

I can wait here if I feel like it.

Snitches are not allowed to stand around in front of my door, says Jameelah.

This isn't your door and I'm no snitch either.

Yes you are.

No I'm not.

I hope you die, says Jameelah spitting on the ground.

Come on, I say.

Come on nothing.

Watch yourself, I say.

What for, says Jameelah, do you think I'm afraid of you or something she says and spits on the ground again.

The spit lands right next to one of my flip-flops.

One more time, I say, and there's going to be trouble.

Jameelah laughs out loud.

Trouble? I'd love to see that you backstabbing Schwein.

She spits again, this time on my bare foot.

Bam.

Just like that. I don't think it over, my brain turns completely off and it feels unbelievably good, my brain is completely shut down and bam, my fist is in Jameelah's face, bam, it's lightning fast, Nico taught me how, you never know when you might need it he said, left, left, right, left, left, right on his punching bag. This time I go straight for a right but Jameelah isn't a punching bag and as she falls down I already feel bad.

Sorry, I say, sorry sorry.

I put out my hand but then she's standing next to me already and in the next second her long nails jam into my cheek. I scream in pain and try to punch her but Jameelah holds my wrist and knees me in the stomach and then I'm lying with my face in the dirt on the pavement a few inches from a big pile of dog shit. I try to pull her down while on my back and for a second it's working but as I start to roll over she gets on top of me and pins my upper arms with her knees.

Snitch! Pig! she screams.

Stop, I scream.

Backstabbing Schwein!

Stop, you're going to break my arms, I scream and then I hear someone call out.

Stop right now both of you!

I'd love to stop but since Jameelah doesn't stop I don't stop either and then comes water, wet and ice cold, and I frantically try to catch my breath.

Who are you, shouts Amir, he's standing next to us on the pavement with a red bucket in his hand, are you dogs or are you my friends?

One of my flip-flops is broken and my bag with my swimming gear has opened up and my bathing suit, sunscreen, cigarettes, and tampons are strewn about the pavement. My face is burning and my arms are killing me.

I'm not going along with this any longer, shouts Amir, you guys need to make up, you hear me!

Slowly I stand up.

Fine by me, I say, I'd love to.

Jameelah looks at me, her hair is all crazy and blood is dripping from her lip onto her tank-top. For a second I think she's going to put out her hand to shake but she just picks up her bag from the ground and says never and then walks off toward the playground.

Wait, I call after her but Jameelah doesn't turn around. In my mouth I taste sand. I spit on the ground.

Nice way to say hi, says Amir grimacing.

Sorry.

The pain in my arms slowly subsides but my face still burns.

How are you doing, I ask.

Good.

Are things working out, I ask. I mean, with everything?

Listen, says Amir, I don't want to talk about it, about any of it. None of it you understand.

Okay.

Good.

Happy Ramadan, I say.

Thanks, to you to. Bajram Serif Mubarek.

Ready to go?

Amir smiles.

Today I'm going to jump off the ten-metre platform.

Swear on your mother's grave, I say and for a second I think I shouldn't have said it but I don't really mean his mother's grave, it's just something people say, you really have to think about your choice of words now and the things you just say without meaning it, but Amir just laughs and smacks my legs with his duffel bag, I swear, he says, I swear on my mother's grave, today I'm going to dive off the ten-metre platform.

At the pool I can see Nico, Tobi, and Nadja from a long way off, laying in our usual spot.

Yo, yells Nico getting up and coming toward us, great to see you.

Amir slaps him five.

Hi, says Nico looking over at me.

I ignore him and put my *Aladdin* towel down next to Tobi and Nadja.

You want anything from the snack kiosk, I ask Amir.

Nah, he says, it's Ramadan.

Are you really fasting, asks Nadja.

I'm trying, says Amir.

Nadja takes a drag on her cigarette.

Isn't it unhealthy?

It's his business, I say.

I know but not eating and drinking all day, it sounds tough to me, you have to have an iron will.

I have an iron will, says Amir pulling a *Star Wars* towel out of his bag.

So, says Tobi, are you living with Jameelah right now?

Amir nods.

So fucked up, Tobi says, that they just threw you in jail like that.

I dig around for my wallet.

Why don't you come with me to the kiosk, I say, then we can go to the diving platform.

Amir stands up. We go together across the lawn and then Amir suddenly stops.

What's up, I say.

Back there, he says nodding his head in the direction of the kiddie pool.

Dragan is sitting beyond the kiddie pool. He's wearing his purple swimsuit, like always, and like always a few of his friends are sitting around him playing cards and drinking Slivovitz. Somebody smacks Dragan on the shoulder, he laughs, but not with his eyes, only with his mouth. Herr Wittner said one time that it normally takes thirteen different muscles to make a real smile and that if they aren't all being used it's not a real smile, but then again what does normally even mean.

He rang the door yesterday, says Amir.

Who, Dragan?

Yeah. Noura answered. He wanted to talk to me.

Why?

He wants to know where Jasna's buried.

And?

They buried her in Visegrad where my father's buried.

Why don't you tell him?

I don't know, says Amir, not yet. Maybe at some point.

At the kiosk I buy a bulette with mustard and a bread roll. I sit down on the sun-warmed tiles next to the diving platforms and watch as Amir climbs up to the ten-metre platform. My face still hurts from Jameelah's fingernails but luckily the wounds in my mouth from getting my wisdom teeth pulled don't hurt anymore, the lead doctor took out the stitches that had popped out and replaced them, but those came out too and things didn't heal so well, that's what the lead doctor said, and he said I should be careful about hard things and spicy things. I bite into the hard crust of the roll. Amir waves at me, I wave back, and then

211

somebody taps me on the shoulder.

Can I sit with you, says Nico.

Leave me alone, I say but Nico sits down anyway.

Don't you get it?

No, says Nico, to be honest I don't. I know you're upset that I went and did it on my own but I had no choice.

No choice? You went straight from the hospital to the police! You didn't think about it for even a second. You didn't give me a chance to think it over.

I told you I was going to go to the cops.

You said you would go to the cops if I didn't.

You were in the hospital, says Nico.

We had a deal, I say.

A deal? What deal?

That you would go if I didn't go, I say, but I never had the chance to go.

Amir was sitting in jail, innocent, and I was just supposed to sit around?

A deal is a deal! You can't just go to the police without talking to me.

A deal. Maybe I should have filled out a form or something, says Nico.

You should have asked me!

I did but you're so stubborn you wouldn't listen. If it was up to you Amir would still be sitting in jail.

Right, of course, now I'm the bad guy.

I thought I was, he says.

I stay silent.

So what are we supposed to hate each other for the rest of our lives now because of it?

That's fine as far as I'm concerned. I'll never forgive you for not talking to me first, and your ring, you can have that back too. I don't want it.

Fine give it to me, says Nico.

Do you think I would still be wearing it? I threw it somewhere in my room and hopefully the vacuum cleaner will find it.

Nico looks at me angrily.

Now get out of here, I say.

Whatever you say, he says standing up.

I look up at the ten-metre platform. Amir is standing on the edge staring down at the water.

Don't look down, I think.

Amir puts out his arms.

Put on Rihanna Burana, he calls, I'm going to do a double-Amir royale with extra cheese and hot sauce!

The security guards look over blankly. Amir jumps and pulls his knee up and holds it against his chest while in midair and then he splashes down in the best cannonball I've seen in ages. People clap and howl. Snorting and with a smile plastered across his face, Amir swims over to the side of the pool.

So, he asks, how was I?

Heavenly, I say, you were heavenly.

It's slowly getting dark and our bags bump lazily at our legs.

It's unfair that I only got to go to the pool twice this summer, says Amir as we walk down the street toward the playground.

Next year is another year, I say.

Who knows what will happen then, says Amir.

Nothing will.

Hopefully, he says and his gait becomes noticeably slower.

We don't have to go that way, I say, we can go around the back.

No, wait a minute.

For a few minutes we just stand around. I'm barefoot, I threw out my busted flip-flops on the way home, and the street is warm beneath my feet but not as warm as a few weeks ago at this time of day, that's one way you know that summer will be over soon, I think, but this is the first time in my life that I'm not sad about it.

Amir lifts his nose.

Come on, he says tossing his bag over his shoulder and marching into the playground. We go through the sandbox and over to the play fort and Amir stops there.

Up there is where you were sitting, right?

Yeah, I say, we were up there.

And it happened back there, says Amir, right?

Yeah it happened back there.

Amir slowly spins and looks all around as if he's never been here before in his entire life, as if this isn't our playground, as if it's the Holocaust memorial on the other side of Tiergarten, and just like the tourists who stand around surveying the memorial looking all serious, that's exactly how Amir looks at the playground now. Back when the memorial was first opened we used to play there, hopping from one stone pillar to the next or hiding in the spaces between them until Noura was worried sick about us, but then the city banned it, they said this is a memorial not a playground but it always remained a playground in my eyes. But now, as I watch Amir looking out over our playground, I realize that our playground is no longer a playground.

Amir goes back across the sandbox and over to our trees. He stops at his linden tree, he lets his bag fall to the ground and starts to climb.

Come on, he calls looking down at me.

I throw my bag down next to his and start slowly climbing up behind him. My bare feet smack against the bark. I have

214

no idea how long it's been since I last climbed something. Strange that you just stop climbing, and you can't really remember the moment when you stopped doing it. Adults always know when they quit smoking or drinking or when they stopped nursing their baby, but you're younger when you quit climbing trees or playing with marbles or Barbies and you don't remember when it happened, you forget long before you're an adult.

The little heart-shaped leaves of Amir's linden tree get denser up near the top of the tree and the branches are thicker and darker. I see Amir sitting on a thick branch above me.

Here, he says pointing to a spot next to him on the branch, here's the proof.

I can't see it, I say.

Amir rummages in his pocket and pulls out a phone.

You got another one, I say.

It's Tarik's old one. It was in my room when I came home, says Amir aiming the light from the phone's display at the branch.

Crazy, I say looking at the short piece of thread hanging down from the branch. The bark looks weird, like an arm that's been bandaged and the skin has grown back around it. I look out through the leaves at the city. It's already dark up here in the leaves but the rest of the city is still lit up, off in the west you can see the radio tower and it looks like it's on fire because the sun is setting behind it.

You can't be angry at Jameelah, says Amir.

I'm not, what do you mean?

Because she didn't want to go to the police, that's what I mean.

Oh.

She didn't want to get involved you know.

I know, I say, but if it wasn't for Nico you'd still be sitting in jail right now.

Tarik's there now, which is just as bad.

But Tarik is guilty.

Yeah, says Amir, I know, but still. Do you still have the box?

No, I threw it away like you said.

Good.

How long will Tarik be in jail?

A long time, says Amir, and when he gets out he'll go directly from jail to the airport and then off to Sarajevo and then Visegrad.

I pluck a leaf and rub it between my fingers.

Have you ever been there, I ask.

Stop that, Amir says taking the leaf out of my hand. He looks past me, off toward the east through the leaves and shakes his head.

Tarik was born there, he says, they lived there, Babo, Majka, and Tarik. Tarik had a red bicycle, there's a photo of him riding a red bike in his bathing suit, the sun is shining like today, can you picture it, he was riding a bike normally, with two healthy legs, says Amir, but then the war came. Babo went to the army, nothing got better, things just got worse and more dangerous. Majka took Tarik. There's a bridge in Visegrad, a very old bridge from the middle ages, and the river runs beneath it. Majka wanted to cross the bridge. There were Chetniks on the bridge. She turned around but they followed her. Tarik screamed and wanted to help her and one of them shot him in the leg.

Amir rips the leaf in his hand and then rubs the pieces between his fingers.

They raped her, he whispers, then they tied Tarik to her body and threw them into the river. Tarik told me the night everything happened. I went straight to the police. On my own. Tarik didn't pressure me at all. Neither did Majka, nobody pressured me, everyone just thinks so because they want easy answers to everything, they want to understand things right away, things that

216

don't have anything to do with each other. But the truth isn't like mathematics, it's always something singular and it's never logical.

The red orb in the sky disappears behind the radio tower, it's nearly nighttime up here in the tree.

Visegrad, I say, the sound of the word is nice. Like a combination of vitamins and ice and grass and glad.

Yeah, says Amir, people think so. But it's always the case that places where bad things happen sound nice, well, either funny or nice, did you ever notice that?

Yeah, I say, I thought that about Fukushima.

Or Auschwitz, says Amir, Auschwitz sounds like Slivovitz, don't you think? It makes everything that much more awful you know, it's like poetry, that combination of tragedy and comedy, life seems to love that sort of thing.

You think so?

Yeah, says Amir, definitely. That's the way life is. When things are going too well something has to come along to mess things up, otherwise it wouldn't be life you know.

Night has descended on his face, just the whites of his eyes, four half moons, glint at me.

Where was she lying, he asks.

I look down at the ground, at the dry dirt around the trunk. There.

Where exactly?

There, I say and point down to a spot next to where we used to play marbles.

What did she look like, Amir asks.

What do you mean, I say.

I mean at the end. How did she look?

I stare at the spot where Jasna had lain. Her tight white t-shirt, blood running out of her left side and soaking into the ground, pinkish yellow puke in the corner of her mouth and her eyes like in that YouTube video where a group of men hunt down a woman and kill her in the street in some hot country.

Go on, tell me.

Peaceful, I say.

Really?

Yes. Very peaceful.

Rainer's taxi is standing in front of the building. I go through the courtyard and up the stairs and look for the key to the apartment but I've barely stuck it into the lock before the door opens. Mama grabs me by my hair and yanks me into the apartment and the next second I get smacked in the face.

Do you know how late it is, she screams, you shouldn't be roaming around like this, how many times do I have to tell you!

I duck out of the way.

First and second period are cancelled tomorrow, I say.

I do not care, Mama screams, after everything that's happened. We get worried.

Rainer comes out to the hall.

When it's dark you are at home, that's what we agreed, he says, and as long as you are living under my roof you will stick to it.

I look him up and down. The way he's standing there in the greasy coveralls that he wears at home like other people wear bathrobes, his thin grey and blond hair pulled back in a pony-tail. I can't help thinking of his porno collection under the floorboards, the way he loves to sit in front of the TV and pick at his toenails, that for him is what it means to be home, the same way he stares at the toilet paper after he wipes his ass, what is there to say to someone like that. Without saying a

218

word I turn around and go into my room. I undress, open the window, and let my legs dangle out the window and smoke a cigarette.

There's a quiet knock at the door.

Nini, whispers Jessi and I can hear in her voice that she's crying.

I just wanted to go to the bathroom and then it happened, says Jessi pointing at a blood stain on her underwear. I flick the cigarette out the window and hop down from the windowsill.

Come here, I say and pull her onto the bed, it's not so bad, are you in pain?

Jessi shakes her head.

No but I don't want Rainer to find out, he said that when I get my period I'll get a white jumper as a gift and have to eat tomato soup, that's what they do where he's from, that's how they celebrate it. I don't want that, I don't want tomato soup, I hate tomatoes.

Come with me, I say and take her hand.

Quietly we creep to the bathroom. I search in the cabinet.

Here, I say handing her a tampon, put one leg up on the toilet seat like this and then you stick it into yourself.

I'm scared, says Jessi.

No need to be scared, it's easy.

No, I'm scared of getting that shock that you can get.

What kind of shock?

From the tampon. Pepi told us about it at school, he said that you can die from tampons. You get some kind of toxic shock and then you're done for. It's right there on the box, there's a warning on every package.

You're not going to get toxic tampon shock, I certainly know better than Pepi.

Are you sure?

I'm sure. You can sleep in my room tonight and I'll keep an eye on you.

Okay, says Jessi pulling down her underwear. You just shove it in?

Yep, I say, just shove it in.

It is easy, says Jessi looking at me with surprise.

See. It gets easier too, at some point you'll be able to put a tampon in while standing at a bus stop or in class without anyone noticing. Just takes practice. And Rainer doesn't have to know, it's none of his fucking business, you hear me.

Jessi nods, pulls up her underwear, and sits down on the toilet seat cover.

Do you know, I say, that you didn't used to want to sleep in Mama's bed when she had her period?

I know. I thought the brown stains on her nightgown were disgusting, says Jessi pointing toward the tampon, why don't you feel it?

No idea, that's just the way it is, it's normal.

That's good.

Yeah, I think so too.

I'm hungry, says Jessi.

There's nothing to eat, I say.

Yes there is, in the refrigerator there's a plate that says *For Nini from Noura Eid Mobarak*. Are you hungry too?

I shake my head.

Go get the plate, I say, but be quiet, I need to go out again.

What if I get toxic shock?

You won't. Lie down in my bed, I won't be long.

I go back into my room, gather the clothes off the floor, and look down at the corner of the carpet where something is sparkling, but it's not what I'm looking for. I open all my drawers and my jewellery box, rifle through the pockets of my jackets and trousers, I crawl around on all fours and look under my desk and my bed and then something occurs to me. Quietly I get the key to the basement out of the drawer in the hallway and go downstairs. With my phone I light up the storage space looking for the guitar case. In the little compartment inside is the ring. I go back upstairs and put the ring in an envelope.

Dragan I write on the front, and on the back flap, *Visegrad.*

I'm tired, the usual condition during eighth or ninth period. Frau Struck is blathering on about the citric acid cycle and diagramming some crazy shit on the chalk board and talking nonstop. Her mouth, that thick pink rubber band, doesn't stand still for even a second. The more complicated something is, the faster Struck tries to explain it, and the fewer questions you're allowed to ask, I know how it is so I just let it go. Normally Jameelah and I play city-country-AIDS during eighth and ninth period but now I sit next to Amir and he takes notes the whole time, what a kiss-ass, it's like he knows I'm completely lost.

Out the window I can see a man in paint-splattered clothes re-painting the white lines of the basketball court in the playground. When he's finished he goes over to the mushroom-shaped gazebo and has a smoke. It makes me think of Nico who is out in the city somewhere in paint-splattered clothes painting something and stopping for a smoke now and then. I look back at Jameelah as inconspicuously as possible. She's playing tic-tac-toe by herself and doesn't notice Struck coming toward her desk.

Wake up there, says Frau Struck snapping her fingers in Jameelah's face, explain this chemical reaction to me.

What, says Jameelah.

This, says Struck going back up to the chalk board and slapping the right side of it with her T-square.

222

No idea, says Jameelah, I don't like acid.

The painter is still sitting in the gazebo smoking. I'm about to put my head down and sleep but then on the other side of the playground the door to the gym opens and Anna-Lena runs out heading in the direction of the girls' bathroom holding something under her jumper. I peek back at Jameelah again, she's stopped playing tic-tac-toe and is staring out the window like she's in a trance. I hold my hand to my stomach, grimace, and raise my hand.

Say you know the answer, says Struck.

No, I say, I'm feeling really sick.

Struck raises her eyebrows.

Really Frau Struck, I need to go to the bathroom.

Well off you go.

I run down the steps and out across the playground to the girls' loos and quietly push the door open. Somebody is throwing up in one of the toilets, throwing up and crying. I creep into the next stall, crying, puking, then silence, then crying and puking again and silence again, over and over again until something is being taken out of a packet, but it doesn't sound like a box of tampons, more like some kind of medicine or something from the pharmacy, and then the sound of somebody peeing. As quietly as possible I climb up on the toilet seat and peer over the stall. There's Anna-Lena holding a pregnancy test in her hand.

What are you doing, I ask even though it's pretty obvious.

Paralyzed with fear she looks up at me, I jump down from the toilet and knock on the door to her stall.

Open up.

No, she says, get out of here.

Open up, I say, otherwise I'll go get the janitor.

The lock rotates from red to green. Anna-Lena is sitting on the toilet seat cover, her face swollen from crying and her hair caked with vomit and snot, Frieda Gaga not looking so freshly laundered. No matter what else happens, I think, I'll definitely mark this day with a red X on my calendar.

Show me the test, I say.

Leave me alone, says Anna-Lena.

I go over to the sink and pull a huge ball of paper towels out of the dispenser and then the door to the bathroom opens. It's Jameelah, she stands there with her hands on her hips and glares at me.

What's going on here, she asks.

I point my thumb at the stall.

She might be pregnant, I say.

Who? By who?

No idea, good question.

Jameelah rushes over to the stall.

Is it true, she says but Anna-Lena doesn't answer.

I asked if it's true!

What business is it of yours, says Anna-Lena.

Where's the test, says Jameelah but Anna-Lena puts her hand behind her back.

Jameelah gasps.

Fuck your test, whose is it, but Anna-Lena squeezes her lips tight as if that will help somehow.

Who was it, says Jameelah again shoving Anna-Lena's shoulder and then grabbing her and shaking her, whose is it, she says, but when Anna-Lena still doesn't answer Jameelah grabs her hands from behind her back, holds her wrists, and shoves her up against the wall of the toilet stall.

Let me go, screams Anna-Lena, you're hurting me.

Shut your mouth, Jameelah screams pressing her harder, look me in the eye do you hear me, look me in the eye and tell me it's not what I think it is!

224

What is going on, I wonder, *Islam will rule the world* it says next to Anna-Lena on the wall, and beneath that, *Men are like toilets either taken or full of shit, Look it's Nutella* and *Here I sit and contemplate shall I shit or masturbate*, and by the time I reach masturbate I finally get what this is about, it's about Italy and Anna-Lena and Lukas.

Oh no, I whisper.

Jameelah slowly lets go of Anna-Lena's wrists and sinks to the toilet seat. Anna-Lena crouches down and covers her face with her hands and as she does the pregnancy test falls out of the back pocket of her trousers and onto the floor. I look at the results and there are two stripes, two parallel pink stripes. That's what life looks like at the very beginning, when it's still invisible to the naked eye.

Jameelah bends down and picks up the test and examines it as if it's hers, then she drops it back onto the floor. She puts her hands together in her lap and they sit there like two people who have broken up but didn't really want to.

Give me some toilet paper please, says Anna-Lena standing up slowly.

Toilet paper, I say looking her up and down, screw toilet paper! You slept with your own cousin, man if that's not some medieval shit, I say, and always bothering us and writing love you my angel on our rucksacks and not meaning it at all, if that's not totally sickening, I say, that's a thousand times more sickening than blackheads and spiders and herpes all put together.

With a long howling sound Anna-Lena lets herself sink to the floor again.

And stop fucking crying, I say but the crying just gets louder.

Anna-Lena, says Jameelah.

Ah come on, I say, forget it.

Anna-Lena, says Jameelah shaking her, Anna-Lena, she says

225

again and shakes her harder but Anna-Lena just cries louder and louder.

If somebody comes in right now we're fucked, I say.

Smack her one, says Jameelah.

What?

You should smack her one. Like you did to me on the street the other day.

Really?

Yeah, says Jameelah, do it.

With pleasure, I say making a fist.

No, says Jameelah, just slap her.

Why?

Because you hit hard.

Sorry about the other day, sorry about everything, I say.

Shut your mouth, says Jameelah, and smack her.

Got it, I say and a second later Anna-Lena gets one across the face.

With one hit the sobbing stops.

Are you two out of your fucking minds, screams Anna-Lena.

Oh stop acting like that, says Jameelah, a teacher could come in at any moment and then you'd have to tell them the whole story.

She grabs Anna-Lena and tries to lift her up.

Come on help me.

Together we pull Anna-Lena over to the sink. Jameelah pulls a bunch of paper towels out of the dispenser, wets them under the faucet, and hands them to her.

Here, clean up your face.

Obediently Anna-Lena wipes her face.

What do I do now, she says softly.

You have to go to the doctor, I say, then you have to wait three days and then you can get rid of it.

No, says Jameelah, you have to talk to your parents.

No, I say, she doesn't have to, there's mandatory confidentiality.

Jameelah rolls her eyes.

Man there's no confidentiality if you're under sixteen, you can't do it on your own, you have to get your parents to sign off, how is it that I'm the only one who knows this stuff? Any idiot can fuck but why can't you people use condoms?

I look at the floor. How does she always know this kind of thing, I wonder, but the fact that I didn't use a condom with Nico she has no way of knowing, but still, I think, I'm not going to sleep with anybody else without a condom and next week I'm going to get a library card, even Orkhan and Tayfun have library cards, but that's just so they can go annoy the librarians when they get bored, but I won't annoy anyone there, I think, I'm going to take something out every week until I finally know more than Jameelah.

I can't tell my parents, says Anna-Lena, if they find out they'll take me out of school and put me in some nunnery in Bavaria, they want to send me there already.

Jameelah looks at the clock.

Come on, she says, we're going to Kottbusser Tor.

Kotti? What are we going to do there, asks Anna-Lena.

We're going to see my mother, says Jameelah, she'll help you.

I've never been to see Noura at the clinic. They only operate on women, women who are pregnant and don't want the baby, or women who don't want to get pregnant at all. They also get some women who have shoved things up their backsides or in the front and can't get them out on their own. Jameelah once told me there's a special box where they collect the things that have been surgically removed from women, everything from screwdrivers to fluorescent light bulbs all of which they have apparently accidentally fallen on. I always find it funny but Jameelah, Anna-Lena and I don't talk as we walk down Oranienstrasse toward the clinic and I don't feel like laughing.

I feel sick, says Anna-Lena holding her stomach, I need something to drink.

You can drink something when we get there, says Jameelah.

No, a real drink. Something cold and clear, like a shot of vodka. I need to get a miniature bottle of vodka.

No liquid courage, only the real thing, says Jameelah.

She grabs Anna-Lena by the arm and pulls her across the stripes of the cross-walk to the entrance to the clinic. She pushes the bottom bell. The door buzzes open.

Let's go, says Jameelah pushing Anna-Lena through the door. We go through the entryway and out into the courtyard. I see Noura through a window.

Mama, calls Jameelah running ahead.

Noura looks up and walks toward the door with a look of shock on her face.

Children, she says, what is it, what happened?

Without a second's pause Jameelah tells her everything. She talks and talks and makes all kinds of gestures with her hands as she does, and Noura nods and pats Anna-Lena's hair, but she also looks very stern throughout, she looks around at each of us with a serious look on her face and saves the most stern look of all for Anna-Lena of course. The way Noura always does things, all at the same time and always properly, Jameelah must have inherited that from her, I think.

Noura puts her arm around Anna-Lena.

You come with me now, she says, we're just going to do a normal examination and then after that Dr Mahmoudi will examine you, and you two, says Noura looking at me and

Jameelah, you wait here.

The waiting room is empty. Tired, I slump into a chair. Jameelah picks up one of the magazines lying on the table and flips through it, flipping the pages, flipping, flipping, way too fast, you can't read that fast, you can't even see the pictures on the pages when you flip through that fast.

Can you please tell me why we're doing this, I ask at some point.

What?

Why are we helping her? Because of Lukas?

Stop it, says Jameelah, I don't want to talk about it, I don't even want to think about him, otherwise I'll kill myself, seriously.

Not over an idiot like that. You don't need him.

Need him? What's that supposed to mean?

Look as of today at the latest he's an asshole, right?

What do you know, says Jameelah.

I'm just saying.

Just saying my ass, you're just saying what anyone would say, Jameelah says letting the magazine drop to the floor.

What's that supposed to mean, I say.

That you have no clue about love, says Jameelah.

And you do, right.

Yeah, because if you really love somebody then you can't change that no matter how shitty that person acts. And you can't do anything about the fact that you can't change it either.

I know, I say, I mean of course you can't do anything about it but you can't really love somebody who hurts you so badly. He doesn't deserve it.

Of course I can, you see, says Jameelah, and anyway what business is it of yours, what business is it of Anna-Lena's, it's not even Lukas's business that I love him, I'm allowed to love whoever I want and he doesn't have to love me back, but I can be in love

229

with anyone and nobody can stop me.

Of course you're allowed. I just don't want anyone to hurt you.

You can't help it, it happens anyway, she says picking up the magazine, but maybe I can keep her from having his baby.

The door to the waiting room opens and Anna-Lena walks in.

So, asks Jameelah.

Nothing, says Anna-Lena, took my blood pressure and that. I'm about to see the woman, what's her name again?

Jameelah frowns.

Mahmoudi, Dr Mahmoudi.

Mahmoudi right.

I look at Jameelah.

Yes, Jameelah says, we're going to wait.

My left leg has been asleep for a while, it seems like forever since Anna-Lena went into surgery. We've been through all the magazines. I look up at the ceiling of the waiting room. Noura turned on the lights a little while ago and I stare at the fluorescent bulbs and at the mosquitoes and fruit flies dancing on them. The mosquitoes and flies try to out-buzz the bulbs.

Look, I say pointing up, they just waste their time up there even though they have so much less of it than we do down here.

Yeah, says Jameelah, they're like real gods.

Gods?

Yeah they aren't aware of time, they know only light and fruit and blood and at some point they'll just die without ever feeling the need to think about their life, whether they lived it well or not.

Do you know this one, I say, two fruit flies meet and one says hey do fancy a fuck and the other says no I have my momentary visitor.

I don't get it.

You know, the fruit fly has its monthly visitor.

I still don't get it.

Come on, a fruit fly doesn't have a monthly visitor, it gets its period for a couple of seconds, not a couple of days, get it.

Oh, says Jameelah still looking up at the ceiling and not really listening.

What is it, I say, what are you thinking about?

Can you remember what Jasna shouted when she was standing on the balcony, what she said to her mother before she jumped?

Yeah she said first you drag me into this world and then you leave me all alone.

I think that's true, says Jameelah.

What?

That we're dragged into this world. I mean nobody asks you, nobody asks whether you want to or not.

Yeah, I say, that's true.

Maybe that's why babies always cry so much, says Jameelah, because nobody asked them whether they wanted to come here and because they're still so close to whatever it was that came before and they can't stand to be here on earth.

True, I say, and when mothers calm their babies it's actually a great big lie because they're trying to make life more bearable, you know, as in hey it's not so bad, here look, here's your rattle.

Exactly, says Jameelah, but the babies know better and they would rather go back where they came from.

Do you mean something like reincarnation?

I'm not sure but anyway you are pretty much brought into this world against your will, says Jameelah.

The door to the waiting room opens and Dr Mahmoudi and

231

Anna-Lena come out.

Well, asks Jameelah.

I have to go home, says Anna-Lena holding up an envelope, I have to speak to my parents.

Are you really pregnant, I ask.

Anna-Lena nods.

What's in the envelope, I ask.

Paperwork for the abortion.

Termination of pregnancy, says Dr Mahmoudi and puts her arm around Anna-Lena but Anna-Lena shrugs it off.

They're going to send me away to the nunnery, I know it.

It's the law, says Dr Mahmoudi, I'm sorry.

Noura comes into the waiting room holding a jacket and her handbag.

It's late we have to go, she says, you know Amir doesn't like to be alone.

You want to stay at our place tonight, asks Jameelah looking at me.

Sure, I say.

Where were you, calls Amir when Noura unlocks the apartment door, Frau Struck is seriously pissed off at you guys, she said you guys are going to have to go before the discipline committee and that you're going to get kicked out of school, that's what she said.

Where's our school stuff, asks Jameelah.

I put it in my locker, where were you?

Everything's fine, says Noura hugging Amir, have you had something to eat?

Amir shakes his head. Noura hangs up her coat and goes into the kitchen.

Where were you, Amir asks again.

It doesn't matter, says Jameelah.

Yes it does, tell me!

No, says Jameelah.

Did you guys make up, he asks.

Jameelah and I look at each other.

I think so, we say at the same time.

Then it doesn't matter where you were, says Amir smiling.

He points at the little table where the telephone book is.

A letter came by the way.

A letter?

Yes, he says, from the immigration department.

Mama, Jameelah yells, a letter came from the immigration department!

Noura comes back into the hall.

There, says Amir pointing at the little table. Noura grabs it and goes back into the kitchen and we follow her. When she sits down at the kitchen table to open the envelope I can see that her hand is trembling.

Well, asks Jameelah.

I look at Noura's shoulders and back which are always straight, even when she's sitting down. She puts the letter down on the table in front of her, braces her head in her hands, and begins to read. Suddenly her shoulders seem to shrink, smaller and smaller, and her normally straight back starts to droop, bending more and more until at some point it looks like Noura doesn't have any bones at all anymore, like somebody removed them one after another. She puts her head on the table and collapses into herself like a hot-air balloon that's spent, a balloon that says I just can't do it anymore, I don't want to inflate and rise up in the air anymore, I don't want to carry you anymore, I don't want to carry anyone or anything, carry yourself.

What is it, I ask.

Yeah, says Amir, what's going on?

Jameelah yanks the letter out from under Noura's head, reads it and then drops it on the floor and runs out to the hall. I hear the door to the apartment slam shut.

Wait, I shout.

I run as fast as I can down the stairs but when I get outside I see Jameelah disappear beyond the far side of the playground. I run across the playground toward the train station. The platform is empty. I gasp for air, for a second I think I'm going to suffocate, that's how bad my lungs hurt. I definitely need to quit smoking, I think, and then I think what a fucked up thought that is and that I'm far too young to be thinking about shit like that. It's not the time for me to quit smoking, it's not the time to quit drinking, it's not the time to quit doing anything, Jameelah and I just started again now that things are better, now that Amir's back and Anna-Lena will soon be off to the nunnery.

I take the train to Wilmersdorfer and run over to the planet. The sky has gone dark, the clouds hang grey and heavy almost down to the roofs of the buildings. There's nobody at the planet except Apollo and Aslagon. They are loading a shopping trolley with all sorts of stuff, old blankets, bottles, plastic bags. On top of it all is a blaring radio. The first raindrops start to hit the street.

Have you guys seen Jameelah, I yell.

Apollo shakes his head.

Haven't seen her, he says and then he looks up at the sky and pulls his hood down over his face.

Come on, says Aslagon pushing the trolley.

What are you doing, I ask, and where are you going?

It's going to get cold, says Apollo looking at the sky again, we're going where it's warm, where we can put on some fresh clothes and have a roof over our heads. Summer is over.

Aslagon nods.

What about the ship, I say, what about Naglfar and the end of the world?

Apollo looks at me and smiles and then takes off his hat like he's making a formal greeting.

We'll see you next year, he says.

Like a caravan in the desert, Apollo, Aslagon and the shopping trolley set slowly in motion. Soon I'm all alone at the planet and I don't know where I should go, the rain is getting harder and spatters down on me. I'm not sure how long I stand there but I'm soaking wet when someone taps me on the shoulder from behind. It's Nico.

Are you crazy, he says pulling me into the phone booth, you can't just stand around in weather like this, he says, do you want to kill yourself?

No, I say, I'm looking for Jameelah.

She was just on Kurfürsten, says Nico.

Kurfürstenstrasse?

Yeah, down where the hookers stand. No idea what she's doing there but she looked really stressed out. Did something happen?

Did you talk to her, I ask.

No, says Nico, I don't think she saw me. But even if she did she hasn't talked to me since all the shit with Amir. She's obviously angry at me.

Probably.

Probably, says Nico looking at me. You were right by the way about just going to the police. I should have asked you again beforehand. It wasn't right and I'm really sorry.

We can talk about it another time, I say, how long ago did you see Jameelah?

Not sure exactly but it wasn't long ago.

Do you have any minutes, I ask.

Nico hands me his phone. I dial Jameelah's number but nobody picks up.

Shit.

I'm sure it's nothing, says Nico.

I have to go, I say.

I run to the U-bahn and take it to Kurfürsten. When I get out it's thundering and there are flashes of lightning. I run half blind along Kurfürsten, the women have gathered under the awnings of the convenience stores to avoid getting wet, but not Jameelah, she's sitting on our electrical box and letting the rain pour down on her. She's holding a Müller milk in her hand, raindrops plop into it, thick drops that are dripping off Jameelah's nose. I climb up next to her. For a while nobody says anything, we just sit there and let life float by, twenty-one minutes past, meaning just thirty-nine minutes of life left, I count slowly backwards from there until I reach zero, until I don't have a minute left to let float by.

What was in the letter?

For a while Jameelah doesn't say anything and I wonder to myself whether she's counting backward from thirty-nine too, because that's about how long it takes her to put the Müller milk container to her lips and gulp it down in one go.

The letter, says Jameelah, the letter said Ladies and Gentlemen, as you have known for a good long time, god's earth is rotten and as a result you can no longer remain here in Germany. Please pack up your things and fuck off back to wherever it is you came from. With rotten regards, your rotten world. That's about what it said.

It can't be true, I say, how can it be so sudden.

My mother went back once after we moved here, says Jameelah, she just wanted to go to her mother's funeral but they found out

236

somehow.

So what, I say, who cares about that.

They care, says Jameelah pulling Mariacron, maracuja juice and milk out of her rucksack and mixing another round, you're not allowed to ever go back once you're here, otherwise you have to go back permanently.

That's crazy, I say.

We have to turn in our passports tomorrow, says Jameelah.

Why?

So we don't drop out of sight beforehand. What do they think, that I'm Anne Frank or something?

Dropping out of sight is a good idea, who is it you said managed to do that?

Anne Frank.

Anne Frank, wait, does she go to our school? The name sounds familiar.

Man the diary! The diary of Anne Frank!

Oh right, I say, we read that in Struck's class. That was boring. And the type was so small.

It was only boring because we read the boring version, there's another one, in the other one Anne Frank writes about her pussy and the guy she's in love with, Peter. It's really good.

I want to read that one. Do you own a copy?

No Lukas loaned it to me, but you can have it. I'm never going to see Lukas again.

Better wait and see, I say.

Do you not get it, Jameelah screams and jumps down from the electrical box, they're deporting us! I have to leave, I'm not going to become German, I'm never ever going to become German!

TODAY I FOUND AN EYELASH AND FOR THE FIRST TIME IN AGES wished for something. When I was a kid I would pull out an eyelash whenever I wanted to wish for something. Why wait for one to fall out when there were so many just lining my eyes and all I had to do was pull the wishes out, I thought, but none of the wishes ever came true, probably because I didn't wait for them to fall out. I have no idea how many lashes I must have pulled out for that alone, just so I could wish for Papa to come home, over and over. That's all I ever used any lashes for whether they fell out or I pulled them out. I know that having Papa come home was a big wish, but none of the smaller wishes ever came true either, not that I expected them to, but still.

I go into the hall and pull on my Chucks.

Let me know when you guys are ready, calls Rainer from the living room.

Yep, I say opening the door to leave.

I walk across the playground and ring at Jameelah's.

Upstairs she's standing in the apartment door barefoot with her hair pulled back, that's how long it's got.

Hi, she says as I make it up the last step.

Hi, I say.

Everything echoes in the empty rooms. No idea how Noura and Jameelah managed to completely clear out the apartment

238

while still going to school and to work. Noura wanted it that way, I want everything to stay as normal as possible until the very last day, she had said, and I don't want anyone to find out, she said, it's bad enough for us without having to be ashamed on top of it all.

Now the apartment is empty, all that's left are the keys sitting on the spotlessly scrubbed kitchen counter and next to them the letter from the immigration office. It's folded twice so that all you can see is the part in the middle. I don't need to read it again anyway, I know it by heart, I must have read it a hundred times, I even copied it by hand and took the copy to Krap-Krüger. Jameelah doesn't know about it, I only went because I was so desperate and Krap-Krüger's a human rights activist. I waited until Lukas and Tobi and Nadja and all the rest had left and then I went in to the tea shop, which as usual smelled like god's rotten earth but I tried to breathe through my mouth so I didn't have to smell it.

Krap-Krüger was really nice at first, he put on his reading glasses and read the text of the letter but after that he looked at me and shook his head.

What can be done to fight it, I asked him.

Krap-Krüger tossed his glasses onto the couch and said, you're just coming now?

I didn't understand what he meant.

Why, I asked, when else was I supposed to come?

It's too late now, Krap-Krüger had said pointing to the letter, you should have come to me much earlier, these bureaucracies, he said, they're cold and uncaring, to them it's not about individual people, this is just a routine transaction to them, with people like that you have to hit them with their own legal language but that takes time, my god my dear, I was here the whole summer.

239

Here, says Jameelah handing me a piece of scrap paper, this is Amir's new address.

At that group home?

Yeah but it's not so bad, I was there, most of the people are out of their chadors but the supervisors are alright. It just takes so long for the whole thing to be resolved, but then he'll be able to move back in with his mother.

Noura comes into the kitchen.

We have to go, she says.

I call home and soon after Rainer is out front in his taxi. He puts all the luggage in the trunk and holds open the door for Noura. Jameelah and I crawl into the backseat.

Have you been to the new airport yet, asks Rainer adjusting the rearview mirror, it's the biggest construction site in Europe.

No, says Noura with a tired smile.

I look out the window. Birds fly past in the sky, I tap Jameelah and point to them.

Cranes, she says with an expert's eye, cranes and back there, she points out the back window, those are swallows.

You can see the airport from a long way off.

Wonder if they'll ever finish, says Rainer shaking his head. He steers the car into the turning circle and pulls to a stop in front of the main building. He gets out and unloads the bags.

Thanks very much for the ride, says Noura handing Rainer money.

No, says Rainer, it's on me, put it back in your pocket. Who knows when you might need it.

No, says Noura, I insist.

I won't have it, says Rainer.

In that case we'll give it to the children, says Noura and hands the money to me before picking up the bags.

Auf wiedersehen and thanks again.

My pleasure, says Rainer and then he sits back down at the wheel.

Wait for me here, I call to him and walk into the airport building with Jameelah and Noura.

Noura looks at the clock.

We have plenty of time, she says, but it's better to be early than too late. Are you hungry?

No, says Jameelah.

I look at the money in my hand and something occurs to me.

We have to do something, I say, just over there at the snack shop.

I'm not hungry, says Jameelah, are you deaf?

Come on, I say pulling her with me.

Large order of french fries please, nothing on them, I say holding out the money to the guy behind the counter.

What's the story, says Jameelah.

I take the tray in my hand and walk over to one of the tables.

Potato party.

I don't want to, says Jameelah.

I don't either, I say sitting down, but then I eat a fry anyway, and then another and another.

Man leave a few for me, says Jameelah reaching for the fries.

Potato, I say, is actually an ugly word don't you think, it sounds bad.

All words that begin with P are bad, says Jameelah with her mouth full, haven't you ever noticed? Prison, priest, pacification, peril, pallbearer, pain.

True, pain, I say, and poison of course.

See, says Jameelah, potato is the same except that it's not really bad it just sounds a bit ugly, like palpitation or puke.

We think of a lot more food items that begin with P, one after

241

the next until the fries are gone. I order another round. A cheesy song from the eighties is playing over the speakers.

I hate that song, says Jameelah.

It's my mother's favourite song, I say.

Really?

Yeah, it's what she listened to when she was around our age. Kind of makes you realize how old grown-ups are.

What do you mean?

Well he's singing about being out in the streets until midnight and drinking seven beers. Like a grandfather.

Jameelah grins.

Staying up until midnight and drinking seven beers, even I could manage that.

And Nico, if he has the next day off he can drink a whole case of beer in a night.

Have you guys talked, asks Jameelah.

Only for a second but not about the whole thing.

Why don't you guys make up?

No idea. Maybe I will.

Yeah, says Jameelah, you should.

Did you ever see Lukas again?

No, she says, and I don't want to. I did hear that Anna-Lena really is going to that boarding school.

We really need to get revenge on Lukas somehow, I say but Jameelah shakes her head.

I don't want to get revenge, revenge is the most disgusting thing in the world. If there was no revenge then Abu and Youssef wouldn't be dead and we would never have come to Germany and I would never have to get deported.

Fuck Germany, I say, what kind of country just sends people away.

Stop, says Jameelah, there are so many good things about

Germany.

Like what?

I don't know, there's a million.

See, you can't think of a single one.

Yes I can. Like the fact that there's always water out front of stores in the summer so dogs can have a drink.

You're crazy.

Seriously, says Jameelah, normal stuff like that, something so idiotically normal like having water out for dogs, that's exactly what life is made of.

She looks at the clock.

I have to go.

We go back. Noura is waiting in front of the departures screen.

Come here my little one, she says bending down to me.

I'll come visit you, I say.

You don't have any money, says Jameelah.

I will, I'll deliver newspapers or something and then I'll come visit. For Christmas break. It's warmer in Iraq than here then, and it's sunny there in winter too right?

Noura smiles.

In winter it's even colder where we'll be living than it is here, you can ski there.

But in summer, I say, it's sunny then right?

Noura runs her hand over my head.

Yes, she says, but where we'll be living the moon is the sun.

Bye, says Jameelah.

Bye, I say.

We hug each other and then Noura and Jameelah go through security.

I'll come visit, I call, whether there's snow, sun, or moonlight, I swear I'll come visit.

Jameelah turns around and raises her little finger.

243

Pinky swear?

Pinky swear, I call and raise my finger.

Rainer is sitting in the driver's seat reading the paper. He starts the engine when he sees me. I slide into the backseat.

Don't be sad, he says turning around to me, all good things must come to an end.

Leave me alone, I say but Rainer won't let it go, he says, come on I'll drive you around a bit and you can take in the pretty sites, the Reichstag and Friedrichstrasse.

No just drive me here, I say handing Rainer the piece of paper with Amir's address on it.

In that disgusting part of town?

Like we live any better, I say.

That's enough of that, says Rainer.

Drive me there, I say, or I'm getting out of the car and I'll take the train.

Fine, fine, says Rainer putting on the radio.

My eyes are burning. I don't want to cry, not in front of Rainer, I fold up the piece of paper with Amir's address, folding it smaller and smaller, I press it together as hard as I can and it helps. When I was younger and I skinned my knee at the playground or whatever, Mama always said it'll be healed long before you get married. Skinned knees and jammed thumbs might heal but nothing else does, nothing on this rotten earth heals. I think I hate Mama and I hate Papa too, much more than Mama, Rainer I don't care about and you can't hate someone you don't even care about.

Rainer turns up the radio. 'When Will The Clouds Part' is playing but it's not the normal version with the normal verses, in this version people answer the question what does happiness mean to you and then in between the singer sings, she sings when will the clouds part and then someone else starts talking about happiness and how they define it. They say stuff like happiness is being free or happiness is never losing laughter, having fun in life, they say happiness is having someone who loves me, or it's wanting to hold onto a moment.

Man how Jameelah and I always hated this song. We hated it because we thought it was stupid to think back on moments in your life that you wish you could hold onto because moments like that somehow never happen, at least not moments like the ones in the song.

The day we first drank Tiger Milk, that was a good moment, when we started using O-language and started going to Kurfürsten, those were good moments too. It's funny, but I can remember all sorts of things from my childhood now but the things that happened just a few years ago, as we started to become adults, I can barely remember those things. Drinking Tiger Milk and going to Kurfürsten, those were good moments but I have no idea who came up with the idea, no idea why we decided to wear the striped stockings, I don't have the slightest idea when it became a game or which one of us came up with the recipe for Tiger Milk. I don't know when and why we started to speak O-language, I don't know why we ended up on Kurfürsten of all streets and with the men there, I don't know any of that, I just know that we always thought nothing would ever go wrong, nothing would happen, as long as we didn't go anywhere alone, never alone.